After leaving school Barbara Kew worked in youth clubs, a community centre and prison after care In London. She qualified as a child care officer and joined a Social Service Department, practising as a social worker and later a family therapist after her children were born. She also supervised a team of social workers. On retiring she became a social work practice teacher and also worked as a private mediator.

She is married, with two children and four grandchildren and lives in the West Country. She now does some voluntary work with asylum seekers and refugees.

Something Must Be Done

Barbara Kew

Something Must Be Done

*To Adele
with all good wishes
Barbara Kew*

Vanguard Press

VANGUARD PAPERBACK

© Copyright 2008
Barbara Kew

The right of Barbara Kew to be identified as author of this work has been asserted by her in accordance with the Copyright, Designs and Patents Act 1988.

All Rights Reserved

No reproduction, copy or transmission of this publication may be made without written permission.
No paragraph of this publication may be reproduced, copied or transmitted save with the written permission of the publisher, or in accordance with the provisions of the Copyright Act 1956 (as amended).

Any person who commits any unauthorised act in relation to this publication may be liable to criminal prosecution and civil claims for damages.

A CIP catalogue record for this title is available from the British Library.

ISBN 978 184386 434 9

*Vanguard Press is an imprint of
Pegasus Elliot MacKenzie Publishers Ltd.*
www.pegasuspublishers.com

First Published in 2008

**Vanguard Press
Sheraton House Castle Park
Cambridge England**

Printed & Bound in Great Britain

Dedication

To Jacqui and Simon

Acknowledgements

"My thanks to Lil, without whose help and encouragement
I would not have completed this story."

Prologue

2000

Every time Bella walked through the kitchen the letter jumped into her line of vision. The open white envelope appeared brighter than those of the circulars and bills lying with it on the table. She wanted to forget it. She forgot things so easily now, but she could not forget this or rid herself of the unease it caused. She must, she knew, respond to it. Make a telephone call. But not now. Later. When she had cleared up. Which she knew was just another way of putting it off. There was no list of priorities in her life today, just the usual things which gave some shape to her day. Ellen, the elderly neighbour who lived a few doors away, to be taken to the dentist at three of course. This was the only fixed arrangement and this was hours away.

She watered the house plants, deadheading the tired geranium on the kitchen windowsill and removing the yellowing leaves. She went upstairs and tidied her bedroom, putting away yesterday's clothes and then, unaccountably, she began to sort through a drawer filled with woollen jerseys, discarding this one and that, wondering if they were good enough for a charity shop, trying to decide whether she would wear them again. She became irritated by the heaps of clothes she now had on the floor and picked them up and stuffed them back into the drawer. This was not what she intended, just a device for avoiding the telephone call she must make.

And then the telephone rang and she was startled and glad. It will be Liz, she thought. Liz ringing to see if I have had her letter. Ringing to talk about it. Relieved and apprehensive, she picked up the phone beside her bed with the words *'I was just going to ring you'* prepared but not needed... It was Maggie, who had lived next door until two years ago, saying it was ages since they had seen her and would she come to lunch a week on Friday. About to say 'yes' Bella hesitated and asked if she could ring in a day or so as she was not sure what she would be doing that week – something had come up – which Maggie was quite happy about and after a little social chat about health and families, the call was finished.

As she put the phone down, Bella realized she was already making assumptions about her life becoming complicated, and because she had her hand on the receiver she decided to ring Liz now and begin the process which would involve her in... in... what? Well, in Martha's life for one thing and bring God knows what difficulties and frustrations in her own. She resented Liz's letter. Liz, her oldest friend. But not writing out of friendship. Still curiously holding me responsible, Bella thought, and yet she needs to tell me. Something terrible has happened to her daughter, Martha.

Bella shook her resentment away and thought of Martha in hospital. Martha, almost another daughter. Born just before her own daughter, Gemma, and somehow a constant disappointment to Liz who found approval and enthusiasm so difficult to convey. She remembered how excited Liz had been when Martha was born. A girl, she had said, I so wanted a girl. Of course I adore Sam, but I feel he is for Matthew and this baby is to be mine. What Liz had meant, Bella now thought, was that the little girl was to be moulded, taught, and influenced to fulfil Liz's idea of what a girl should be, and I... well, I looked for the free spirit, I suppose. Encouraged self-confidence which sometimes seemed too deflated, which was so easily deflated, until now. This awful thing happened. But I still don't really know anything. I must ring.

But she didn't ring. Not then. She had to go downstairs for the number and yet when there she paced around, removing an old newspaper, shifting a photograph to another shelf and then shifting it back. She even went into the garden and stared at the borders which needed weeding. But not now. Now she was thinking about what she would say to Liz and what Liz would tell her and, exasperated with herself, she went back indoors and dialled Liz's number.

Later, as she toyed with the sandwich she had made for her lunch, Bella felt the coldness of anxiety and the doubts about what she had offered to do. Liz, of course, had given her the problem as Bella had known she would. She thinks me culpable and perhaps I am, she thought, but the distracted voice expressing fear and despair echoed in Bella's head as she shared the emotion.

"Can you imagine the shock? And when they said she might have damaged her liver irreparably... Matthew was distraught. Well, you know what he's like. He doesn't think the horrors of the world have anything to do with our family life, and it was that dreadful case at work. If there's an inquiry it might be in the paper."

A moment of panic shot through Bella at these words. The letter had not mentioned any of this. Just depression because a child had died. This was going to be dreadful, and Bella was filled with dread and anxiety when Liz said they had met the Director of Social Services at the hospital and he was very kind, but he had recommended that when she left hospital she should be looked after away from home in case the media became involved. Bella knew, before Liz said any more, what was coming – Martha wants to come here to me. And she was right. Liz went on to tell her that Martha's daughter, Beth, had told her that Martha said I would understand better than anyone, but of course, she couldn't ask me, and didn't want anyone else to ask me.

She didn't mention that in the letter either, Bella thought, but she knew it would hurt Liz to tell her this and managed to mutter something about families seeming too close at times. But Liz wasn't listening. She was saying that "Beth wanted to look after her mother but that Martha had been quite adamant that she couldn't impose on her daughter, which Liz felt rather rich as she thought Martha should have thought about her daughter before taking an overdose, which was such a selfish thing to do."

The mixture of anger and misery in Liz's voice could not be soothed and Bella remembered herself saying: "Well of course she can come here if that's what she wants. But if I'm not supposed to know, how do we handle this?"

"I don't think she has any right to make conditions at the moment," Liz had said. "Whether she likes it or not we have to make some plans." Bella heard Liz begin to cry as they talked. Liz doesn't cry, she thought. I don't think I have ever heard her cry before, so she heard herself say: "Yes, yes, of course. Of course. And if I can help…"

As she wiped the surfaces in the kitchen and threw away her half eaten sandwich, Bella realised she had not asked about the child who had died or why there might be an inquiry, but she filled the gaps with her knowledge and imagination. This was child abuse and Martha was the social worker. A child had died and Martha was so implicated she had tried to kill herself.

Bella went upstairs and changed her slacks for a skirt and fiddled with her hair. She went to fetch Ellen early because the time was passing so slowly. She drove to the dentist and then parked the car and waited outside for Ellen to come out. She coped with Ellen's news about the cat's behaviour and the discussion heard on the radio about taking cod-liver oil for arthritis. She helped Ellen in and out of the car as they stopped at a convenience store for Ellen to make some purchases and later, as she helped to put the shopping away, she noticed a packet of sausages on top of the fridge which she was sure they had bought last week. She saw the sell-by date had passed four days before and thought of slipping them into her bag, but Ellen had noticed she had picked up the packet. "I thought I would have some of those for my meal tonight," she said.

Bella explained about the sell-by date but Ellen was dismissive saying that we didn't have sell-by dates in the past and went by the smell. If they smelled alright, they would be alright. She took the packet from Bella's hand and sniffed it and nodded. Quite alright. She had that steely look in her eyes which Bella knew, meant that she had no intention of changing her mind, so she didn't argue. When Ellen made decisions she brooked no arguments. It was about holding on to her independence, asserting her rights. One never quite knew when she would become obstinate and stubborn, but Bella knew the signs. She gradually extricated herself from Ellen's kitchen letting her eyes slide over the newspapers piled on two chairs, the table covered with small heaps of letters and circulars, and the plate and dish left from Ellen's lunch without her usual urge to help Ellen tidy up. She colonises every surface in the small house, Bella thought. Each room, she knew, was filled with the things Ellen was saving for something or someone or had just put down for the time being. Usually Bella attempted to bring a little order – her order – at least to the kitchen, but today the tension in her stomach and the awful sense of knowing that something had happened which could not be undone allowed no space for attempting to organise Ellen's life, and she left, knowing, but not able to care, that Ellen really wanted her to stay.

Later as she turned off the television which she had watched but not heard, Bella decided that it would be best if she wrote to Martha and told her she could come if she wished. Martha would find telephoning difficult, especially as the suggestion would have come from a tight-lipped Liz whose messages could be so mixed. She wrote carefully without referring to either the overdose or the probable cause, simply saying she was sorry Martha was very low and asking if coming to stay with her for a while might help. She had always felt close to Martha. They had been able to talk easily since she was quite a young child and this was probably what was needed now. And it's what I do, she thought. Talk and listen, listen and talk.

Gemma rang at eight, full of the news that her daughter Susan and boyfriend Martin had decided definitely to get married once the baby was born. She is already planning the wedding, Bella thought, and realised she too was pleased. A granddaughter's wedding and a new baby was something to look forward to and she surprised herself again in realising she was about to become a great grandmother. But the bad news interrupted the pleasure felt by both women when she told Gemma what she had agreed to.

"But do you really want to get involved?" Gemma's reaction was predictable. Martha, she said, was a depressive, whose life was always going to be a problem and this sounded very unpleasant. "I mean, Mum, do you really need this? With the baby coming, I thought you would be coming up here soon."

It was often difficult to explain herself to Gemma, who was so practical but she tried. "I suppose I feel I must react positively to Liz and Martha. After all, Liz has been a friend all my life."

Gemma knew that. "But I've always failed to understand how it is that you are friends. Martha was always rather a pain when we were children, always unsure, always apologising and as for Liz... well, you know I've always thought she was pretty awful. Critical, bossy and not the sort of mother I would have wanted. I mean, I'm sorry Martha is in such a state and that something terrible has happened and of course, you'll be much better for her than Liz, but take care, Mum. Don't get too involved."

Bella said she would be alright but was left thinking how from the first she had responded to Martha, born just a few months after Gemma, with the enthusiasm and warmth that Liz found it so hard to provide in her anxiety to control and influence. That was when their closeness had begun to weaken. Becoming friends is easy to understand, Bella thought. In our early years of adolescence and the twenties when being friends was sharing the awful things that disturbed the progress of life and the wonderful things that brought expectation and excitement. It was talking, at school, at home, on the phone, in the cafés and with the first babies, about everything. It was simply part of what one did with people who seemed to understand what you were saying, whose bodies presented the same mysteries and discoveries and who laughed at the same things and enjoyed the same things you did. Staying friends was an altogether different matter, a habit which no longer depended on mutual understanding. Separate lives weakened the bonds of affection. Motherhood placed us on different tracks, Bella thought, but some kind of inner compulsion exerted the pressure which reminded us we had been friends for years and must try to ignore the bad bits and keep going. Bella supposed, not for the first time, that one could actually come to dislike old friends like Liz, but she couldn't argue the point with Gemma.

Before she went to bed she sat down and wrote to Liz, enclosing the letter to Martha, and attempting some comfort in saying that while these cases could be very unpleasant, they did not always result in publicity. Then she added a bit about talking to Gemma, who, she said, sent all her love. This is why we are still friends, she thought, because I tell all these lies.

Chapter One

1969

Rensham was a small town which had expanded from the hamlet which had once served the surrounding farming area. As it grew it divested itself of the marks of its rural past, rather as it had once divested itself of its Roman ancestry, which was now only to be found in the form of odd bits of mosaic paving beneath the concrete and brick, when there was the need to dig up foundations to see to the drains.

There was a large square at the centre of the town, fronted on one side by the City Hall, which, erected in the early 19th century had replaced the wool market, now only remembered by the plaque which said "Once the site of the 16th Century Wool Exchange". Indications of the more distant past were opposite, where an 18th century edifice stood with an imposing frontage. Its original function was proclaimed in the carved letters above the portico which stated this was "The City Market". Inside it was indeed still a market with stalls neatly displaying fish, meat, cheese and vegetables, as well as rolls of fabric for curtains and clothes, children's shoes and toys, cut flowers and confectionery.

Next to City Hall a concrete block of offices squashed a small timbered house up against the corner of a road. Curtains hung in the windows and it seemed that this was still a private dwelling, but on the other side was a low timbered building housing the City Museum. Other assorted buildings, of various ages and sizes, which sold a variety of things such as houses, shoes, china, coffee and newspapers stood beside the City Market and together with a post office and a Woolworths, filled all other available spaces around the square. Unaccountably, but probably the result of a rush of patriotic blood to the head of a past local councillor, in the middle of the square stood a statue of George V affectionately stroking the hair of a small girl with the dates 1914 – 1918 carved on the base.

Once there had been a wall enclosing the town. One could come across pieces of this, carefully preserved, at the end of streets, but the town now spread beyond them and was continuing to grow outwards, with small factories and large housing estates eating up the countryside.

In common with all other towns and cities in the country, the local council of Rensham had incorporated a Children's Committee after the 1948 Children' and Young Persons Act was passed by parliament. As with most legislation concerning the welfare of children, this Act had been passed after the scandal of a child being abused. Local authorities across the country had been authorised to set up Children's Committees, managed by a Children's Officer, charged with ensuring that children within each locality were properly looked after.

The Children's Committee of Rensham was peopled with councillors who were earnest in their desire to see the children of the town receive the care and attention they needed. The Children's Officer had taken advantage of the various new courses which offered training in all aspects of child care (and which incorporated the newest psychological theories) in appointing her staff, although in Rensham, as in other local authorities, it was not always possible to find qualified persons. Those with related experience, such as teachers, ex-employees of the NSPCC, and residential institutions were taken on, often with the promise of secondment to training at a later date. Expertise was consequently uneven and constantly running to catch up with the latest theories on child development.

Children's Department staff were know as child care officers and their tasks were complicated and varied. In the early days they recruited foster parents and, with the new knowledge that small children fared best in family situations rather than in institutions, set about moving young children from residential nurseries into family homes. They still made use of the large institutions run by Barnardo's and the National Children's Homes for older children but gradually these were seen as far too big and impersonal to meet the needs of older children and by the 1960s, small family group homes were being established and run, for the most part, by a husband and wife or one of the unmarried childless women once the mainstay of child care for children who lacked parents, or whose parents lacked parenting ability.

The fact that each local authority was more or less autonomous meant that the welfare services across the country were themselves idiosyncratic and varied considerably in the services they offered. It was not surprising therefore that as concern grew relentlessly during 1950s and 1960s for the welfare of children, the elderly, disabled and the mentally ill, the press and eventually parliament noticed that there was on the one hand a variety of different organisations trying to meet needs, and on the other hand, an alarming lack of uniformity in the quality of services on offer.

Apart from the Children's Department, most had a Department for the Mentally Ill, a Child Guidance Clinic, a Welfare Department for the elderly and those unable to care for themselves (for which there were special institutions), a Home Help Department providing domestic help for the elderly and disabled. There were also Hospital Almoners (later called Medical Social Workers) working for NHS concerned with the social needs of the sick, and an office of the National Assistance Board responsible for paying benefits. A Housing Department managing the area's council accommodation was the final organisation concerned with the welfare of its clients and its officers, together with the workers from all other agencies, visited people in their homes in response to their needs or their failure to keep to the rules each organisation had seen fit to make.

It was a confusing state of affairs, with workers literally tripping over each other on doorsteps and while there was some attempt at collaboration and sharing of information, this was not in any sense mandatory. Good communication was consequently extremely hit and miss, a fact which the press became increasingly keen on making public whenever a member of the public appeared to be suffering.

Bella, driving her car to her new job as a child care officer in Rensham's Children's Department, knew the welfare system was under review. She had been working for nine months in the Children's Department at Woodbridge, a large city with a population of some 300,000 where everyone was Waiting for Seebohm. She knew that when she worked at Rensham they would be waiting for Seebohm as well, because the government had responded to the unease about the welfare state by setting up a Royal Commission, under the chairmanship of Frederick Seebohm, to study the welfare provisions of local government and make recommendations for the future. The study was now published, and although the waiting was partially over, parliament had not yet passed the legislation which would create the new Social Services Departments, which were going to rationalise the welfare services under one heading in accordance with Seebohm's recommendations. In this sense, people were still waiting to discover how their work would be reorganised.

In fact, Bella was more anxious about the day ahead and the work in which she would be involved than the future shape of the organisation. Working at Woodbridge had not really given her a great deal of experience of child care. She had been temporarily employed as a duty officer and had simply logged the referrals made over the phone and seen people who arrived at the office, filling out forms which gave details of their problems. Everything was then passed to a senior child care officer who usually allocated the work to one of the permanent workers and only occasionally suggested that Bella attempt to help the client herself. In future, she knew she would be one of those workers who had to do the work and then it would be about casework methods. Casework?

When she had been at Liverpool, training, she had been puzzled about the word 'casework'. They were being trained to be caseworkers; they would be doing casework. She had originally thought it implied some special formula or theory, but when she asked someone to define it, they had simply said it meant one worked with individuals and called them cases, which was both a disappointment and a relief. But there seemed to be a great volume of theories to apply to one's work, and Bella was not sure she would know how to proceed. They had studied Freud and obtained some knowledge of the unconscious mind. And then Skinner, who didn't worry about the unconscious and developed the theory of Behaviourism, and then there was Group Work, and Crisis Intervention. Bella found it all intensely interesting, but practising…?

At Woodbridge she had not heard much about methods, except she got the impression that one did not talk too much about Freud or the unconscious mind. She had read Melanie Klein, the Winnicotts, even Freud himself (although not very much), and then found Erikson's Childhood and Society which immediately appealed and seemed far more relevant to the business of rearing children (even although it was mostly based on studies of American Indians) than digging away into the unconscious. And then there was Bowlby. It was from John Bowlby she began to understand the significance of the relationship between children and their natural parents and what happened when this was broken. But at Woodbridge she had become aware that most of the people coming to the office were poor, badly educated, badly housed or depressed, which convinced her that the most important factor in welfare work was improving social conditions. So theoretically, she thought, I am very eclectic, or perhaps just a bit of a mess.

When she arrived at the detached house in which Rensham's Children's Department was housed, Judith Naseby, the Senior Child Care officer, who had interviewed her for the job, fetched her from Reception, and led her upstairs, explaining and describing as they went. "We are very squashed up," she said, "because of last year's expansion which had been necessary after the two new housing estates had been built on the north side of the town. It had been decided they must divide the town in two and employ two teams to cover the work." Bella understood she would get the south side of the town – clients were allocated according to where they lived. "But," said Judy, "it is not as bad as it had once been." She laughed and remembered how it was when she started. In 1951 in City Hall, in the basement. "We had had a coal fire, would you believe, and one of my first jobs," she said, "was to stoke it up during the day. There were only three of us and we sat round one of those great boardroom tables. Now we do have central heating, thank goodness, and one gets a bit of privacy."

She opened a door and ushered Bella into a very small room with a desk and chair by the window, a filing cabinet against the wall and another door opening into another room. There were a variety of hooks on the walls.

"I think this must have been a dressing room when it was a proper house – plenty of choice about where to hang your coat – and Harry and Jan's room, through there, that must have been the master bedroom." She pointed to the other door. "The others who work Area 1, Evelyn and Jennifer, and the typists' room is across the passage, and I have a room next to that, which I think was once a bathroom, because it has two pipes running up the wall and the lavatory is next door which can be rather noisy, but this is you. The child care officers working Area 2 are on the top floor, and the Admin Officer is next to Reception below, opposite the waiting room."

As she spoke, a woman's head appeared round the door by which they had entered and told Judith that she was wanted on the phone. There was a hurried introduction. This was Marian, Judith said, who would probably do some of Bella's typing, and then she excused herself and left, promising to return to talk to Bella as soon as she could.

Bella chose a hook for her coat and sat down at the desk on which there was a new pad, a stapler, a wire tray and a shiny notice on blue paper with orange letters announcing the news that the Seebohm report had recommended an amalgamation of welfare services and the establishment of generic social workers who would work with all client groups. As she glanced at this, a young man – twenty something – in crumpled jeans and a red pullover, with long amber-coloured hair dangling round his neck (which matched his eyes, Bella thought), came in and introduced himself as Harry Briggs. He told her how good it was to have her working with them and wasn't it good about Seebohm, and he and Jan Wrayburn were only next door and Jan was making coffee and Bella must come in and join them.

So she did, and she met Jan, a bit younger than her, in green mini skirt and white polo necked jersey, with long straight black hair in a pony tail. There were two desks littered with papers, a filing cabinet, several chairs and a small cupboard on which there was a kettle, several cups, an opened bag of sugar and a bottle of tomato sauce. In a corner, a cardboard box spilled an assortment of toys onto the floor.

"You're going to have to use our phone, I'm afraid," Harry said. "It's extremely inconvenient and Kate used to drag it into her room – it just reaches – and sit on the floor inside the door to make calls. We keep asking for one for your room, but nothing happens. Don't worry about it. We're used to it. Marian, our clerk, fields most of our calls and takes messages."

Drinking coffee they talked about the office, and gave each other brief accounts of themselves. Bella heard that Jan was divorced, with twin daughters and a mother living nearby who was a godsend. Harry had worked for the youth service before starting as an unqualified child care officer at Rensham and was hoping that one day they would second him for training. Bella told them about Woodbridge.

Harry enthused about the Seebohm report which, he thought, would shake some of the stuffiness out of the department. "It's constipated with rules and very sensitive about its image. On no account must we upset the Children's Committee who are the Chosen Ones, and we mustn't forget we are public servants specially appointed to save the offspring of the poor and inadequate and make them into nice middle-class children."

Jan laughed and told Harry to stop, but he went on, "That was what Kate forgot. Oh, do you know about Kate?" he asked Bella, but before anyone could go on the door opened and Jennifer Penn and Evelyn Lambert arrived.

As she shook hands, Bella wondered why Kate leaving was something she should know about, and then she concentrated on the tall, bony woman with short grey hair, dark grey mid-calf skirt and matching jersey who had just come in. She beamed at Bella and said she was Jennifer Penn and she believed she was going to look after Bella and help her settle down.

"I expect Judy has told you," she said.

Bella felt some relief. Jennifer was older than her, so she wasn't the oldest member of the team. She smiled back and said Judy had not had time to say anything yet, but she was pleased as it was going to seem very strange. Jennifer consulted her watch, apologised and then left and Bella was introduced to Evelyn who looked rather like a health visitor in a blue buttoned-through dress. She remembered how at college they had been told they should wear clothes that blended in with their surrounding. She had put on her rust-coloured trouser suit this morning and felt she blended in with no one.

Evelyn had a shy, self-effacing manner and seemed to be hiding behind heavy rimmed glasses, but she also told Bella how glad they were to have her. Kate had left so suddenly, without warning. They had found it difficult, and as she left she turned and said, "We must get to know one another... have a talk."

"She sees you as a potential recruit for the Bible group," Harry said, and was immediately shushed by Jan who said, "Evelyn is a lovely lady. Very serious but extremely conscientious, but I'm sure you will like her. She used to work for Barnardo's and her husband still runs one of their small homes."

Bella returned to her room and sat at the desk, opening drawers and removing odd scraps of paper and old memos, and putting the sandwiches she had made for lunch into the top one. She put her diary, a notebook and the elephant pen holder which Gemma had given her on the top and stood the small calendar up. The 3rd March was ringed in red. The day I start work at Rensham, she thought. Today. She looked out of the window and saw her car lined up with others in the space which had been the garden. An old leafless tree and a laurel bush restricted the parking space on one side. She wondered why these had been saved. On either side the original back gardens of the houses were filled with small buildings and sheds and more cars. But her thoughts were interrupted by Judith Naseby poking her head round the door, apologising for the delay and asking Bella to come into her room.

When she returned to her room later, she deposited the pile of files she carried on her desk and stared out of the window again. The last half hour was blurred with information only partly absorbed. Judith Naseby, the Senior Child Care officer, was dressed in a dark brown suit and Bella knew she had dark brown tights on her legs fitted into lace-up brown shoes. Her skin was very pale but her cheeks glowed red and her eyes darted about beneath her spectacles. She seems to be very healthy, Bella thought. Probably likes long walks. There was a pile of brown case files on the desk in front of her and on one side a pint bottle of milk and a green apple, Bella wondered if this was Judy's lunch.

Judy began with a burst of friendliness. "Please call me Judy. Everyone is so informal these days, have you noticed, although we still observe the formalities with Miss Bateson, the Children's Officer of course, and the Admin Officer is rather a stickler for the proprieties – that's Miss Henderson."

All this was said with a breathlessness that made Bella wonder if she was really comfortable with this degree of informality. Then there was a little social chat. Was she settled in her new house? How was her daughter liking Rensham? Followed quickly by a correction. Of course she was at college so hadn't been here very much. Studying law, I think you said. So useful.

They talked a little about Bella's work at Woodbridge which Judy thought must have been so productive, she would have increased her knowledge base. Then, patting the pile in front of her, Judy said they must get down to work. There were seventeen cases – Bella counted them later – and they were rather neglected, Judy said. Response only. Clients had been told there was a staff difficulty and there would be a delay. But she wasn't going to go through them all now.

"Have a browse. I don't want you overwhelmed and Jennifer Penn is going to look after you for a while. She's very experienced, and I will see you tomorrow, or the next day. I must confess I am a bit concerned about the reviews. You probably didn't do reviews at Woodbridge, being on duty all the time. We have just started them for all children who are in care in foster homes. There is a form – Marian will show you – and you arrange with the foster parents to sit down and see how things are going. You may want to invite the school and occasionally, if it seems appropriate, we invite the mothers. I shall see the forms when they are done and will talk things over with you. I think Marian has put a note on the files where reviews are due. We are going to do them every six months and they are in addition to the usual visits under the Boarding Out Regulations – Miss Bateson is very fussy about Boarding Out Regs, especially bedrooms! You'll soon get the idea."

Bella hoped so. At present she was wondering why Miss Bateson was fussy about bedrooms but she expected the others would know. She began opening the files.

There were seven files with a note pinned on the front which said REVIEW DUE. Bella listed the names of the children involved and then began to look at the other files. Rita Hollis's file had been open some nine months and there were a number of referrals from neighbours who reported the fact that they believed Rita left her three children (the oldest only seven) alone in the evening. Bella's predecessor, Kate, had visited Rita on each occasion, when she vehemently denied that she ever left the children and said the neighbours – and she could guess who they were – were vindictive nosey parkers and liars. The last report on the file said that Kate had visited the next door neighbour (who made most of the complaints) and told her to ring the police if it ever happened again. That was three months ago and it seemed nothing had occurred since. Bella added Rita's name to the list thinking that if she introduced herself, this would serve to warn Rita that the Children's Dept were still concerned.

She added Margaret Wright to her list. A rather large file originally opened a year ago. Masses of debts which Kate had tried to help her manage, warding off the creditors, assisting her with budgeting. Now her electricity was going to be cut off.

Jennifer had seen her a week or so ago and had started to negotiate with the electricity board for a meter to be installed. Maureen Banford with six children needed to be re-housed, but Kate's last note said the Housing Department would not consider her until her rent arrears were paid off. Bella thought she sounded seriously overcrowded with five girls under eleven and a boy of thirteen in a three-bedroom house. Bella wasn't sure, but thought there was a law about overcrowding. She would find out.

There is so much I don't know, she thought, and will have to find out. Judy may have imagined my knowledge base was useful, but I doubt it is useful enough.

She read through the file on Jacky Martin who had three children, all of whom appeared to have had behaviour problems which Kate had helped her to survive. But now the three-year-old was, apparently, totally beyond her control. Kate had written more than once that Jacky had said this little boy would have to go into care. She just couldn't cope. When she last visited, Kate had devised a star chart for Jacky to use as an incentive for her and the boy. Bella wondered whether star charts were going to help such a young child. She would have to see how it was going. She added her to the list and was relieved when the door opened and Jan came in with another cup of coffee and pulled a chair up to the desk.

"After a session with Judy and a pile of work, I thought you could manage another one."

She is really very pleasant, Bella thought. She heard how Jan had been on her own since her husband left for Dubai some four years before. She had returned to work two years previously as her mother lived nearby and helped to look after the girls.

"But I remember how awful first days are and you mustn't be disheartened. It's really quite bearable here. Judy is rather picky but she's helpful and good hearted although she is rather obsessed with doing things according to the book – always reminding us about the law and the fact that we are responsible for keeping to the rules. She seems to need to please Miss Bateson, who is really rather a pain in the neck. Constantly reminding us we are local authority OFFICERS. Personally I can't bear being called an officer."

As they talked and laughed together, some of the confusion and desolation left Bella. Then Harry came through the door exclaiming loudly, "Would you believe it? Just had a call from the police in Liverpool to say they have picked up Stephen Holder. Slippery Steve. Apparently they picked him up yesterday but it wasn't until today that he decided to tell them who he was. Little toe-rag. Now I have to go to Liverpool to fetch him and I'm supposed to be seeing Mrs Hamley and Bernie after lunch. God! I wish our clients were on the phone. I can't leave here until one because I'm on duty. Jan, darling, would you be able to go and tell her I shan't be coming?"

But Jan had other things to do and she was very sorry but sweet talk would get him nowhere. She simply couldn't do it. She explained to Bella that Stephen was in Farrington House, which was a small children's home, and he was always absconding. "Why can't staff from there go and fetch him, Harry?"

"Why indeed? They never retrieve the children they lose. They say they don't get the mileage allowance and haven't got the staff available."

Bella hesitated a moment and then offered to take the message to Mrs Hamley. The prospect of getting away from the office was very tempting and Harry was full of gratitude although Jan told Bella she was not here to do other people's work. Harry went back into the master bedroom to write a note to Mrs Hamley and Jan eventually followed him, saying to Bella as she left that they must have a meal together sometime, and she would love to see Bella's home.

Before he left for Liverpool, Harry told her that Mrs Hamley had trouble with her thirteen-year-old son Bernie, who frequently truanted from school, refused to help in the home, smoked and swore and was generally beyond her control. "She won't be very friendly, I'm afraid, and will tell you she has had enough and she wants him taken into care. Actually, he can't go to school at the moment because he's suspended for swearing – not a very good idea for a boy who truants, but that's schools for you, and he learns most of the wicked words from his mum and dad who don't have a good word to say for him. I'm trying to work on that but haven't got very far."

After lunch Bella took a map and drove past the Victorian houses now occupied by solicitors, estate agents and dentists, into the narrower street of a residential area with tidy semis and neat front gardens, and then on to the council estate at the edge of town where few gardens showed signs of care and some were squares of concrete or scattered with oddments of iron and paper. Her destination, No 18 Mangrove Road, had a mixture of debris, including the remains of a chair and several bottles and tins, battling for space between the front door and the gate. Mangrove Road. She wondered what flight of fancy had overcome the official that named the road. There wasn't a tree in sight.

Mrs Hamley was, as Harry suggested, not friendly. As Bella began to explain her visit and hand her Harry's note, a boy standing behind her pushed past Bella shouting to his mother that he wasn't bloody staying in any longer if Mr Briggs wasn't coming. Mrs Hamley shouted after him that if he wasn't back for his tea he wouldn't get any and then told Bella she could tell Mr Briggs she had had enough and if he didn't do something about it soon she would have the boy put away. Bella promised she would and listened to Mrs Hamley's complaints which flowed from her with a mixture of anger and frustration. Bella said she was sorry she couldn't help and promised that Harry would visit tomorrow, and then backed away from the door and returned to her car.

In the car park outside the Department a tall curly haired man in corduroy pants and a yellow pullover stopped her and asked if she was the new Area 1 worker. He introduced himself as Tim Moore.

"I work on the top floor in the servants' quarters. I used to be with Harry and Jan, but I've been moved to the new team for Area 2. We heard you were coming but don't tell me they have had you working already?"

Later, at home, she sat at the kitchen table and kicked off her shoes. She felt extremely tired, but thinking back decided that people were being pleasant and friendly. She thought of the files and the work to be done and then pushed away the anxiety this caused and began to get herself something to eat. She opened a tin of soup and took the remains of yesterday's chicken from the fridge and made some salad, then she went upstairs. In her bedroom she stepped over two boxes which still lay on the floor unpacked and remembered she was going to do that this evening, and then tackle the mess in the spare bedroom which was filled with packages and bags. Perhaps when she had eaten... but after she had washed up she found some music on the radio and sat with her feet up on the sofa and let her mind drift until she realised she was likely to fall asleep. Then she forced herself upstairs and began unpacking the boxes.

49 Lovelace Avenue
Rensham

22nd March 1969

Dearest Gemma

It was good to hear from you yesterday. I'm so sorry it was so short. You can reverse the charges you know – I don't mind – I know you won't do it every day.

So I'm now in my third week and beginning to feel slightly more at home, or perhaps I should say, less anxious and insecure. Everyone has been very pleasant and welcoming but I have a tremendous pile of work. As I told you I am being looked after by Jennifer who rushes about with an air of exasperation and who has taken me out to various clients and agencies. She seems to have no time for health visitors who, she says, always expect us to DO something about the cases which cause anxiety and who don't, she thinks, understand the limitations of the law But she is full of knowledge and tells us stories about children for whom she arranged adoption years ago and who are thriving. I think she believes that most of the children she sees would be better off adopted! As you know, I am not at all sure about adoption, but I am keeping this to myself at present!

The team are a mixed bunch and I miss Sim, but I have rung her and told her my troubles. Jan and Harry are the most friendly. He is in his twenties, fairly radical with long tawny hair and eyes to match. He looks a bit like a lion! She is a bit younger than me, a divorced mother of twins. Her ex is working in Dubai. Apparently she refused to go there with him and the marriage died years ago. Her mother lives quite near and looks after the twins whenever necessary. I think they are about fourteen, and she is fun to be with. We had a bad afternoon on Tuesday when one of her cases created a scene downstairs because she wanted some money we couldn't provide and I had to go down and help calm things down which wasn't entirely successful. The woman, who was rather large, shouted at Jan and threatened to report her to the MP before leaving. Afterwards we went to the pub to recuperate. We asked Evelyn to join us. She is about my age I suppose and is rather a serious, shy woman who has asked me if I would like to join her Bible reading group, which, you will not be surprised to hear, I declined – nicely of course. She declined the pub nicely which was not surprising either. Jan says she thinks she is rather against the drink but is very caring and competent. I doubt Jennifer is the type to frequent pubs either, she probably wouldn't have time – and although Harry would have joined us, he was out. He seems to spend his time chasing boys who have run away.

They have given me 17 cases 'to be going on with'. These all belonged to Kate, whose departure was apparently very sudden for reasons which I have just discovered. Everyone was very cagey about her but there was an occasional sniff of disapproval which I thought must mean something. I now know what. She was apparently having an affair with a man in Area 2 and they were caught in flagrante one evening in the office. Judy, the senior child care area officer, returned there quite late and walked in on them. Can you imagine! Kate never returned and sent in her resignation, but the man, Tim, is still here. I gather he was temporarily suspended and the news crept out via one of the clerks. I suppose I should be grateful to them as Kate's leaving created the vacancy.

The work is quite different from Woodbridge because now I have my own cases and spend my life shooting in and out instead of just sitting in the office dealing with callers and passing the work to someone else. And after Woodbridge, the town is quite small, but it has its grotty side. In fact, several grotty sides like little self-contained areas dotted around estates of semis and occasional detached houses where people mow their lawns and clean their cars on Sundays – like the one we live in except mostly in better condition and I haven't cleaned the car for weeks. The middle is just offices and shops and it appears to be, as you pointed out, dead as a doornail after 6 p.m. – or perhaps there are hidden delights which will emerge over time? I believe it is quite old but traces of its history are hard to find. An occasional timbered Tudor building but mostly large Victorian houses on the north side – interspersed with squares of unlovely concrete and brick offices filling in the holes that were made, I am told, by air raids during the war.

Of course I am pleased you will be bringing your new friend Jane down for a weekend. I will try to finish painting the bathroom and I have bought a sofa bed to go in your room so you two can talk all night. It fits quite well – a sort of greyish-pink that looks right with the carpet and curtains – at least I think so.

The good news is really in the garden. There are bulbs appearing – mostly daffodils I think, but also snowdrops are already blooming. The grass is much too long and I'll try to cut it when I've had the mower sharpened. Most of it will have to wait. I'll try to deal with it gradually, it is so overgrown – as you so elegantly put it – there are probably gorillas in the undergrowth.

And I forgot to tell you – the people next door in that rather battered Victorian house, have called. Maggy and Brian. Very pleasant. I am to be invited for a meal.

Talk to you again soon, darling – I am going to Gran's at the weekend. Had a long call from her worrying about Granddad's cough.

Now I must go to bed...!

It was four weeks before Bella was summoned to meet the Children's Officer during which time Jennifer took her out to see some of her clients and introduced her to some health visitors and the head of one of the local primary schools. She was becoming familiar with the paperwork and the procedures she must follow. Jan had invited her to a meal and Evelyn kept saying she must come to them but had not yet fixed a date. She had met the workers in Area 2 and seemed to keep bumping into Tim Moore whom she now knew as the man who had had an affair with her predecessor Kate, and she had begun to visit the families whose history she had absorbed from her seventeen files. Even so facing Miss Bateson made her feel a little nervous.

"A good deal of your work will be with children in foster care, of course. I know this is something you have not really done before but we are lucky to have Miss Penn, who is experienced and will, I am sure, help you. Have you been out with her yet?"

Miss Bateson was a thin woman in her fifties. She had smooth shiny skin like a nun, Bella thought, well scrubbed and faintly pink, and her hair had been tightly secured in a bun but was now descending in odd strands which floated round her face. She was wearing a brown suit partnered with a cream blouse buttoned to the neck. Clothes to make one anonymous, rather like Judy, Bella thought.

Together with the Chief Finance Officer and various people in secretarial and administrative positions, to whom Bella had been introduced, the Children's Officer occupied a suite of offices on the second floor of City Hall. Now sitting facing her Bella could not at first equate Miss Penn with Jennifer. No informality here. Then she nodded. "Yes, she is being very helpful and I am looking forward to extending my experience." Thinking as she spoke that the formality of the occasion was influencing her speech.

Miss Bateson nodded. "Good. And then Miss Naseby will be your supervisor so you will be surrounded by good experience." She looked out of the window, appearing to study the traffic. "Of course it is most unfortunate that you have had to take over Miss Menton's work. No doubt you will have heard about the way she left us. I expect tongues have wagged."

"Well, yes, I have heard."

"As I have already said, in this work we must be beyond reproach. It is of the greatest importance that people in our position observe a strict moral code. I hope you agree." She turned and looked at Bella. "I have been very distressed by this occurrence."

Bella nodded. Miss Bateson continued. "Of course, we all have problems but our training should help us understand the difficulties which some people face and as I repeatedly say, our behaviour must always set an example to those less fortunate with whom we deal. Now your experience as a widow will be, I am sure, invaluable to you in your work. You clearly know something about loss."

"Yes, I suppose I do," Bella replied, trying to connect her widowhood with being beyond reproach and then suddenly thinking that perhaps the loss of her husband was an important part of her CV.

Miss Bateson studied the traffic outside again as if unsure how to move from this sensitive subject to something more mundane, then she turned again to Bella with a bright smile.

"It's very nice to meet you, Mrs Wingfield. I'm sorry it has taken so long to arrange but of course we are delighted to have you and I do hope you are happy here. I am the legal guardian of all the children in our care and I like to know about them so I shall read the files and talk to you whenever I think necessary. There are going to be changes in the future now we have had the Seebohm Report and I have to say I am not very enthusiastic about it at present, but we all have to deal with our reluctance to change. Now is there anything you would like to ask me?"

Bella could not think of anything and after thanking Miss Bateson for seeing her, she walked back through the town to her own office where Harry immediately offered to make her some tea.

"Sit down and breathe deeply," he said. "And tell me if she talked about Kate."

"Yes, indirectly. She told me our behaviour must be beyond reproach."

"Of course she did and quite right too. Good old Miss Bateson, spreading the word. Did you agree with her?"

"I think I nodded."

"She probably thinks she must keep an eye on you – merry widow and all that."

"She seemed to think that it's an advantage that I've lost my husband."

"God! Did she say that? She's very deficient in social skills. When Tim was back – he was suspended for a month – she sent round a memo saying she was sure we were all very upset by recent events and she didn't need to remind us that child care officers have a duty to model good behaviour at all times for the benefit of our clients who often have weak moral values. She couldn't cope with the smudging of boundaries between us and them. Personally, I blame the weather. It was unreasonably warm and as Byron put it, 'What men call gallantry and the gods adultery, is much more common where the climate's sultry'. Of course, you missed the other memo which came before you arrived. She had had a complaint, she said, from the Chairwoman of the Juvenile Bench about the way men dressed for court without ties, wearing jeans, and with unbrushed, long hair, and that women frequently wore mini skirts or trousers. It showed no respect for the court, she said, and in future we should all be properly dressed. You don't need to worry though. Very respectable in a skirt and jacket."

Bella laughed. "I think I'd better confess. It's probably my middle-class background or my age, but this morning I thought I'd better wear a skirt for my interview."

"God, Bella! A conformist at heart. We must do something about that."

Bella began to sort through papers on her desk and looked at her diary, when Harry interrupted again.

"There was a call from Mrs Bickford for you. She needs you to go immediately. Lee has been arrested for shoplifting and Mary is suspended from school. She wants you to do something. You are a big hit. Much as she liked Kate she said she could tell you have more experience of Life."

"I'm not sure about that and I can't go today, it will have to be next week. She is very loyal to her children, isn't she? She told me Mary was being bullied at school and that her children were picked on all the time."

The Bickford file was the thickest Bella had, going back some six years. Mrs Bickford, whom Bella had met, was a large formidable woman with a very assertive manner and five children. Her eldest was in prison (taking the rap for someone else, his mother said), the second eldest was on probation (which won't do any good); her nineteen-year-old daughter was pregnant with her second child (Mrs Beckford herself had taken her to the family planning but that Dutch cap was obviously no good); Lenny, the one recently caught shoplifting, was second to last and Mary was the baby at fourteen (and always getting the blame for some other girl's bad behaviour).

"There is something in that," Harry said. "The police go there first and the school will tell you they have marked the whole family out as trouble since they were infants. They are expected to misbehave and so they do."

Bella knew she could not visit Mrs Beckford today. She had had a telephone call from Tracey Meredew's foster mother, Mrs Cummings, to say that Tracey wanted to go home for the weekend which was highly undesirable and not part of the agreement they had about home visits. Bella knew she should see Tracey's mother first but she said she would call as Mrs Cummings was very demanding. She thought she should talk to Judy about it, but Judy was out for the rest of the day, and so, rather unsure about what she would be able to do, she had agreed to call and see them. She told Harry Mrs Beckford would have to wait until Monday as she didn't want to be late that evening because her daughter was coming and bringing a friend for the weekend.

***

In fact, she was rather late and the visit had left her feeling uneasy and unsure, but she peeled potatoes and scraped carrots and pushed disquiet and anxiety away from her head in the effort to prepare a meal for Gemma and her friend before they arrived. But the session with Mrs Cummings and Tracey kept intruding. Tracey now fifteen, was subject to a Care Order made some twelve months earlier following referrals from the school where her attendance was very erratic and Kate's several visits to the family home where she usually found various men and boys lounging about, watching television and often drinking. Tracey's mother was part of the general disorder, and sometimes, Kate thought, the worse for drink, and although she was always telling Kate she was just about to throw everyone out and get Tracey to school, made no effort to do so; on one occasion, in fact, she thought it amusing that Tracey, sitting on the sofa with the arm of a young man wrapped round her shoulders, shouted at Kate to get the fuck out as she was not going to that bleeding school again. It was after this event that Kate had applied to court for a Care Order on the grounds that Tracey was in moral danger.

Mrs Cummings told Bella it was arranged that Tracey should visit her mother every Saturday afternoon from two to six but she was certain that Tracey had been to see her mother without permission during the week and as she was so often in late, Mrs Cummings thought sometimes she had been drinking. Tracey, she said, did not respond to any form of discipline and had now apparently told her mother she would be home for the weekend.

While Mrs Cummings spoke, Tracey, wearing a mini skirt, patterned tights and platform shoes, sat stony-faced staring at the wall, sighing loudly from time to time.

Bella had tried to mediate and to look at some of the positives. Tracey was now going to school regularly, she said, so there had been some progress. Tracey said it was so unfair. She was leaving school at the end of the term and was almost sixteen and her mother was expecting her. Mrs Cummings said that Tracey was very bad at coming in, was very untidy and did little to help in the house, and she had been told that overnight stays depended on some improvement in her general behaviour, which had not occurred. Tracey supposed that Mrs Cummings thought she should be middle-aged before she could go home and Mrs Cummings said there was no need to be rude. They went round and round and back and forth.

Bella knew she should have seen the mother before this conversation and she suggested they had a joint meeting. Mrs Cummings said that Kate had arranged joint meetings and they did no good at all. Bella said she would see Tracey's mother next week anyway and perhaps the best thing was to allow Tracey to go home this weekend and… well, be home by nine on Sunday? And see if Tracey could keep to these arrangements, to which Mrs Cummings said, "Well, if that is your decision, Mrs Wingfield, there is nothing more to say."

Bella kept thinking that Tracey should be given some contraceptive advice, but felt this would not go down very well with Mrs Cummings. She was not sure if one actually made these suggestions or not. Perhaps it would be best to talk to Tracey's mother about it but Tracey left the room with a triumphant smile after which Mrs Cummings said, "Her mother is a bad parent. No control at all and all manner of male visitors always at the house I believe, and if you don't mind me saying so, Mrs Wingfield, I don't think it's a good idea for Tracey to think you are on her side. It doesn't help girls like Tracey if the adults take different views."

Bella knew this was true, but she suggested to Mrs Cummings that it was probably better to let her go this time as she might take matters into her own hands.

Mrs Cummings reminded Bella that Tracey came into care because she was considered to be out of control, and the whole object of her living away from her mother was that she learned to observe some rules. Allowing her to make her own rules was exactly what they were not supposed to be doing. However it was her decision although perhaps Mrs Wingfield did not appreciate that the home was not exactly desirable. Men frequented the house and Tracey was known to be staying out very late with older boys.

Bella appreciated what Mrs Cummings was saying but suggested that these were difficult years. There is always a tension, she said, between the young feeling grown up and wanting to do their own thing, and parental fears for their safety. She would see the mother next week and see if they could manage to make a new set of arrangements. That would be better, wouldn't it, she said, than Tracey going off without permission today.

"Well, it's your decision." Bella heard the disapproving words again as she laid table in the dining room. Then she heard the front door open and Gemma and Jane came in scattering bags and coats and pressing a bunch of daffodils into Bella's hands. Suddenly everything was warm and satisfying and the anxiety gave way to the pleasure and the noise and confusion as Gemma rushed around the house, introducing Jane to each room and talking non-stop.

"The carpet is great. I couldn't have chosen a better colour myself and the sofa fits in, and dinner smells fantastic. Meat. I'm sure I can smell meat. We need meat, our haemoglobin is very low, we can't afford meat and we are both starving. We haven't eaten since two revolting sandwiches for lunch and one bar of chocolate between us, and while I remember, don't let me go back without looking at Daddy's law books. The library is impossible, one waits for ever for the books we need and he might have something…"

James' law books. Still in the box where they had been packed when she moved from Woodbridge. Yes of course, they might be useful again.

As they ate dinner she heard about the shower in the flat that didn't work, the awful bus service, the nine o'clock lectures which were so crowded one had to get there early to get a seat near the front, which was really the pits because it was so hard to get up in time, and Professor Tompkins who was so obscure, and the seminars and presentations and the Union where they debated fiercely about the Vietnam War – ("And you've heard that the US is now bombing Cambodia, haven't you?") They teased each other about Jason and Phil who seemed to be the new boyfriends and Bella asked about Tom.

"Oh, do you mind? Yesterday's news, Mum. He is so… well, he actually wore a suit to our seminar last week with black shoes and black silk socks. He is a complete prat. The rest of us, including Jeff, our tutor, were wearing jeans. Jeff had bare feet. Tom said he is defying convention and dressing as befits a barrister. A barrister! He said he's going to define himself as part of the legal system. Jeff said that was fine but what about defining himself as a student first."

This is what I have missed, Bella thought. There were always two or three girls coming in and out when Gemma was at school. There was always chatter and gossip and argument. She realised she felt a contentment that had been missing since Gemma went to college.

"Tell us about your job, Mrs Wingfield. Social Services sounds so interesting," said Jane.

Gemma interrupted. "And tell us about the office affairs. What is this man Tim like? Has he made a pass at you yet? Has anyone made a pass at you?"

"Certainly not," she said, laughing, but she tried to explain what it was like and told them briefly about the variety of work she had to do. Children in foster care for many different reasons: mother's illness or mental health, parents' death or desertion, parents' inability to cope with behaviour, non-school attendance.

"We do try to keep children at home, of course, that's when we try to help parents learn how to manage – techniques for coping with difficult behaviour, that sort of thing. And then there are the children who have committed offences and are subject to Care Orders, and then... then... all those cases where people come to the Children's Department with financial or housing problems. We all spend a lot of our time," she said, "haranguing the Housing Department, or trying to find ways of keeping people's gas and electricity supplies working. So many problems seem to be about money, or the lack of it.

"I really shouldn't gossip about cases. Confidentiality and all that, so you mustn't repeat anything. But some situations are difficult. I saw a girl who wanted to go home for the weekend which was against the rules we made when she came into care and the foster mother was very opposed to the idea. I felt the girl would probably go anyway and that it was really quite reasonable that she should be allowed to stay with her mother.

She is over fifteen and has only been in care some twelve months so the bonds are very strong. Of course I should have seen the mother first, but I hope to do so next week and perhaps then I can draw up a new contract between them all. But I wasn't very popular with the foster mother and, actually not very sure I did the right thing."

"Draw up a contract. Oh, my God! Don't mention contracts. I'm writing an essay on Contract and I can't bear the sound of the word at the moment. I have just been immersed in the Misrepresentation Act! Whatever you do, Mum, be careful of misrepresentation. Don't misrepresent fraudulently."

Contract. Conveyancing. Law of Tort. It was strange to realise these words were coming back into family conversation. Bella had always found it difficult to appreciate that law relating to land, mortgages and leases had so fascinated James and now they apparently attracted his daughter. She recalled challenging James. "I don't understand how a dyed-in-the-wool socialist like you wants to deal in property. I thought all property was theft." To which James had replied, 'Ah, but one must know one's enemy.'

"So what do you think could go wrong if she goes home for the weekend?" Jane asked.

"Well, she might mix with her mother's dodgy friends and stay out all night. When she came into care she was considered to be in moral danger!"

"Gosh! Just as well we haven't got any child care officers at college. Nearly everyone is in moral danger there."

"I think the Children's Department is in mortal fear of the teenagers in care getting pregnant. I get the feeling that the management thinks we should try to get them to eighteen at least. But she could get pregnant while she is fostered, couldn't she? But there are many other kinds of foster children. Most of the foster parents are fine, I think. The department depends on them. Better than putting children in children's homes, which is what they once did."

So they cleared the table and washed up, made coffee and finally settled in the sitting room which made Bella feel she was being re-attached to the world which had receded when Gemma went to college. It was rather disappointing when Gemma announced that they intended to go back to Woodbridge on Saturday to see old friends and look at the old house.

"I rang Myra and she and Sal will be there and they want us to go to lunch, and I thought you might like to come too. There must be plenty of people you could visit... but... but if you don't want to, I wondered if we could have the car... please?"

Bella had been back to Woodbridge twice since she had moved and each time it had been good to see friends but had left her with an ache, partly of regret and partly of anger. She wasn't sure of the cause. She had avoided driving past the house. She needed more time before looking at the place where she and James had lived. She had been so happy and so sad in that house. And she didn't want to go this weekend, and especially not with Gemma. Gemma had been upset when they sold the house and moved. Not that she had said very much. She knew Bella had to find a job somewhere and had been earnestly supportive and practical. "Of course you must take this job and we must move. After all I am at college – almost left home – and you have to get your life worked out properly." But Bella had found her in tears as she packed up the room she had slept in since she was born. They had, in fact, wept together as they took the posters off the wall and found boxes for the woolly toys and remembered and mused over the past, Bella filled with guilt at Gemma's hurt and Gemma wetly insisting that it was really quite alright and moving would be full of new opportunities for her mother and being sad was OK too.

Now she said she thought she would stay at home, and yes, they could take the car. She had been there recently and it would be very short notice for friends if she was to land on them. It would be like old times to be left without the car for the day, and she asked, "Will you be back for a meal in the evening?"

Nothing is ever quite as one planned, Bella thought when she saw Gemma and Jane off in the morning, reminding herself that Gemma's idea of a weekend at home was obviously going to be different from hers. And she had plenty to do, especially as she now had to walk to the shops. So the day was filled with the usual Saturday domestic tasks and after lunch she sat and wrote a report on her visit to Tracey, in spite of Jan's advice that she should never take work home. She had already found the writing helped her to keep her mind clear and she needed a clear head when having a session with Judy.

The day passed, and she was preparing an evening meal when they arrived back with news of old friends and a glimpse of the new residents in the old house, "who have painted the front door a rather bilious green and cut down the hedge in the front garden. We stopped the car and were staring when a woman came out and stared back, so we thought we had better move." Gemma laughed and then said quietly, "But it was rather sad and I wished I hadn't gone."

Later, on Sunday, when they unpacked the box in which James' law books had been stored there was a wave of nostalgia and a sudden shock as Bella found herself looking at a page of notes. Handwriting is like a personal message from the past, she thought, smoothing the surface. Almost like a voice. She felt sad as she slid the notes between the pages of a book and lifted out Obligations: The Law of Tort and Constitutional Law, while the girls picked out the books they wanted and repacked the box. But I have *now*, she thought, Gemma is here even if I have to accept that she will continue to come fleetingly and then go again.

***

When she saw Judy a few days later, she found herself facing a lecture on setting priorities, interlaced with kindly words about how well she was doing. Judy clearly needed to take a didactic tone, telling her she must manage her work according to the seriousness of the problems which arose even when this meant constantly changing her priorities but, apparently also anxious that she was being too hard, saying she understood how difficult it must be for Bella considering her lack of experience. She had all Bella's files on her desk and was opening them one by one.

She seemed to think it necessary to emphasise that they worked in a clear legal framework. As if I am not already aware of that, Bella thought. Then Judy went on about the 1963 Act which gave the Children's Department responsibility for helping people with financial difficulties and so preventing children coming into care. This work was also very important and must always have priority, she said. Bella wondered if Judy had forgotten she was trained and had already had some experience, but she nodded obligingly as Judy talked, although she felt her hackles rising when it came to Tracey, with whom, Judy said, Bella must persevere.

"She has a superficial and lazy parent as I recall, and is subject to a Care Order until she is eighteen. If she is beyond control we might consider taking her back to court and applying for an Approved School Order."

Bella protested that this was surely too drastic; Tracey was not committing any offences. But she stifled her inclination to talk about contraception. She felt this would not appeal to Judy, who immediately informed her that the law was there for a purpose and their task was to prevent Tracey becoming the same kind of woman as her mother, which Bella felt was a silly remark. Tracey was to some extent already like her mother, and

Bella wondered if Judy really believed if she stayed in care she would actually change into someone else.

Then it was Rita Hollis, who left her children alone. Bella had been to see her and found her outraged that the neighbours had made allegations, but Judy said this was very important, and must have priority. She noted that Kate had asked the neighbours to ring the police if it happened again, but Bella must visit regularly.

They discussed the reviews, Judy again saying that the fact they were overdue was not Bella's fault, but they must, of course, have priority, and, she said, "You must see the bedrooms." She knew it could be embarrassing and that child care officers were reluctant to insist, but it was important, and Miss Bateson was very particular about this. One could gauge so much from bedrooms. They should be clean and tidy, but one should look to see if they were really used. Toys, books, the foster parents were mostly marvellous, but one never knew... She was sure Bella understood. Bella nodded, thinking of the posters on the walls, the knickers and tissues on the floor, the general chaos of Gemma's room. Yes, she understood.

As Judy worked through the files, Bella understood these were not the last ones needing priority treatment. There were those with housing problems facing possible eviction, Margaret Wright with six children about to have her electricity cut off. Two cases referred by Education about children who were often absent from school, and appeared neglected, smelly and disruptive when they did attend, and of course the Bickford family, "who are a department cross we have to bear, I'm afraid," said Judy. "So much work and such poor results."

As Judy closed the last file, Bella thought that the only case which did not require immediate attention was Mary Jenkins, already at the end of Bella's list. This was a girl, subject to a Care Order, who was mentally handicapped and was at a special school in Dorset. Bella had noted she needed to be collected from school at the end of term and then taken back at the beginning of the next term in a clean school uniform and, Bella read, decent and clean new shoes, something her mother found difficult to provide and which were usually purchased by the Children's Department.

Back in her room she put the files on her desk and sat down feeling her brain had become paralysed. She wanted to leave the building and walk in the fresh air. She could hear Marian's typewriter, but otherwise it was quiet. She walked to the window, looking out on the tree isolated amidst the cars then sat down and began to list her cases in terms of priority. Overdue reviews first, telephone foster parents... but not now... this afternoon. Then she noticed a memo on her desk. Mrs Bickford wanted to see her about Mary. Bella had arranged a meeting with Mary's headmaster for next Tuesday, so there was no point in seeing Mrs B today who always had a long list of problems which she was still discussing as one got into one's car. She looked at her watch – twelve-forty. She had no sandwiches and was hungry. I will need to go out for lunch, she thought... but perhaps I had better ring the electricity board about Margaret Jennings' electricity to see if there is a way she can be reconnected... but first I should write to Mrs Bickford or she will ring again. She put her writing pad on top of the files and then looked for the Bickford file for the address. Her desk was a chaotic heap of papers and files. She moved things about at random, achieving nothing. I need a break, she thought. I can't think straight... I want to give all these cases to a senior as I did at Woodbridge.

The need to leave the office had become compelling. She collected her coat from the hook on the wall, picked up her handbag and walked out of the room, down the stairs and out of the front door. No one saw her go and she did not mark herself out at Reception.

She walked towards the centre of the town, past the Victorian mansions converted into offices; past the rectangles of brick and concrete occasionally inserted between them "in the spaces left by the bombs we had during the war," someone had told her; past the shop on the corner which seemed to have been left over from another time, and eventually past City Hall and through Memorial Square, named apparently to commemorate the First World War with the statue of George V in the centre, the sight of which irritated her; she felt isolated from the town and desperately lonely. She came eventually to the main shopping street where she began looking into windows but saw only her own reflection in the glass until she came to a window through which she saw people sitting at tables, which was familiar. She and Gemma had been here in the past. She went inside and ordered coffee and beans on toast.

As she waited for her food the feeling of panic began to subside and looking round she told herself that she must begin to feel she really lived here, remembering how she and her daughter had talked about the excitement of getting to know somewhere new. I just need more time, she thought, and when the coffee arrived her mind began to clear. There was no point in being overwhelmed. She had to cope. There was no alternative. And by herself. A wave of loneliness surged up and could have brought tears if she had not been in so public a place. She knew crying would not help and as she drank her coffee and forced herself to eat the baked beans she thought of Sim, her supervisor at Woodbridge, saying: 'You can only work through every unforgiving minute and the fact that there are not enough minutes is not your fault. Just plan your day, don't panic and when you have done as much as you can, go home and do something else'.

Planning. It always helps to write a list. She would go back and finish the one she had started.

"I thought I saw you here, can I join you?" Bella looked up and saw Tim Moore smiling at her. "I saw you through the window," he said.

For a moment Bella felt found out truanting, but she smiled and said, "Oh, hello. Yes, do sit down." She was also thinking of being found out with the man with the reputation.

"I'm running away," she said. "I needed to get out for a bit. I should really be working as I'm very busy and running away won't help."

"Oh, but it will. Running away is very important. I do it often." They both smiled and then Tim asked, "So tell me, why do you do this job?"

People always want to know, Bella thought. We all want to know why we do it and it is never easy to give a clear answer.

"Well I do it now because I need to earn my living and this is the only qualification I have. Why did I qualify in the first place? Harder to say now. I was full of hopes for a brave new world after the war and managed to get to Liverpool on the new Child Care Course. I think I believed – perhaps still believe – that social conditions and class prevented a lot of people from coping properly with life and there was a need for a service that would understand how hard it was to bring up children properly. I was very political in those days... but... but then I think I began to realise that people were not just the result of social conditions that could be engineered."

"The dilemma of the Marxists which they never really understood," Tim said.

"I suppose so. I think I began to be interested in personal psychology and then my own psychology, or was it biology, interfered with the course. I got pregnant and I didn't finish. Women have babies and take them to college now, but then somehow getting pregnant put you in an entirely new category and the ethics of the course were very much about children being looked after by their mothers, so I stayed at home."

"But you qualified eventually?"

"Not until after James died. Gemma my daughter was over seventeen and I went to Liverpool and did a Letter of Recognition for a year. That was about four years ago. I worked for a bit at Woodbridge, where we lived then, but that was only a temporary job as duty officer, and there was nothing there when that contract ended so I had to look round and finally came here."

"So what happened. How did James die?"

"He had a heart attack. Actually he had two and didn't recover from the second one. He was thirty-five."

"God! I'm sorry. That was too young."

"Thank you. Yes, it was."

They sat silently for a few minutes and then Tim asked if the work was measuring up to her expectations.

"Well, yes. Or rather, no. I mean I do enjoy it, but I guess it's different from the dreams I had at college. For a start there is so much. But that's enough of me. Why do you do it?"

"Not for the lofty reasons you do. I did a BA and the bits of sociology were interesting but I had a mate who was doing child care who was of the opinion that this was the new career for men because it was filled with women who were all following their vocation and were without greed or ambition. He reckoned a man could get on, and I wanted to get on! I came here as an unqualified worker and they seconded me for training after two years. I think another year and I shall look for a senior's post."

"The Department is certainly run by women. I believe there is a senior man in City Hall but I haven't come across any others."

"That is sadly true but things will change. When we have Seebohm and bigger departments we shall have a better career structure. Of course, I shall have to live down my bad reputation first. I didn't really count on that." He paused and looked at Bella with a slight smile. "I suppose you know all about that?"

"Well, people do talk and I know there was rather a scandal, but I have mixed feelings because if Kate hadn't left I wouldn't have had her job."

"Wonderful. We did some good." For a few moments neither of them spoke and then he said, "Actually it was all a bit crazy and probably just as well we were caught. It wasn't going anywhere, not for me, and it had begun to leak out, but at the time we both felt driven. Do you know what I mean? And then it was over. As soon as we were caught my priorities reasserted themselves. All I could think of was how Nancy would feel if she knew and how we would live if I lost my job. Money, you know. It is important."

"I didn't know you were married."

"Oh, yes, 'fraid so. We've had a bad time. I was sure Nancy would find out and so in the end I confessed. I think we shall make it, but she's hurt and sad and so of course is Kate, who said she couldn't bear to come back and work in the same building as me, so sent in her resignation. A total disaster really… and yet… well, I wouldn't have missed the good bits. Are you shocked?"

Bella didn't think she was. She thought she was supposed to be impressed but she said nothing. She thought he was presenting his story like a trophy. She said she must be going back now. She felt better. He had not drunk his coffee so she could go alone. Talking had helped, but it always did she mused, as she walked back to the office.

***

49 Lovelace Avenue
Rensham

26th October 1969

Dearest Gemma,

I tried to ring over the weekend but no one answered the phone so I guess you were all out enjoying yourselves. I am so looking forward to the hols – only two months now and I have taken 5 days leave after Christmas. I can't believe it is already 9 months since we came here and 8 months since I started this job, although sometimes I feel I have worked here forever. The work never stops coming and I think they have stopped protecting me.

Our holiday was great. I'm so glad Jane came with us. She is such a pleasant person, and such fun to be with. I don't know about you, but already I could do with lying on the beach again soaking up the sun, but I have cheered myself by making decisions about Christmas and booking some leave. Gran and Grandad want to come and I just hope it won't be too boring for you in a strange town with only your mother and grandparents for company!

I've just had a letter from Martha – Liz's daughter, remember. She will be doing teaching practice at Wickham, which is about 30 miles north of here, and she wonders if she could come here for half term in February, as apparently Liz and Matthew are going to Italy and she seems to anticipate being totally exhausted after half a term of ten-year-olds. I have said this will be OK although I shall have to work and leave her alone a good deal – but we have always got on well and she knows I will listen and not criticise like her mother always does. One thing I shall have to do is clear up the spare bedroom before she comes, so she can get to the bed, so that is probably a good thing.

Work is still pretty frantic most of the time, although I think I am getting used to it. There always seems to be some disaster to prevent, and I am coming to dread hearing that someone's electricity is about to be cut off just as I decide to close the case! But I am about to place a baby for adoption (when it is born). The prospective adopters are very pleasant, and holding their breath and although I still have mixed feelings about adoption, it is probably for the best. The mother is only 15, but I am still slightly apprehensive. It's one thing to think you want the baby you are expecting to be adopted, especially when your mother keeps telling you this is the right thing to do, but quite another to give up a baby you have just delivered. Judy says she thinks I am more concerned for the young mother than for the baby and I must think hard about this, but thinking hard doesn't really help.

My social life is improving. Maggie and Brian (next door) have had me to dinner and introduced me to a lady called Ellen who lives down the road. A sprightly sixty-year-old, who rides a bicycle and helps with reading at the local primary school. And I have been to Jan's a couple of times and she is coming here next week.

Evelyn (at work – the Bible group one) keeps saying I must visit them, but so far has not actually invited me. I think she and her husband are always very busy because he runs a small Barnado's children's home. For the rest I spend what free time I have in the garden, which is gradually coming under control. I have bought three large pots in which I intend to plant bulbs for the spring. I thought they would look good on the patio.

Must close now darling. Too tired to write any more. Take care of yourself.

Much love

Chapter Two

1970

Thinking about it afterwards, Bella knew that it could have been the crisis with Rita Hollis, who had a tendency to leave her young children alone in the evenings, that began the process which so altered Martha's life. It never occurred to her at the time that the incident with Rita had had such dramatic significance. That Martha was disenchanted with teaching was obvious. As soon as she arrived at the beginning of the half term holiday looking pale and tired, she told Bella that she was no good at teaching. She could not inspire interest, she could not keep order and she found it quite difficult to keep her temper. Bella let her talk and tried to find some positive things to say about the way one always had black spots on courses and how she herself remembered considering working for Marks and Spencer's in the middle of hers. But they cooked together and had a long walk into the countryside which bordered the town to the south and where Bella had already discovered Middleton Hill. It rose unexpectedly from the flat fields and farmland and amid the trees which grew thickly almost to the top one could lose sight and sound of human habitation within minutes of starting to climb.

Out of breath they collapsed to the ground and remembered other walks and expeditions when Martha and Gemma were young, and then thought how middle-class those childhoods had been and how impoverished by contrast were the families with whom each was involved at work, who didn't, or perhaps couldn't, go for country walks and climb hills.

"Perhaps I could suggest some kind of outing for my ghastly ten year olds," Martha suddenly suggested. "We would need a mini bus or something. Of course it's all about money. There usually isn't any. When I think of the cost of the Americans going to the moon and what could be done with that sort of money that would improve things in the world…"

"It was rather amazing though, wasn't it?" Bella said. "I set the alarm and got up and couldn't really grasp what was happening. Did you see it?"

"Well, yes, of course it was amazing. We watched it at college, but it did seem a dreadful waste of money."

"I think most people at work thought that as well, but one couldn't not be excited. Going to the moon. It seemed quite incredible."

"Sam wrote to me in quite a fury about it. You knew he went to India. Much to mother's disapproval of course. She was glad he left the commune where he was living with Marina – did you know about her? – she's a Hungarian girl he met in London, and they were living together – but I think he hopes she will join him. He is working on an ashram. Mother and Dad are always in despair about Sam, but I rather envy him. He has got away! Heaven knows what he will end up doing but when he wrote to me he said it would do the Americans good to see something of the poverty in India and find some of the inner peace he had found through meditation. I showed the letter to the parents and they said it was a pity he didn't try to save the world by getting some qualifications and a proper job."

At home later, Martha was more relaxed and insisted on getting the evening meal while Bella sat down, but as they began to eat the telephone rang.

Miss Bateson was crisply sorry to disturb Bella but she had no option. The police had been on to her. Rita Hollis's children were at home alone and the police wanted the Children's Department to take over. They were in the process of getting a Place of Safety Order and felt they should now take the children into care. Miss Bateson said she had tried to contract Miss Naseby, but she was out and as she had remembered this was Bella's case, she was afraid she must ask Bella to deal with it. Bella said she had a visitor but this simply produced another apology and the request – given in the tone of an instruction – that Bella would have to sort things out. She assumed Bella would know how to get details of available foster parents – there was a record in the office and she expected Bella would know how to use it.

Bella did know about the record in the office but protested that taking three children into care, the youngest only about two, would be difficult as she was alone. Miss Bateson assured her that she would not be alone. The police were there and would act as escort when she removed the children, and if she could get hold of Miss Naseby she would send her down at once.

"But can she really do this?" Martha wanted to know. "I mean, supposing you were out?"

"If I wasn't in, I wouldn't be able to do it," Bella replied. "She would ring someone else I suppose. I know the others have to go out sometimes. I suppose it's my turn. The trouble is the neighbours have been told to ring the police if it happens because it has happened before."

She felt angry and apprehensive as she got ready. Martha wanted to go with her and she nearly gave in to this request, but issues about confidentiality and qualifications crossed her mind. She was sure this kind of thing was not allowed. She nearly rang Jan, but decided this would not be fair so she had to apologise to Martha for leaving her alone and set off for the office.

It was a long evening. At the office she found the foster parents' list and began ringing people up, but she couldn't find anyone who could take all three children, Mrs Belshaw could take two, and Mrs Joseph could take one. It seemed most unsatisfactory but in the end she accepted these offers, wondering how she would split the children up.

She also wondered what she would do if the mother returned while she was there. The police had taken a Place of Safety Order but if the mother returned the children would be alright so perhaps it could be cancelled. If she didn't come home the police would have to notify her about calling them in and tell her where the children were. And if they had to be moved what would be the best way? The eldest and the youngest together? The two youngest together? Perhaps that would be best. The oldest girl, about seven years old, Bella thought, would be best on her own.

She saw the police car outside the house as she drove up. Several people were standing in the garden next door talking. There were lights upstairs in several neighbouring houses with heads poking through the open windows. All waiting for the drama of seeing three small children taken away. Bella thought, God! What a bloody job this is.

A WPC opened the door and said she wondered if a Child Care Officer was ever coming. She had been there already over an hour. As she led the way into the living room she said they were all ready to go and she had got some of their things together.

Michelle, the oldest, was cuddling five-year-old Trudy on the sofa and shouted out that there was no use Bella coming in as they weren't going anywhere. They were waiting for their Mum and she would tell her Mum that the policewoman had gone through their things which were private and none of her business. The youngest, Darren, was on the floor beside a young policeman, and they were playing with some cars. He looked at Bella and said, "Fuck off you," and then turned back to his game.

The WPC stayed standing, clearly expecting that they were all about to move, but Bella managed to ignore her and sat beside Michelle and Trudy on the sofa attempting to slow down events and explain as carefully as she could that it was better to go to a foster home than be left alone. She said she could see Michelle was being very grown up and responsible looking after Trudy and she hoped she would help the little ones to get ready to come with her. She felt very unsure about being too reassuring but nevertheless did say it would only be for a short while because Mummy would want them back at home.

Michelle burst into tears and Trudy joined in the weeping as Bella spoke, and for a few minutes Bella felt she was losing all control and purpose. She kept visualising taking the children out of the house by force, but watching Darren play and relate to the policeman, she decided that he seemed to be able to relate well to other people and perhaps would not be too upset to be separated from his sisters. She joined him on the floor and talked about going to stay with some nice people on his own without the others. His reaction was surprising. He got up from the floor and went across to Michelle and hit her leg saying, "She horrid. She bossy," before returning to his game.

"I think we should get going now. Delaying matters will only mean they get more upset. Now I expect we will go in your car, but I shall come along." The WPC was getting impatient. Bella was hoping the mother would come back, appalled at the prospect of taking the children against their will. And yet they shouldn't be left alone. But if the mother returned they could be left with her, couldn't they? Her indecision confused her. I should know what to do, she thought I feel helpless.

Later, when she got home, she told Martha the mother had returned and the children were not moved, and she was so glad because she would have had to separate them. Martha asked a lot of questions and Bella answered as best she could without giving many details. She was very tired and glossed over the pain the event had caused. She wanted to talk but not to this over curious young woman who she thought could be upset and probably ought not to be involved. The matter was, after all, confidential and the kind of conversation Bella needed was with colleagues from whom she could get both advice and comfort. She made hot chocolate and forced herself to be cheerful, but later, in bed, she went through the evening remembering how she had decided to take the two girls to Mrs Belshaw and Darren to Mrs Joseph. Explaining this to Michelle caused tears again and a protest that Darren couldn't go anywhere by himself and no one was going to separate them. Bella remembered that the WPC had pulled her to one side, and speaking quite softly said she should tell them they were all going together and then separate them when they got to the foster homes. Bella knew she was aware of Bella's inexperience and was trying to be helpful, but still felt this was quite inappropriate. She had been shocked and remembered choking back her anger and saying nothing. She had gone back to the sofa and tried to talk to the girls about their favourite toys. She knew she had been playing for time and could feel the impatience of the WPC who walked about the room.

Michelle had told her that Darren always took his rabbit to bed and that if he had to go anywhere, he must have his rabbit. Bella looked around for this, but Trudy said it was upstairs on his bed which interrupted Darren's game. He stood up and began to cry, wanting his mother and his rabbit.

Bella wondered what she would have done if the mother had not then returned. The commotion at the door and the sudden appearance of Rita, confused and frightened, brought a wave of relief, and although the WPC immediately threatened Rita with losing her children and for a few moments Bella had wondered if they were still going to move them, she had not opposed Bella, throwing caution to the wind and saying that they were not going to move them this time, but if there was ever another occasion...

Before the police left, the WPC said the children would most certainly be moved if it ever happened again and she would have to consult her chief about the present situation, but since Mrs Wingfield was happy to let them stay tonight, they could stay.

She had to have the last word, Bella thought, and clearly disapproved of me.

***

The following morning Judy called a meeting in her office with everyone in Area 1, except Evelyn, who was out for the day. They must work out a clear strategy for this case, she had said, for it was bound to crop up again. She said she was very doubtful about leaving the children with Rita. She wondered if they should take the matter to court and ask for a Supervision Order. Miss Bateson had been talking to her about the case and although she said Bella had done well under the circumstances, she had spoken to the police and they were concerned. They had already visited Rita that morning and warned her, Miss Bateson said, and she agreed with them that they would have the children in care eventually. The mother was most unsatisfactory. Judy made it clear she also agreed with this prediction.

Bella was relieved that there was no argument about the children staying at home and although she did not express an opinion about going to court for a Supervision Order, she was, she realised, glad it was decided not to do so at this stage. She felt very ambivalent about things. She knew she did not want the children to come into care. Rita had been very shocked. Angry at first, she had calmed down and sat crying with all the children before Bella left, and there seemed such real affection between them all.

"But do you really think the children would be better off in two different foster homes, Judy?" Jan asked.

"But she has been warned before and still goes out. I can see us removing them eventually, and one could say the sooner the better," Jennifer countered.

"She clearly loves them," Bella answered. "She was devastated at the thought of them being taken away and they clung to her and cried and cried when she came in."

"But one has to think about the future," Jennifer continued. "This woman wouldn't keep leaving them alone if she really cared. What is the youngest? Not yet three, and the oldest eight. Rita's social life obviously takes priority when she wants it to."

"Aren't we imposing our middle-class values on the situation?" Harry suggested. "Working-class children learn to look after each other and they survive."

"I think we should think about our responsibility to improve the quality of people's lives, Harry," Judy replied. "We can't continue to accept that because things have always been done a certain way that it has to be right, surely."

"I don't think we should support the idea of children going back down the mines,' Harry said. "But do you really think it improves the quality of their lives to be taken away from the mother they love and fostered in two separate foster homes. Come on, Judy!"

"Yes, I do, Harry. Not always of course, but given the kind of mother we have here – and don't forget she has been doing this for months – I think the quality of the children's lives could be improved, although I agree they should eventually be together. And next time, if there is a next time, and I am sure there will be, we will have to take the matter to the court."

"We took the Brampton family in when their mother died, remember. Five children, two different foster homes and the oldest in a children's home. And they are still there, although I know Jennifer keeps them all in touch – you took them all out for the afternoon last Saturday, didn't you, Jennifer?"

"Well, yes, I did. The oldest girl is always so sad about not being with her sibs. We must keep them in touch, but where will we find a foster home that will take five? I think it would be best if they were all together in a children's home. I was going to ask you Judy whether we shouldn't apply to National Children's Homes, or Barnado's."

"Yes, I think that might be a good idea. I did hope that some of the relatives might help, but no one has offered. The trouble with going to one of the big institutions is that they may finish up too far away for their Dad and other relations to visit. We must talk about it and I will have a word with Miss Bateson, but you will be glad Bella didn't have to use Mrs Joseph for one of Rita's children, because we have earmarked her for Timmy Watford when his mother is confined."

Judy turned to Bella, "So do you agree, Bella? We leave them for now and you continue to visit very regularly – perhaps find out where it is she goes and what arrangement she might make for someone to sit in – we must be practical – but if there is another incident like last night, we must remove the children and take the matter to court."

Bella nodded. "Yes, although I believe Kate did try to get her to find a sitter... yes. I see that we must do something although I do believe she has had a very bad fright... yes... I think that is the best plan."

As the meeting ended and Jennifer, Harry and Jan left the room, Judy told Bella that she understood how difficult it was to face taking children into care and she thought, perhaps, it was the first time Bella had faced the possibility. Bella said it was, and she had found it very difficult. She said she knew it would greatly upset the children and wondered if in fact causing them distress was worse than leaving them at home. But Judy reminded her that there could have been an accident to any of them, and Darren was particularly at risk. "We are responsible for the welfare of children, Bella. That is our job and we have to think of the whole situation. Rita simply should not leave her children alone and we have a duty to safeguard their welfare." She smiled, and said Bella had done very well and it was a nasty case to deal with. She was sorry she was not available to help her.

As she left the room Marian called her and said Rita Hollis had arrived. Judy encouraged her to be firm and authoritive, offering to join her if she would like this. Bella thought she could cope. Halfway down the stairs she remembered she had meant to ask Judy for money from the Section 1 fund which was available to prevent children coming into care or before the courts. She had just taken on Anne Meadows, whose gas was cut off and who had four children and a cooking problem. Bella had obtained a camping stove (using Section 1 money) and had now received a message that it was not working properly. Bella felt she must provide some food and then negotiate with the Gas Board about reconnection and had promised to call after lunch. Before, she remembered, she saw a couple who had applied to be foster parents. She knew this was a priority as well, especially after the conversation they had just had.

At the door of the interview room she paused for a moment and pushed Anne Meadows and the foster parent application from her mind. Now it was Rita.

Chapter Three

1972

Bella adjusted the date on her desk calendar. March 17th. She suddenly recalled the red ring around March 3rd in 1969. My God! she thought, I've been here three years – and I've survived.

The room was large but crowded with desks. Last October they had at last stopped Waiting for Seebohm. The changes took place. They were now the Social Services Department and she was a social worker. A generic social worker at that. No longer concerned only with children, her workload could eventually include the mentally ill, the elderly, the disabled and whatever else came through the door. Or so it seemed. At present she was still doing much the same work as she had before. The new Director had said they would not rush people into new areas. The idea was for skills to rub off. Get to know each other, learn to cope with new situations.

Nothing much has rubbed off yet, she thought, but we are getting to know each other, and we have had a lot of team meetings which mostly expressed everyone's anxiety.

They had moved from the detached house and were now in teams which she was not sure she really liked. It was good having other people around to talk to but in her little room – the dressing room – she had had quietness and privacy. She was not sure how she would do any work in a public arena – but she did have her own phone. Jennifer, whose desk was nearest to hers, also had a phone, whereas Jan and Evelyn had two desks pushed together and had to share one.

On the other side of the room Adrian, from the community mental health department, had his own desk and a phone, but next to him two more desks were pushed together for Don, originally the welfare officer for Renshaw, who shared a phone with Meg, the team's new social work assistant. The newly qualified worker, Charlotte, had a desk squashed into the far corner, also with a phone.

The room was housed in a building which had originally held workers in the Health Department and now housed all the members of the Social Services Department. The new Director, Mr Mervyn Clarke, who had previously been Chief Welfare Officer at Stanthrope, was upstairs. He was very self-effacing about himself, telling staff he knew absolutely nothing about children or the mentally ill – which everyone thought very encouraging. His deputy, Miss Agatha Simpson, was in a room next to his. Like Adrian, she had also come from the Mental Health Department. Also upstairs, were the Administrative Officer, Mr Geoffrey Owen – previously from the Children's Department, whom Bella already knew, the Finance Officer, Mr Billington, who apparently came from the Planning Department in City Hall and whose first name was not encouraged, and Mrs Henderson, who had been with the Children's Department and was also fussy about first names. There was also a Residential Services Officer ('call me Joe') who had previously managed an old people's home and someone known as a Development Officer called Ben Dixon whose purpose and previous life was still a mystery. Judith Naseby, with the new title of Principal Child Care Officer, was upstairs as well. There were other rooms on the first floor which were rumoured to be waiting for occupation by the Home Help Service. They were still in their old premises at the back of City Hall and it was said they did not want to move, although rooms were waiting for them.

Marian, now called Team Clerk, shared a small room on the ground floor with a woman called Betty, who was Team Clerk to the Area 2 team who were housed in another large room on the other side of the Reception and Waiting Room area. There were also three interview rooms opposite Reception and clients' and staff toilets nearby. Rachael Henley, Area 1's new Team Leader had a small room next to the toilets which she shared with Betty Hudson, who was Team Leader for Area 2.

There was some uneasiness when they assembled in their new team room. They were wary of each other, each very concerned with their own work and reluctant to admit they had any interest in the work of others. Bella had detected a little atmosphere between ex-Children's Department workers and those from Mental Health – each apt to imply their work and training was superior to the other, although there seemed to be a general agreement that both were far superior to the ex-Welfare worker, Don, who was, nevertheless, considered a delightful, if elderly, man who constantly reminded everyone that he knew very little.

Rachael told them they must set about team building and had suggested that at first they pair up occasionally taking each other out on joint visits. This was working rather slowly. Bella had been out with Don to visit a man applying to go into residential care and had watched him fill in a financial statement and then put his name on the Waiting List – kept in a special brown file which noted the date of completion or the date of death – whichever comes earliest, Don said. It didn't seem very exacting although Don had attempted to find out if there were any relatives who could help or any services that could be supplied that might tide him over for the present. Don said he visited all applicants who were waiting about every three months to see if anything had changed. "Well, sometimes they become incontinent or senile, and our homes can't cope with those things."

"What happens if they are incontinent or whatever?" Bella asked.

"Oh it's a medical problem then. Hospital usually, but not us. Get in touch with the GP. But if they are still OK and a place comes up in a home, I usually take them for a visit and then arrange a date for them to go in. I'll take you to one of the homes so you can meet the Matron and see what they are like."

But today Bella was on duty. She had hoped she would not have to see anyone as she had records to write up and lists to make. But she had just begun to sort out her files, when Meg brought her a cup of coffee and the telephone rang to say a lady was waiting in Reception who wouldn't give her name and said she just wanted to see a policeman.

As Bella opened the door of the interview room, the elderly woman who was seated inside stood up hurriedly clutching a brown carrier bag to her chest. She was wearing a plain grey cloth coat and a grey hat which sported a large red bow on the side. Her face was lined and agitated. She frowned at Bella saying, "Are you the police? I've been waiting here for hours. It's disgraceful."

Bella smiled and explained she was a social worker and this was the Social Services Department, and asked what she could do to help.

"I don't know why you are here," the woman said crossly. "They are never here if you want them. They won't have the man who took it. I can't keep wasting my time. I have to get his tea... kippers, he likes kippers."

"Perhaps you could tell me your name first," Bella suggested, "then we can see how I might help. You sound as if you've lost something."

"Names, names. They always want names. That's how they find out who you are." She got up and then sat down again, both hands still clutching the bag.

"Well, I would like to know what I should call you. My name is Bella. Bella Wingfield."

"Bella, Bella. Is that short for belladonna? That's a poison."

"No, not belladonna. My real name is Isobel, but I've always been called Bella. I think my mother started it." She smiled encouragingly. "So what shall I call you?"

"They do. Mothers do that. Call you something different from your real name. My mother called me Edie. Edie. Always did. But Jimmy didn't like that. He always called me Dee."

"So your first name is Edith, I expect. What's your surname?"

"Like I told you before, Curtis. Curtis. Write it down so you remember. That's what you people do, isn't it? Write down our names."

"So, Mrs Curtis. What can I do to help? Did you say you had lost something?"

"No, I haven't lost it. It has been taken. They have taken it as they did before."

"What has been taken?"

"The pension book. The pension book. It's all been written down at the police station. Can't you look it up? Not that you'll find it now it has been washed away in the stream."

"So you think your book has been stolen and you have reported it to the police?" Bella felt her grasp on reality beginning to slip.

"It won't be found. That stream takes it right inside the castle walls. We'll never get it back now, but I can't stay here all day talking." She got up from her chair and moved to the door and resisting Bella's attempt to detain her, she left the room with Bella following. As she crossed the reception area, Adrian, tall with shoulder length black hair, wearing blue jeans and a black sweater came towards her, smiling in recognition.

"Edie. It is Edie, isn't it? How are you?"

But Edie glared at him. "I don't know you. Never saw you before and I'm not stopping here." As she spoke she dodged past him and made for the door.

"Adrian, you know her!"

"Yes. I know Edie. She's inclined to be very confused and confusing. Did you have difficulty with her?"

"She had a story about losing her pension book. It's been washed away and she thought I was the police."

"That's Edie. It is usually her pension book, although I remember once it was her bus pass. People steal things from her!"

"But she is alright? I mean, she sounded quite mad."

"She copes very well on the whole. Annoys the neighbours. They call the police and the police used to call the Mental Health Department and I used to go and see her. But by the time I arrived she'd usually forgotten what she'd lost."

"I felt confused," Bella said, laughing. "I'm not used to mental illness. But is she alright? I mean, can she look after herself? And what is actually wrong with her?"

"I don't think I can give you a definite answer to that. Probably the onset of dementia, it takes various forms. Apparently she was perfectly OK until her husband died. I think she's very lonely. No children and as far as I know, no relatives around."

"Well, I'm glad to know there is nothing dramatic to do. Thank you."

Adrian smiled. "You must come out with me. We are supposed to be teaching each other, aren't we? What did the boss say – 'now we are all together we shall proceed by the process of skills rubbing off'. I could do with some child care rubbing off on me for that matter. Perhaps we should set up our own training programme!"

"Well, yes. Sounds a good idea." Bella walked with Adrian back to the team room where her telephone was ringing and

Reception was waiting to tell her that the Housing Department wanted her to ring about Maureen Banford who was now in her new house but again accumulating rent arrears. Bella cursed under her breath. Now I shall have to start collecting money off her every week – again. God! she thought. How can I get this woman to pay her own rent? Perhaps I shouldn't. Perhaps I should let her be evicted with all her children. But Jan interrupted this fantasy reminding her that they were all going to the pub to celebrate her birthday after work and Bella remembered she had no cash and had meant to go to the bank the day before and now she couldn't get out as she was on duty. Perhaps the garage would cash a cheque. She lifted the phone and called Housing.

***

They had pushed two tables together in a corner of the lounge bar and were sitting squashed up around the glasses of beer, lager, lemonade and wine in a haze of smoke, eating crisps and nuts and talking.

"Hopefully when we become an adoption agency that will spell the end of the Diocesan Council preying on unmarried mothers for their babies." Jan was talking and Bella knew she had a thing about the Diocesan Council.

"Is that what they do? Prey on unmarried mothers?" Adrian asked.

"Oh, that's nonsense Jan, they have been doing a very good job for years," Jennifer protested.

"They have a great hunger for babies. I know that. I had a girl come in a few months ago who was pregnant and confused about what she should do and we went through the options. She'd been to the Diocesan Council but didn't seem too keen to go back to them. She seemed to think living at home was going to be impossible, and we talked about how she might cope in St

Margaret's House where they would help her manage the baby. I took her there for a visit which went very well, but when I went to visit her in hospital after the baby was born there was Miss Robeto-Dobson from the Diocesan Council, sitting by the bed chatting away about the nice adoptive parents she had found. Molly – that's the girl's name – had, as I said, gone to the Diocesan Council before coming to us. Girls so often don't know what to do and she seemed very pleased to see me and rather confused by Miss Whatshername Dobson. She immediately said she didn't know what to do and what did I think?"

"And don't you think the baby might be better off in a good home instead of being brought up by a seventeen-year-old girl who has fallen out with her family?"

"No, I don't. At least I don't know. But I do know that seventeen-year-old girls can make good mothers and they should be allowed to make free decisions and not pressurised to give their babies up. It doesn't end there for either mother or baby and can be very disturbing for both of them in later life."

"So who won?" Adrian asked.

"Well, in a way, I did, but not because of anything I said. While I was there Molly's mother arrived and insisted she take Molly and the baby home. She was so kind and loving and Molly was overwhelmed. It may not last, I suppose, but babies can help to mend the breaks in relationships and... well, it just seems right that the baby will be with its real family."

Bella noticed that Jennifer shook her head and turned away but said nothing more.

"All this child care is rather daunting. How do you feel, Don, coming into this lot? There were only three of us in Mental Health and we hardly ever saw a child." Adrian spoke to the grey-haired man in spotless white shirt and green tie, sports jacket and grey flannels, who had the scrubbed neat look that Bella associated with her father.

"Three of you! There was only me and Jim Bazely in the Welfare Department, and I don't think we ever talked about children. Not the young kind anyway. The only ones I saw were middle-aged and trying to find a place for their aged parents instead of looking after them themselves – the 'something must be done with mother brigade'. Can't see myself becoming a child care person now."

"No fear of that, Don. No Child Care officers here. We are all social workers now. You heard the Director today… 'We have an exciting time ahead. Learning from each other and developing a real family service. Skills rubbing off', he said, although I thought that bit sounded a bit like housework."

"Yes, well, I don't know how we are going to do that. Takes me all my time to deal with the Waiting List."

"Don, you will have to tell us about the mysteries of that. I keep hearing about the Waiting List. Can I come out with you one day or perhaps visit an old people's home? Rachael told me that she thought welfare assistants would be very useful in welfare situations."

Meg is always so enthusiastic, Bella thought. So helpful, even too helpful sometimes in her rush to please. She wants to do everything and especially she wants to be seconded for social work training.

"So are you going to come out with me one day?" Adrian asked Bella, who smiled and was about to answer when there was an interruption and a sudden scurry of activity and talk.

"Harry!"

"We didn't know you were coming?"

"I kept it secret in case he didn't make it."

"How is the course? Are you nearly qualified?"

"When are you coming back?"

"Are you coming back?"

"Harry, you haven't met Charlotte and Don and Adrian, oh and Meg. Our new team. Charlotte, this is the man you've been hearing about. He's coming back soon to shake us out of our elitist ways. Harry, Charlotte is really ahead of you. She finished training last year and is already a force to be reckoned with."

"What Jan means is that I have a thing about the Housing Department. It's appalling. Half the people I deal with are either homeless and in B&B or living in buildings that should have been pulled down years ago." Charlotte smiled and shook hands. "And I don't know what your course is saying, but we were engulfed in the 1969 Children and Young Persons Act and the things it has missed out. We still have approved schools and borstals. In addition we have the implications of Intermediate Treatment – yes, I know it's not called that in the Act, but it is supposed to be Intermediate – something between prison and staying in the community."

"Oh, yes… we are supposed to be recommending the courts make orders for special activities at special times in order to keep the young out of trouble, which is quite a good idea. I was never sure what to do with kids I had on Supervision Orders. I think they now have in mind youth club type activities, but the delinquent young have already tried ping pong and billiards and rejected them, so we shall to think of something more exciting – like stock car racing or trips abroad to climb mountains." Harry and Charlotte laughed. Then Harry went on, turning to the others. "What about the 1970 Chronically Sick and Disabled Persons Act? Are you involved with this yet?"

"Don't mention it, Harry," Jan protested. "We had a memo from the new deputy – she is Agatha Simpson, ex-Mental Health – she said that meetings are being held with various voluntary organisations concerned with the disabled, and the first thing we are going to do is compile a register of all the disabled people in our area. She said that services for them would depend on finances being available and they were still waiting to hear what the government is going to do about this. Of course, the disabled themselves have heard all about it from the newspapers and TV, and we are getting referrals all the time, but apart from making lists, we have nothing to give, and we are waiting for the occupational therapists to join the teams."

This is the first time we have been together socially since we re-organised, Bella thought. So they told Harry that Rachael Henley had become Team Leader and Judy had become Principal Officer for Children upstairs, and that the Chief Welfare Officer from Stanthorpe, Melvyn Clarke, had become Director and how when Harry came back there wouldn't be any room because one of the Home Help organisers, as well as an occupational therapist, were going to join them… and anyway, why hadn't he been to see them before.

A new woman in his life was partly why. And then there were the Union meetings and protests. He seemed to be spending a lot of time protesting against the Vietnam War and about Bloody Sunday and Bloody Friday.

"I finish in March next year and I suppose I shall rejoin you then, although I'm doing my last placement at a Child Guidance Clinic and it doesn't grab me, especially when half the time my supervisor wants to analyse my feelings and hang-ups, and where we spend our time with nice middle-class families looking for the reasons why their kids pinch smarties in Woolworths. Mostly we seem to find it all depends on whether the child was breast or bottle fed when a baby… stuff like that."

"So what does she make of your hang-ups, Harry?"

"Oh, I have an identity problem. I'm angry with authority figures! Actually I wind her up by telling her what a great guy my father is and how I loved school. She had decided I'm in denial. But I have to pass the placement so I don't tell her I think she talks psychobabble crap and the real problems in the world are about poverty and class and people like her who are elitist and patronising and, of course, how I used to pinch stuff from Woolies myself because it was so easy and part of the business of being accepted by the gang."

They talked and argued and drank more beer and wine and Bella and Adrian arranged to take each other out to visit clients, and then Harry pulled his chair up beside Bella and asked what she had been doing and how her daughter was.

"We had a wedding," Bella said. "She was married in May to a young solicitor. He's rather nice and has just joined a practice. She qualified this year and is working at one of the new Law Centres where they give free advice, so they only pay her a pittance, but she seems very happy. They live in Stockport which is rather a long way away, but I see them quite often."

"I'm deeply shocked. I thought she would wait for me. You know I always fancied you as a mother-in-law."

"Oh my God! I'm not old enough to be your mother-in-law," Bella protested. "But I shall be glad when you are back. I'm waiting to hand back Mrs Bickford. Mary, who leaves school any minute, has been suspended again and, would you believe, Lee, who's about nineteen now, has just been caught shoplifting again. I think they must have a shoplifting gene; but after two Supervision Orders and Probation, I think this time he will go to prison. I have to confess I have been completely unsuccessful."

"Oh, God, nothing changes, does it? But I can't have the Bickfords back. Mrs B thinks me much too young... But I'm glad Gemma's doing the right thing about work, even though she's married to a blood-sucking solicitor. At least she's not fleecing the public. But tell me, what of the office Don Juan? Who is he sleeping with now and has he made a pass at the gorgeous widow, the bastard?"

"He's working in the team for Area 2. He tried to get Team Leader with us but Rachael beat him to it. Quite right too, I thought. Tim hasn't got enough experience. But I'm afraid I don't know anything about his love life."

"So do you like it? The new system? This generic business? What do you think?"

***

What do I think? At home Bella reflected on Harry's question and her rather waffling response. She asked the question of herself quite often but the work drove her, interrupting contemplation with activity and although she had been keeping to her lists, she was beginning to realise that one rarely finished anything. Cases that closed often re-opened and as she ticked off the names at the bottom of the list, new ones appeared and some of the old ones appeared again.

The re-organisation had been exciting, but she was not sure how she would fit in learning about mental health, the elderly, the disabled and so on. She often thought of Edie, lonely and confused and clearly unhappy and yet apparently OK to be left. She wasn't sure that was right but had no idea how it could be rectified.

It was late when she got home but she was wide awake and wanted to talk. She thought of Sim at Woodbridge, always available, always able to listen but now in Canada, and wanted to talk to her. She sat at the kitchen table and began to write.

Renshaw

17th March

Dear Sim,

It was good getting your letter and what wonderful news – a baby in August. I am so pleased for you and of course you are not too old. Most women have their babies later now and they will take good care of you. I am extremely cross that you will be going through this pregnancy too far away for me to visit, but I am still extremely cross that you went to Canada in the first place. I really need you here! Perhaps I can save enough to visit in a year or so. Certainly not at present. Gemma's wedding, which we had here, was quite low key, but very enjoyable, but it still cleaned me out and then my friend Liz's daughter, Martha got married two months ago and I've always been very fond of her so I couldn't scrimp on the present. I just hope they both wait a while before producing young, while I try to recoup. Of course Martha's wedding was very posh. I was in the minority who didn't wear a hat and Liz didn't approve of Martha's husband Luke. He is working for an Estate Agent and Liz thinks he is a parvenu. He buys and sells antiques and even mild Matthew murmured that he seemed to have a lot of irons in the fire. I found him rather pleasant, very good-looking but perhaps rather too fond of himself. Martha however, was deliriously happy, even when she told me that of course Mummy doesn't really approve, but then Liz hardly ever approves of anything Martha does. By contrast I have a nice son-in-law called Josh and feel he and Gemma have a really good relationship.

You ask about our re-organisation. The new Social Services Department! Where do I begin? My old team is more or less intact which is a relief but we now have Adrian from the old Mental Health Dept (who is rather dishy), Don from Welfare, who is a sweetie but over 55, and Meg who is a frightfully keen Welfare Assistant. She is very useful but her enthusiasm exhausts me. Then there is Charlotte, newly trained and very political, very attractive and very fiery about our dreadful Housing Department. She talks about the squats that are occurring all over the country and thinks we should have one here. I am tempted to agree. Housing is one of the great problems for us.

We have a new team leader, Rachael, who was in Area 2, and I like her and feel I can talk to her. Judy who has become a Principal Child Care Officer, was so prim and not really my type. But we are only just getting going and I still have my caseload of families, although I have to cope with anything that comes in on duty – the mad, the bad and the halt and the lame. Then we have something to look forward to! The Chronically Sick and Disabled Persons Act. Have you heard about this? Does Canada have something of the sort? We are going to have to provide telephones, transport, home adaptations and walking sticks etc. It has just come in and the press are very excited about it which means the public is already knocking at the door. We are going to have an OT join the team soon (if we can find another chair) and I guess this work will go to her, but of course, there is no money for all these goodies and we are being told not to promise anything for the moment, so we are creating another waiting list. As you see... plus ca change...

And no, since you ask, I have no new lovers. My brush with Tim was fairly brief and I was rather bitchy. I said that just because I took the place of his last passion, did not mean I was available to be his next. He was not offended, which he should have been, but I think the fact that he wasn't indicates how superficial he is – just looking for an easy lay I guess. Although (for your eyes only) I won't say I wasn't tempted. It has been so long, but on the other hand I do rather enjoy being on my own... AND I nearly forgot. All us social workers are now on a Standby Rota for emergencies out of hours. I've had a phone put in by the bed and heaven knows if I'll cope if I'm called, but we are having a list of resources we can use if we need them. Think of me going out at 3 in the morning to deal with Rensham's dramas!

I am writing at nearly midnight after an evening at the pub, where, incidentally I arranged to go out on a mental health case with the handsome Adrian, so you see life does still have attractions... but now I must go to bed. Do write again soon and look after that baby!

***

They were waiting to start the Allocation Meeting. Rachael had been called away to the Director's office to talk about Battered Babies. There had been another government directive about communication between agencies and the importance of holding case conferences whenever there was an alleged or suspected incident. As someone had said, Battered Babies were now flavour of the month.

"I think the most difficult thing is facing quite different ideas on child management to what we are mostly used to. I mean, it's a cultural thing, isn't it? Some people hit their children for anything. They always have, but we can't take away all the children who get hit. And the people we deal with, let's face it, mostly working-class with problems and with low thresholds when it come to anger... well, they've always belted their kids and they'll tell you that their parents smacked and beat them and that it never did them any harm." Adrian was speaking.

"I agree," this from Jan. "But I disagree that it's just a class thing. Of course we don't see much of the middle classes, but that's because they are better at concealing their nasty habits. Think of the public schools where they encourage the older boys to beat the younger ones."

"The press isn't concerned about them. It's battered babies that get the headlines at the moment. I mean, since the case of the Simpkins baby, and that was neglect as well as injury, the press jumps around looking for someone to blame – besides the parents of course," Bella said. "I heard from Rachael that it has worried the boss. A couple of weeks ago he had the Team Leaders in for a pep talk about vigilance. Rachael was quite sorry for him. Apparently he kept saying how he didn't really know much about the child care field but he knew it was very difficult work and attracted so much public attention. She said the poor man was quite frightened and thought the News of the World would be ringing him up any day. Judy was there in her new job as Principal Child Care Officer and he kept saying how he relied on her and how she would always be there for us."

"I think it's crazy to appoint a man as Director who doesn't know anything about child care," Jennifer said. "I know Judy is his child care person, but we really don't want someone at the top who is nervous. What sort of support will that be if we need it. I mean, in that Simpkins case, it wasn't the Director who was in the headlines; it was the social worker and the health visitor. I can't imagine Mr Clarke taking the responsibility if anything happens here."

"It's very important to discuss any anxieties we have with our supervisor, isn't it – and our colleagues. If one is worried about anything one should talk about it," Evelyn said. "I think we are so busy trying to cope with our cases we are apt to think it a sign of weakness if we admit we are anxious or unsure. We always feel we must cope, don't we?"

"Quite right, Evelyn." Rachael had come in and heard the last remark and she pulled up a chair beside Adrian and put her papers on his desk.

"Sorry I'm late. But we must get on. I have quite a lot here."

She dealt with the new referrals first. They each did a day on duty, but passed the new work to Rachael who then allocated it to whoever had the capacity to take it, or who was most appropriate. That anyway, was the system. It was not working very well, Bella thought, hoping nothing would come her way today. Everyone was already busy and although Rachael was still giving out the work according to the workers who were familiar with the client group – child care cases to ex-child care workers and so on – cases did not present in tidy categories. Today Charlotte took on two children whose mother had just been admitted to the local mental hospital with manic depression. The children were staying with their grandmother, and the hospital referral indicated that this lady was very unsympathetic to the mother's problems, saying to her daughter when she visited without the children, that she should pull herself together. "So it's about child care and mental health," Rachael said. "It seems the main task at first is to arrange for the children to visit their mother and then there's work to be done with the grandmother."

"Tell her that suggesting a depressive pulls herself together, is like suggesting an amputee should go jogging," Adrian commented.

Charlotte smiled at Adrian and agreed to take the case and then Jennifer agreed to see what was needed in the case of an elderly woman who, according to neighbours, was wandering about inadequately dressed. "An assessment needed here, by the sound of it," Rachael suggested and thought Jennifer might have to liaise with Don and she would probably need to speak to the GP.

A woman who was being discharged from hospital after taking a overdose was known to Adrian, and he agreed to take her on, commenting that this lady overdosed fairly regularly when she and her husband had a row, which caused him to be very frightened and apologetic. "It's a problem-solving technique she's developed. Somehow we've got to find another way for them to manage their disagreements." And then Rachael confirmed that the two applications for residential care which Don had already seen should stay with him, but, she suggested, perhaps Jan or Evelyn would like to do joint visits with Don on one of those to familiarise themselves with assessing for residential care.

"And there is one I thought you would take Bella. I think you would be right for Amber Jackson, who can't let her three-year-old out of her sight in case he gets run over like her first child was a year or so ago. Janet was about four when she ran into the road outside the house and was killed. I'm sorry it sounds so sad and grisly, but the health visitor is worried that the little boy, Jamie, is kept indoors too much and is generally very over-protected. One can hardly blame poor Amber – it was a dreadful business. I don't know what we can do, but perhaps you could visit and assess the situation."

They were then all reminded about the reviews for children in foster care and about the meeting which had been arranged for next Thursday at 4 p.m. with the head teachers to talk about liaison between Social Services and Education. She said she wanted at least two people from the team to go as it was important that communication between the two services was improved. Two workers from Area 2 would also be there.

"Oh, God," Charlotte exclaimed. "They don't like our Care Orders or our Supervision Orders and want us to send them all to approved schools."

Rachael thought that rather an exaggeration, but agreed that there was a tendency to push their difficulties back to Social Services if they knew they were involved but went on to say that she thought perhaps they should start talking about the time when there would be no more approved schools or borstals and all children would be placed in community homes or foster care whether they were delinquent or not, because that time was coming. It was going to be about taking off the labels, getting rid of stigmatisation and treating all children as having needs which they had to try to meet.

Bella wondered if teachers thought about meeting children's needs. She said she sometimes felt it was the teachers' needs which were paramount. She said that Mrs Broadbent from St Hilda's Primary told her the other day that Mark Jones was disrupting the whole class and was in danger of being suspended. Suspended! Mark was only five years old and not very bright. She, Mrs Broadbent, said she had had his older brother two years ago and he was just as bad. You can see them coming, she said, and Mark should either be in care or in a special school.

"They don't seem to think about the trauma of removing children from home and have little understanding of the law. They seem to think," Bella continued, "that we can just swoop down and tidy the Marks of this world away."

Rachael nodded but said that that was why they were going to have a meeting. There was a lot to discuss and, she said, we had to help them to understand we are not just a receptacle into which they could put the children who presented with problems. She started to collect up her papers but then stopped and suggested that it might be a good idea to put down some of the things we wanted to raise with Education… make an agenda for the meeting… everyone seemed to have a lot of feelings about this. So let's have some ideas that she could translate into nice positive suggestions… show them how reasonable we are…

As she went back to her desk after the meeting had broken up, Bella knew she would have to cancel her morning plan to visit Jilly Berkshire at twelve. Team meetings always ran over time and she had a review at 1.30.

Bella had met Jilly a year ago, when her husband had left her. He had paid no maintenance for her or for her child and Bella had assisted the negotiations with the DHSS that resulted in Jilly receiving a weekly allowance. Yesterday, Jilly had rung her to say the DHSS had taken her book away because they believed she was living with a man. Jilly told Bella this was not true and she now had no money. She had a boyfriend, Bella knew this, and she knew he stayed the night from time to time, but she also knew that he had no intention of taking on Jilly and her seven-year-old son, and Bella knew Jilly knew this as well.

But the poor cannot have casual relationships of course and she knew the DHSS would tell her that the man was leaving the house after breakfast because they had been watching and this was proof enough for them. But before she began fighting for the return of the payment book, Bella knew she must get a

Section I grant from Rachael to keep the child fed. She had better go today, so it would have to be after the review.

***

"A Sister Phillips rang to speak to Don and when I told her he was off sick she said it was very urgent and she must speak to the Duty Officer. I said you were expected."

The receptionist's tone emphasised her disapproval and Bella said she was sorry she was late and would contact the hospital.

She had wanted at least half an hour's peace, her mind still full of the telephone call from her mother which had interrupted her breakfast at eight. Christmas arrangements. God! It was only October.

"She said it was urgent."

"Yes. Alright, I'll ring her straight away."

Sister Phillips was quite explicit. It had been arranged that Don would collect Mrs Sinclair and take her to Apperly House Old Peoples' Home, where she would stay until her broken leg was sufficiently mended to allow her to return home. She would be ready to leave by 10 a.m. and there was no question of her staying. Her bed was needed. Sister Phillips had taken it upon herself to ring Apperly House and they were expecting her, so could someone fetch Mrs Sinclair as soon as possible? Bella enquired about ambulances but was told they were needed for emergencies and it was anyway understood that transport would be arranged by Social Services.

As Bella put down the phone Rachael arrived at her desk and told her Don had rung in and was worried about Mrs Sinclair. Bella said she knew. Rachael said it would be interesting for Bella to do some welfare work and that she would cover duty while Bella was out.

It *was* interesting, Bella told Adrian afterwards when they were driving to a pub he knew on the edge of town. Mrs Sinclair was very disagreeable, Bella said. In some pain, she thought, complaining all the time. It was difficult to get her into the car with her leg encased in plaster up to the hip and in the end she and a nurse and a porter had to take the front passenger seat out completely so that Mrs Sinclair could sit in the back with her leg extended.

"Good grief. How did you do that?"

"With great difficulty and with the help of the porter's tool kit."

"What did you do with the seat?" Adrian asked.

"I had to leave it at the hospital. Mrs Sinclair is a large woman who seemed to occupy the whole of the back seat. That didn't make me very popular either. The girl on Reception said they couldn't take responsibility for people's possessions, so I told them to throw it out if it bothered them and shoved it behind the desk. They were in the process of reporting the incident to someone when I left. But the most enlightening part was at Apperly House. Mrs Sinclair grumbled all the way there and when a member of staff and I wrestled her out of the car into a wheelchair she let out a great cry which was so loud we nearly dropped her. But the really interesting bit was when we wheeled her down the corridor, a very fat woman emerged from a room which I later found was the office, and called out imperiously, 'Put her in the first lounge' to which Mrs Sinclair replied, 'I want a cup of tea before anything else.' This was answered by the fat woman, who I discovered was the Matron, who said, 'She can have tea when everyone else has tea, which is after she has had her dinner.' She then disappeared into her room again without making any attempt to speak to Mrs Sinclair who wasn't in the least pleased; but when we got to the first lounge, she saw someone she knew, thank heavens, and we were able to leave her recounting her misfortune to that poor lady. And then the best, or worst part of my first visit to Apperly House... I went to the office on my way out and the Matron – Matron, God, doesn't that word sum up the world of institutions? The Matron made me very welcome in a condescending way, you know, 'Of course you are new to this kind of work aren't you? What were you? Children's?' Obviously very low in her estimation, and then she sent for tea. I nearly took my cup to Mrs Sinclair ..."

"It's like operating under the old Poor Law. The Matron as head of the workhouse," Adrian said.

"I remember a lecturer we had at college saying. 'try to get inside the head of the client when you offer a service. See if you can feel what they feel.' I still feel very indignant and angry. How do we change things like that?"

"I guess, very slowly," Adrian said. "But what about your car seat? Have you got it back or did the hospital throw it away?"

"No, it was still there but the receptionist was still very cross with me and the porter had disappeared and I only just got it into the car with some difficulty. No one offered to help. They watched me struggle to get the bloody thing through the double doors, calling out to be careful not to break the glass. I was seething by the time I got into the car and then I went to my garage and they put it back."

"It's good to know you can get angry."

"Oh, I'm so glad I'm pleasing someone. Does that surprise you, that I get angry?"

"Well, yes. I think it does. You are always so calm and well organised."

"That doesn't sound like I feel at all. I'm always getting angry at something. In fact I started the day being irritated with my mother who rang very early to see what arrangements I was making for Christmas, which made me late for work and that made me angry as well."

"So what are you doing for Christmas?"

"Please! Don't mention it."

"So. OK. Before we get to the Dog and Whistle, I'll tell you about Mark Gregorio, who is, according to his wife, becoming manic again and may need hospital. You and I are going there tomorrow, remember. He has these episodes about twice a year and probably wouldn't have them at all if he didn't stop taking his medication, but his wife recognises the symptoms and tries to get him treated before he gets too bad. He has been talking now for two days and not sleeping and he's planning his next business move. They have a newsagent's in Merton Street, which does quite well, but he's apparently decided they must move into general groceries and is seeing agents and the bank and God knows who else, and is so busy he's not helping her in the shop. She's worried that he will get involved in some financial mess if he isn't calmed down, and of course he doesn't take his medication because he says he is so well. These episodes sound almost amusing, but they are not in the least funny. Apart from the obvious fact that he could spend all their money he's driven by such a strong urge to follow the ideas which seem to chase themselves through his head, he could in fact do himself harm or do someone else harm. If one argues the point with him over an idea he can and sometimes has become quite violent and terribly reckless. The bipolar disorder is, of course, probably responsible for some of our greatest works of fiction and amazing inventions. Dickens for one, Van Gogh another. Both turned out an incredible amount of work and were difficult to live with. Once on a roll, the patient thinks and talks faster and faster and doesn't sleep. They can accomplish tremendous feats of work."

"So what will you do when you visit?"

"Good question. I shall try to persuade him that going to hospital is a good idea and that won't be easy. Dr Linwood knows him and says I can take him up any time but he doesn't like going and will tell me how well he is. He has been taken in by force in the past and I certainly want to avoid that. People don't forget when that happens and it makes it harder to get them to go again. But the thing with people with psychotic symptoms is that they usually do know they're not really well and one has to try and reach that bit of them. It helps if they already know you and important that you try to keep the contacts from being oppressive. I shall introduce you as someone who is in training, if you don't mind. That will interest him because he's quite knowledgeable about the mental health services and will give you a lot of advice."

"I'll look forward to it," Bella said, as Adrian parked his car round the back of the pub. "And before we actually have lunch, I think we should go Dutch. I will pay for myself."

"No way, I invited you. No arguments."

"Well, alright then, but it will be my turn next time."

"I'm glad you said there will be a next time. Perhaps we could work ourselves up to dinner one evening?" Bella smiled.

"Yes, perhaps we could."

***

Christmas Eve 1972

She replaced the receiver and told herself that it was foolish to mind about this one short period when Gemma would not be coming for Christmas. She forced herself into activity. A bag to be packed. Food to be sorted and taken and the presents, of course. Thank God she had wrapped them. Then the indoor plants to be watered. The house to be secured. She saw it was already seven and she had said she would arrive about nine so she must telephone her mother and say she would be late and she must telephone Maggie next door and tell them she would be away until the day after Boxing Day.

She left eventually at 8.15 and drove out of Rensham with the uneasy feeling that she had forgotten something, thinking she should have given herself more time and not stayed at the office where Harry had suddenly appeared with bottles of wine and Jan had brought a cake.

They had spent the morning distributing the parcels of toys which had descended on the office during the week from various churches and charities. There had been the usual objections and long discussions as to how they could avoid this avalanche of goodwill which came once a year.

"This isn't about giving stuff to the poor and needy," Charlotte said. "It's about satisfying the donors who feel all warm and cosy because of their generosity."

Bella agreed, "I saw Councillor Mrs Petherington two days ago. She brought a small bag of goodies but told me to be sure to give them to the needy folk and not to people who didn't make an effort to help themselves. I wondered to whom she was referring... needy folk! The whole question of giving things is uncomfortable and complicated. I mean, Tracey Mansfield has given me the most awful necklace and earrings and she usually hasn't enough money to get her through the week, and here I am giving her a bag of second-hand toys for her children. I have decided I don't like being a bearer of gifts. I don't think that's what we are here for."

"Oh please Bella, don't start wondering what we are here for," Gordon said. But the team room was full of wrapped and unwrapped toys so they piled them into their cars and took them round to their clients.

***

The house, always badly lit, seemed small and dismal and her parents, pleased to see her, were full of regrets that she was too late for a meal – her mother waved sadly at the cooked lamb chops on the dresser – and regretted Gemma was not with them.

"It won't be the same," she said. "I do think they should have gone to you as you are on your own."

Her father, already in his dressing gown, thought Bella probably had too much to do looking after all those people who couldn't look after themselves, to manage Christmas. "So how are the great unwashed?" he asked.

Bella ignored this and reminded them that Gemma not only had new in-laws but was going to visit James' parents who lived near Stockport. She prattled on about Christmas not being so important, there were other weekends.

She helped her mother stuff the small turkey and forced an enthusiasm she did not feel about the Christmas Day arrangements to counteract her father's determination to tell her how tired her mother was after all the work she did at the Day Centre. "She goes there three days a week now and comes home exhausted." A statement her mother immediately denied. "They are very shorthanded," she said. "And I enjoy going there."

Bella met her mother's exasperated expression and thought we've had this kind of conversation so often. Her father believed that people took endless advantage of his wife who was constantly thinking of other people rather than of him. And he thinks much the same about me, she thought, except he is more angry with me because I have joined the welfare state which he decided long ago is ruining the country.

When she had lived at home, she and her mother prepared Christmas dinner while her father took a short walk before opening a bottle of wine and pouring them all a glass of sherry. Nothing had changed, Bella decided on Christmas morning as she laid the table, placing a cracker beside each mat. Except that she had changed. The three crackers used to be an excitement, now they seemed absurd.

But in a way the rituals which took them through the day were comforting. No need to think what she should be doing or worrying about what she had forgotten. Watching her parents dozing through the Queen's speech, protesting that she could not possibly eat any cake which her mother produced at 5 pm, making turkey sandwiches at eight which they ate while watching an old film on TV and finally allowing her father to talk her into a late glass of whisky before she went to bed – a sort of acknowledgement, she thought, that she had grown up, and although misguided, that he still loved her. All restfully predictable.

Chapter Four

1973

Adrian and Bella were driving in her car to see one of her clients. Bella felt a little uneasy. Working in front of someone else... she knew he liked her but today felt shy and tense. She asked him about Christmas.

"I took the boys to my brother's on Boxing Day. Yes, it was a good day. Five young lads, football on the common. A large lunch, TV and then a fairly long walk. My sister-in-law is a great believer in exercise but I'm sure it did us good. We went back to my place fairly late so Jason and Julian didn't get up until lunch time, but it was OK. We played monopoly and talked. I'm glad they can talk. But Jason suddenly asked me if there was any chance of his mother and me getting back together. I wasn't ready for it. He said Maurice, her boyfriend, was alright, but he didn't want him to live with them, which brought on a load of guilt when I said there was no chance at all. It's always there for them, particularly Jason."

For a moment he stared into space, saying nothing, then, "They went back to their mother the following afternoon. My turn to have Christmas Day next year. What about you?"

"Oh very quiet. My first Christmas without Gemma. Just the parents and not very exciting. My father sniping at me and my mother getting meals according to the time rather than our appetites. On Boxing Day next door came in for drinks. A couple in their sixties which livened things up for an hour or so.

Dad told them I was working for the welfare state and spent my time with people who were living on benefit who were too lazy for work. It actually backfired at bit. Brenda, the wife, was immediately fascinated. 'We just don't know', she said, 'how the other half live, and do you come across people who don't have enough to eat? And criminals? And those poor children whose parents don't love them?' She thought it all must be so rewarding for me. It seemed a pity to tell her I wasn't rewarded nearly enough, so I told a few stories about fostering and homelessness. I went on rather about the shortcomings of our Housing Department while Dad muttered about the cost to the ratepayers!"

"Tell me about it! This morning I was greeted by Jessy Radford. She went into hospital a week before Christmas, very low, suicidal I thought. She was discharged yesterday back to the bed and breakfast place Housing gave her six months ago. Madeley Road. Disgusting place. Room too small to swing a cat and furniture falling to pieces. This woman needs somewhere decent and today she was so low I rang the doc who said the hospital thought she was OK for discharge because she had been fine on the ward. Of course she was fine on the ward. They had a Christmas party and there was company and they made sure she took her pills. What we need is sheltered accommodation for the Jessy Radfords. They keep talking about it, but so far nothing."

"Ah, but it's so rewarding!" Bella said, smiling. But she had been thinking about Adrian's sons commuting between parents, still hoping for a reconciliation, but Adrian went on, "I was wondering whether to ask Meg to visit her. Perhaps take her shopping or for advice. Welfare assistants are supposed to do that sort of thing, aren't they?"

"Good idea. Meg would like that."

"It's not a real solution but it might help. The situation is so frustrating."

"Well, you are about to visit another frustrating situation," Bella said and tried to describe the family to Adrian. Peggy Stringer worried her. Married to a man more often drunk than sober. Peggy's apathy was, Bella felt, a kind of permanent depression. She couldn't seem to get the oldest two to school, or take the two youngest to a mother and toddler group, in spite of all the arrangements she and the health visitor made, and according to the school, if they did arrive, they were dirty and smelly. Bella also worried about them being badly nourished. They seemed to live on fish and chips and sticky buns, she told Adrian, and although Peggy was full of good intentions, Bella said she found it impossible to motivate her. Adrian asked about the husband and Bella had to confess she had hardly ever seen him. "He's either in bed or down the pub," she said.

An unfriendly girl in a dirty dress and unbrushed hair yelled, "It's the welfare," when she opened the door. A voice answered from an inner room, "Well, bring them in, bring them in." Bella and Adrian followed the girl into the sitting room where a large fire was blazing in front of which a thin, pale woman sat smoking and burning her bare legs into red blotches. A baby was strapped into a large pram next to the woman and a small boy, wearing only a blue striped jersey with a large stain down the front, stood sucking his thumb and staring while a slightly larger girl was wrapping a doll in a grey cloth which Bella thought had once been a nappy. The floor was littered with broken toys, old chip paper and cigarette ends. There were two battered armchairs which contained an assortment of clothes, and a large wooden cupboard stood against the window bearing a television set which was making a hissing noise while the picture raced down the screen.

Bella introduced Adrian, who squatted down beside the boy asking him his name. He didn't answer. "Tell the gentleman your name, Lenny. His name is Lenny, but he's shy, ain't' you?"

his mother said, and then, "An' the baby's is Billy, and then Tracey is my big girl, ain't you, and Goldie came next. Her real name is Marigold, but we always calls her Goldie, don't we, eh? I know what you are going to say," Peggy went to say to Bella, "but I couldn't get them to school because she was bad. Tracey was poorly this morning, wasn't you?"

Tracey agreed. "I was sick," she said.

"But you're better now?" Bella asked.

To which Tracey replied, "I didn't have no dinner."

"What about Marigold? She could have gone to school, couldn't she, and the little ones could have gone to playgroup?"

"You don't expect me to leave Tracey when she's bad and go out with the others?"

"What about Jack? Wasn't he here?"

"Dead to the bloody world he was. Came home last night out of his skull and snoring like a pig this morning. Can't leave her with him."

"I'm not staying with him," Tracey said.

"Is he still in bed?"

"No, he's off out, isn't he? Down the betting shop I wouldn't wonder or playing them machines, and don't tell me to talk to him, Mrs Wingfield." Her voice began to whine. "Real nasty he gets if I start. Says the children is my responsibility."

Bella moved to the pram where a pale-faced infant with a dummy in his mouth put a hand out to touch her face. "Can I pick Billy up?" she asked.

"'Course you can. Mind you, he'll be wet."

Bella took the child onto her lap, sitting in one of the armchairs on top of the clothes, where she sank nearly to the floor and became conscious of the wet nappy which was gradually seeping into her skirt. She held the boy up so his feet rested on her thighs and bounced him gently. His feet made no response. They should be feeling the pressure, she thought. He was making no effort to stand. She placed him on the floor on his tummy where his head flopped to the ground and although he wriggled, he made no attempt to brace himself on his arms or move his knees. As he began to cry she picked him up again and continued to bounce him on her lap. He began, slowly, to put some pressure on her legs with his feet and when again on the floor, with help, he pushed himself up a little on his arms.

"You see, Peggy, he needs to have the chance to move about," she said, and seeing Marigold becoming interested spoke directly to her. "Babies need to be able to practise moving, see? He must begin to think about standing up. We must help him." She placed his feet on the floor and again bounced him gently until his feet began to respond and make small attempts to stand. "You really shouldn't keep him strapped in the pram so much, Peggy," she said. "He needs exercise. At this age he should be moving a lot more. Now if you take him to the toddler group they will give him the opportunity to learn to crawl and then to walk. What is he now? Fourteen, fifteen months? And it will be nice for you to meet other mums." She turned to Marigold. "And you enjoy going to school, don't you, meeting your friends and learning to read and write?"

"I ain't got no friends there," Marigold answered.

"Well, I think that's because you don't go every day. If you went every day you would make friends, wouldn't you?"

"Dunno."

More interested in the baby, Marigold took both hands and jiggled him up and down, making him laugh and Bella lose her grip, at which his legs collapsed and he fell face down, letting out a loud cry.

"Now you've upset him. Give him here." Peggy levered herself from her chair and picked him up. "Tracey, get us a nappy, he's soaking." And to Bella, "It's no good having him on the floor, he only hurts himself." Bella didn't give up.

"But he needs playing with, Peggy. Can't you see? If you played with him he would learn to move about himself. He needs encouragement now, but he would soon learn to crawl and eventually to stand. The others did now, didn't they?"

She looked round the room, trying to identify the medley of clothes, toys and clutter. "What happened to the blanket I brought you for the baby to play on?"

Peggy looked round and then called out, "What you done with that blanket, Tracey? The one Mrs Wingfield brought?" Tracey, returning with a nappy nearly as grey as the one wrapping the doll, said, "I ain't got it. Goldie had it on her bed."

"Well, you go and fetch it, Goldie. It weren't for you. Go on now, but I can't get down on the floor. I had a fall and hurt me back see. But we has a game at bedtime, don't we? He likes being tickled." The baby giggled as she poked him gently and stuck a dummy back in his mouth, and Bella watched as she changed him. He smiled at her and tried to grab her hair.

I've been here before, she thought, and it makes no difference. But she went on trying and Adrian joined her, sympathising with the painful back and asking Peggy how she had fallen. Peggy said that she had slipped on the stairs. Bella noticed that Tracey stopped fiddling with the control on the television set at his question, stared at her mother and then went and stood at her side, putting an arm around her shoulder. Peggy said nothing more but she shook her head at Tracey and gave her a hug. She then said four children were hard work. Adrian agreed with her and then he joined Bella in attempting to fire Peggy's mothering towards getting the children out of the house. The blanket was recovered and Bella suggested it was given a wash as it seemed to be rather damp and dirty and she then made the suggestion which had been hovering in her mind and which she was trying to ignore. If Peggy agreed, she said, she would try to help them get into a routine by fetching the older ones for school next week, if Peggy could get Billy and Lenny to the nursery. As she was making the suggestion she was thinking how she did not want to do this.

Peggy was delighted with the idea but for Bella it would mean getting to work earlier and it would be creating dependency. But she made the arrangement anyway and said that if Peggy had the two girls clean and ready when she arrived at 8.30am she would take them to school in the car and Peggy could get the boys ready to go to the toddler group when it opened.

Peggy directed her enthusiasm towards the children. "That'll be really nice, won't it? You'll be going in Mrs Wingfield's car. You'll like that, won't you?" to which Tracey nodded and Marigold asked if she could sit in the front. Lenny, who had been sitting silently on the floor moving the little car back and forth suddenly came to life and shouted, "Car. Car... I go in car," and then threw his toy car across the room and turned and hit Adrian's leg, shouting incoherently until Adrian picked him up and held him above his head, which made him laugh.

***

They talked in the car on the way back to the department.

"Apart from the offer of transport, that was almost a complete replay of my visit before Christmas and the two visits before that. I don't know how to achieve a change. It's always the same and now I've committed myself to early mornings. How to motivate her? I'm crazy. Tell me I'm crazy."

Adrian told her she was crazy. But he couldn't think of anything else that would make a difference. All those early mornings. And yet he thought that the only way to get things moving was to become more involved. He agreed Peggy was deflated. Probably very depressed and not very bright, in fact the whole family was not very high in intelligence. He said he had begun to think, while they were there, that when one works with people who were handicapped – and the awful husband plus low intelligence is a handicap – the only thing to do was to model behaviour. That way Peggy would get to see the advantages and then carry on herself, which, he supposed was what Bella had in mind.

"But they won't be clean and the school will complain and how long do I keep it up before she gets them to school herself? Really one should move in with them."

"What a ghastly idea! It's a bit malodorous in there – the colour of those nappies! But in spite of all that I think there's affection there. Perhaps not the obvious kind that hits you in the face, but once you get under the disorder and the dirt... yes, it was there."

Bella knew that Rachael would not approve of her new arrangements and she knew it would be difficult to organise herself in the coming weeks, but when she and Adrian returned to the office there were messages waiting and other things to think about. Foster mother Hilary Bentham's mother had been taken ill and Hilary had to go to Chester to look after her, so her foster child Bobby Webster, aged four, would need to be moved while she was away. Bobby was waiting for an adoption placement and, Bella thought, the last thing he needed was to be moved at this stage. And the Housing Department had left a message about Betty Bishop's rent arrears which were apparently getting bigger.

She found Rachael who said, "If Hilary Bentham had a four-year-old of her own, she would take him with her, wouldn't she?"

"Well, yes, I suppose she would, or she'd make an arrangement with a relative or friend."

"Well, not that, Bella. If the child was to go to anyone we didn't know, they would have to be approved and all that and I guess there wouldn't be time. I think you should suggest she takes him with her."

Bella didn't get around to telling Rachael about her plans for the Stringer children. She forgot them for the moment. She phoned Hilary Bentham and wondered if she could, perhaps, take Bobby with her as he was so settled.

She was met with surprise and hesitation. Bella emphasised how well Bobby had done with her and said how important it was that he continue with her if he was to be eventually moved to adoptive parents. "They do so much better if they have bonded well, whereas moving them about…"

But Hilary interrupted. "I'm sorry, Bella, I do understand and I'm very sorry but you must see that my first priority is my mother and she's very poorly. Bronchitis and probably developing pneumonia. I shall have my hands full. I really should be going today but certainly must go tomorrow. I shall talk to him about it, of course, before I go. He's such a sensible little fellow. I'm sure you understand."

So Bella understood and said she would do her best to find another placement, visualising picking up the happy little Bobby from the home to which he had become accustomed and putting him down, with no preliminary introductions, in a strange place which she had yet to find.

It was 6.15 when she left the office, taking three files with her in the forlorn hope that she would write reports during the evening. She had made phone calls to several foster parents before Melanie Hollis said she would have Bobby. "But please don't bring him before five as I'm at the dentist with Jo Jo at three."

Which to Bella meant nearly bedtime and *bedtime* was the wrong time to move children. When she told Hilary of these arrangements, Hilary complained that her husband would not be pleased at having to stay home with Bobby, as she had to set off before lunch.

She had rung Housing about Betty Bishop's rent arrears and had been told by the Manager that in her opinion Betty Bishop's children should be taken into care as the woman was quite incapable of managing her money and they had no choice but to evict her. Bella's protestation that the Department was not happy about taking children into care because of homelessness had made no impression and had elicited the response, "Well, if you think they will be better off in bed and breakfast, that's up to you. We can do no more." She had just put the phone down when Adrian looked in and told her it was time to go home.

"Opportunity would be a fine thing," she said and then, "Sorry, but I'm in the process of cursing the Housing Department and a foster parent. Better leave me alone."

***

She remembered she had not bought a card or a present for Liz's new grandchild. Her son Sam's partner, Marina, had just given birth to a boy. Liz had written of course, with scarcely veiled disapproval, to tell of the birth of her first grandson and express her doubts about Marina's mothering ability and her distrust of a situation where a couple who were not married produced a child while living in some sort of commune.

There was a letter from Martha waiting for her, giving more news of the new baby but also other news about which Bella felt some doubts and anxiety. Martha had decided to train as a social worker and was starting a course in a week's time. Her new husband was happy to finance her and she sounded excited and delighted to have been accepted on a post-graduate one-year course at Birmingham. "Since that evening when I was staying with you and you had to go out to that family, I began to think that kind of work was what I really wanted to do. Teaching was just not me. So many children need more than school can give. I'm sure you know what I mean."

Oh yes, I know what you mean. You want to rescue children. Bella poured herself a glass of whisky, extracted a trout from its damp wrapping paper and put it under the grill. She found she had no vegetables so cut some bread and buttered it and sat with her glass at the kitchen table remembering the night when Martha was with her and she had had to go out to the Hollis children. A remark James had once made came to mind: 'External circumstances conscript you.' Is this what had happened? Had the drama of that evening – and Martha certainly saw it as a drama – influenced the decision Martha had now made? Would she have pursued the idea if they had spent the evening indoors? Was this her doing, telling Martha about the situation – perhaps dramatising it herself? But why was she getting herself in a state about it? It wasn't my problem and Martha might be a very good social worker. But a one-year course which she could take because she was a graduate teacher? Not long enough.

She ate the trout and found a dish of apples and custard in the fridge to finish her meal and was just washing up when the door bell rang. It was a surprise to find Adrian on the doorstep, clutching a bottle and saying he knew it was late but she had seemed rather down and he thought perhaps she needed some company.

As he sat at the kitchen table and Bella finished the dishes, she dispelled her first reactions. It was too late. She was tired, the house was a mess and did she really want this complication in her life? Thoughts that jumbled through her mind in opposition to the pleasure that was there as well. Anticipation.

He talked rather fast and filled the space between them with questions. Where had she lived before? What did she think of the neighbourhood? When would she be seeing Gemma? Easy social chit chat. Inconsequential. Almost artificial. She found a bottle opener and he poured the wine. Then he remembered he had brought a record. Pink Floyd's The Dark Side of the Moon. She suggested they could play it in the sitting room so they took the wine and sat on the sofa listening. When it finished conversation became suddenly difficult, pointless...

"Shall I get some biscuits?" She started to rise but Adrian's hand restrained her.

"No, we don't want biscuits." He slipped his arm around her waist and bent forward and kissed her neck. "I want you." She turned towards him letting herself slide back to his shoulder and he kissed her hair, her eyes and then her mouth.

***

She took tea upstairs and found Adrian already dressing. She suggested getting breakfast but he said tea would be enough. It was all he ever had and perhaps he should go home and have a shower and get a clean shirt. "I'd rather stay. I wish I had the nerve to call in sick and stay all day. Would you like that?" He pulled her towards him and kissed her gently and then pressed his face against hers. She let herself sink towards him but then pulled back, smiling.

"I think I would but… well, I'm not good at lying about being sick either. My mother used to tell me that it was tempting fate to say I was ill when I was well. I grew up thinking that if I ever did, I would get some awful disease."

"My God! You are still in thrall to your mother."

"Do we ever get free? There are always words that come back. But no. I'm, not in thrall as you put it, to my mother. If I were, you wouldn't be here now."

"She would disapprove?"

"Well, actually, I don't know whether she would or not. I suppose I just assumed she would. Her world always seems so narrow and constrained by self made rules, and anyway, I have a child to move and a woman being evicted and God knows what else. No, you must go. We must both go."

Chapter Five

1975

Bella collected her coat and bag and prepared to go out. The team room was full. Harry had arrived back three months earlier and now had a desk next to Charlotte at the end of the room where they were able to revile the Housing Department together. Next to him (with just about room to slide past) was Jeanette Fraser, the occupational therapist who had joined the team during last summer. Two Zimmer frames rested against her desk on the other side causing Jan and Evelyn to be moved nearer to Jennifer, who had been pushed up nearer to Bella. Three filing cabinets stood against the wall at intervals round the room and the kettle, sugar, a carton of salt and four cups stood on an old cupboard between Adrian's desk and the door. At right angles to the door was a blackboard on an easel on which various messages were written in chalk. Team Meetings were held on Tuesday mornings at 9.30; Dr Watkinson was giving a talk on dementia at the hospital on the 24th May at 11; The staff of Wendover Elderly People's Home was holding a tea party for Mrs Hobbins who would be 100 on 19th May and all were welcome, and in large letters across the bottom 'IS IT URGENT OR SHALL WE GIVE IT TO A SOCIAL WORKER?' An occupational therapist's joke which had caused laughter and a little cringing. But they worked so hard, Bella thought. Jeanette it seemed, was never still. Delivering aids, collecting them, modifying people's homes with a long waiting list which was constantly growing.

Under the Chronically Sick and Disabled Persons Act people could apply for telephones as well as other things such as walking sticks and bath aids. But the money for telephones ran out during the first four months of the financial year, which meant requests for phones comprised the longest waiting list of all. Bella realised she had never really thought about the importance of phones for disabled people. Now she always felt very inadequate when telling people about the long wait, after they had told her they had to walk half a mile to the nearest phone box if there was an emergency.

Jan caught her up in the car park and Bella told her she was going to see Amber Jackson and hoped that they would then take Jamie, now four years old, to the mother and toddler group in Granville Street. "I often remember Miss Bateson saying to me that my experience of loss would be useful. I would like to tell her it's not in the least useful when dealing with a woman whose first child was killed in a road accident. There's really no way to adequately deal with that. I've been visiting her for nearly a year and for the first months I just listened to her talk. It seemed most people had told her she must put it behind her and get on with life. But she needed to go on grieving and really it's time that has helped her, not me. But that's what dealing with death is like, isn't it? One gradually covers the grief with layers of new events and experiences and it begins to sink down out of immediate consciousness. But even that doesn't stop the fear that it could happen again."

"But she is getting over it?"

"Well, I got Housing to move her to a quieter street and I've spent months persuading them to erect a high fence round the front garden, and I've got her out with the child a bit, largely by taking her out to the park with Jamie, who was, of course, well secured with reins most of the time, although we have got them off so he can have a go on the swings! Today we are both going to the playgroup. She has been there with him, but hasn't been able to stay or to leave him. Today we are going to stay."

And they did stay. Amber was very shy with the staff and other mothers but she was able to relax when she saw how Jamie enjoyed himself, and Bella enjoyed the morning with the under fives, thinking how much more satisfying it was to play with small children than struggle with the inadequacies and problems of the adult world. When they left, Amber thought she would like to go again, and Bella said she would pick her up again next week, and perhaps she would be able to stay by herself.

She stopped at a garden centre on the way back and bought two tree peonies. Last month she had seen them at the centre but decided that she could not really afford to spend any more on the garden at the time. She realised she was rather pleased that Adrian would not be coming round this evening so she did not have to think about a meal and could spend time in the garden. Not that he would mind, but he wasn't really into gardening, preferring to play music and talk. He always had a new tape to listen to or had marked out a radio programme that he wanted to hear. Not that she minded. Bella enjoyed music too, but they were both ambivalent about the relationship, she thought, and it was largely because of his boys.

Jason, the youngest, didn't like her. That was obvious. He didn't like her because he was scared she and Adrian were going to be a permanent fixture. It was the relationship with Adrian he didn't like not her, she thought, and Adrian... Adrian was... well, it wasn't his fault, but he seemed frightened too... dreadfully worried all the time about Jason's feelings, but wasn't that right? Wouldn't she worry, she thought, if Gemma was upset about her having a relationship with someone else? But that didn't fit somehow – history and circumstances were too different.

She shook away the discomfort of thinking about Adrian's boys and thought about the last year, which had been good. They had had two weekends away in a cottage belonging to a friend of Adrian's in Somerset, and although they were not actually living together, Adrian came round several times during the week and stayed, and every month or so they had the boys with them, which had been rather hard work, but was not so bad as to alter her feelings for Adrian.

The test, she thought, is how would it feel if he did not come any more. The mere possibility made her cold and empty. She thought of how he loved her, cherished her, and filled her with a passion that had been absent for so many years. He was very untidy and teased her out of the routines which had become part of her single life. He made her laugh – they were good together, she knew that.

Later, when she left work and went home, she climbed upstairs to change her clothes for gardening. On her dressing table was the letter from Sim that had come a few days ago. In it, she knew, was the suggestion that she went to Canada and stayed with them for a holiday and took Adrian with her. "We want to meet this man of yours, see if we approve…"

She had mentioned it to him and although he seemed pleased with the suggestion there was a hesitation in his manner that made her wonder. He said something about talking to the boys. She wasn't sure what he really felt.

But once in the garden she became absorbed in her plants and it wasn't until it was getting dark she remembered she had not eaten.

***

Harry pushed the window and it opened slowly inwards. He heaved himself up to the sill and squeezed through, jumping down to the floor.

"You see, it's easy. Give me your hand." He leaned forward extending his hand to Charlotte who was gazing nervously over her shoulder. "Come on. No one is coming. It's OK."

Charlotte took his hand and thought how climbing through a window in the dark in an empty house was different from sitting at a desk in the office complaining about the Housing Department. But he pulled her up until she got a leg across and slid herself through onto the floor. In the dim light of dusk she could see she was in a room which had been a kitchen. It smelled sour and musty. There were cupboards against the opposite wall and an old fridge stood with its door open next to a shallow and stained sink. The floor was littered with paper, bits of broken china and rags. As she got to her feet, she kicked a saucepan which scuttled across the floor with a metallic clang. "Oh, my God. Someone will hear us."

"Don't panic. No one will hear. These old houses are pretty soundproof and if anyone did they'd think it was a cat or something. Now we are in, we haven't committed a crime. We haven't broken anything so it isn't breaking and entering and there is nothing to steal, so it isn't burglary. Minor trespass, perhaps but don't worry so much. Come on. I'll show you around and we must open the front door. Bob and Arlene will be here in about fifteen minutes."

Showing Charlotte around did not take long. It was a small Victorian terraced house with two rooms on the ground floor and a kitchen built on to the back in the small yard through which Harry and Charlotte had entered via a broken gate. In the front room the only furniture was a table, two broken chairs and a dilapidated armchair sagging in a corner. There were scraps of torn lino still covering dirty floorboards; the fireplace was filled with paper and cigarette ends and the window was half covered with the remains of a net curtain. There was a damp, musty smell mixed with the smell of stale cigarettes. In the back room which also smelled of dirt and ash, there was nothing but a torn rag rug partly covering broken floorboards in front of the fireplace which, in the half light, also appeared to be full of ash, paper and cigarette ends.

"Oh, Harry, it's awful. Filthy and falling to pieces."

"It's not exactly your des res, I grant you, but it wouldn't be empty if it was and it will clean up and be a lot better than sleeping in an old car. Come on, I'll show you the bedrooms."

In the small hallway Harry opened the front door and they made their way up the narrow stairway where it was completely dark. At the top there were rooms to the right and left, one of which was completely empty except for a suitcase spilling old newspapers. The other room contained a single bed frame without a mattress.

"There's no bathroom."

"Ten out of ten for observation. As you say, there's no bathroom. But there is a privy outside the kitchen door. I was saving that 'til last. Actually I have only peered in so far. I saw there was a broom handle and the frame of what looked like a pushchair. I though I'd wait until I had some support before I investigated further in case I fainted. But as I told you, there is water. The tap in the kitchen gives out a nice stream of cold water. I don't know why but the water hasn't been disconnected, so hopefully, the privy works."

Back in the kitchen Harry took two candles from his pocket and sticking them on pieces of broken saucers lit them and put them on the fridge. "It'll be OK to have a light in here, I think. Can't be seen from the road. But until they are actually in I think we should be careful so no one notices the occupation."

Charlotte went to the sink and turned on the tap which immediately sprouted a jet of brownish cold water. "You see, cool clear water," Harry said. "Well, it will probably be clear once it has been run for a bit. Can't understand why it's still operating, but it flows. With water they can cope."

"Without light or gas or electricity. This oven is gas."

"We can get some light. Camping stuff and a camping stove. Come on, where's the blazing revolutionary spirit you had when we discussed it? Don't despair. Remember this is space and better than what they have got, which is nothing, and coping with relatives who don't want to help. And we will have help. Jan and Bella and Adrian. They will help – and probably the others as well when we tell them."

"What about Rachael? What sort of reaction will we get from her? I mean, she hates the Housing Department but she is management."

They were interrupted at this point by a noise which made them jump but Harry went to the hall and met the two people who had just come in. "Great. You got here. Are you OK? Come on in."

Bob, a pale thin man in his thirties with long straggly fair hair, wearing jeans and a sweater with holes at the elbows walked into the kitchen followed by Arlene, nervously wide-eyed, her dark hair fiercely backcombed and rather overwhelming her small face. She stood on her platform shoes beside him, her eyes darting round the room while she fiddled with the buttons on her jacket. "Is it alright, Harry? I mean, someone might see us."

"It's not breaking and entering. The door was open, wasn't it? It's squatting in an empty house, or it will be if you still want to do it. It's not illegal. They can't turn you out without a court order. We'll have to get a new lock for the front door so you can get in and out, and there's a back door here we can lock up as well. I expect you could fix them, couldn't you Bob?"

"Don't worry – easy job."

"Come on, then. Let's look at the rest of it. It isn't exactly Buck House, but it will clean up and once we have some furniture in... well... come and see."

So they went round the house, now almost completely dark. Harry lit one of the candles briefly in each room which brought gasps of dismay from Arlene but a growing reaction of optimism and enthusiasm from Bob, who suddenly seemed to be an expert in DIY. They talked about the need to clean up and the way they would get some furniture in – in the early mornings or evenings, Harry thought – and the way they would equip the family by begging and borrowing. Bob became quite animated. He said he could get stuff and he had mates who would help. He presented as a fixer with a finger in many pies. Arlene was not so easily enthused.

"There's no bathroom. How shall I bath the kids? I must bath the kids," she said, but eventually, even she began to make some suggestions, agreed they could still use her mother's bathroom and it would do somehow. So they decided that they would start cleaning up as quickly as possible, perhaps actually getting one room fit for them to stay in, if they could get a mattress on the floor. Arlene thought her mother would have the children for a couple more nights. She had them already of course, while the parents still slept in Bob's brother's old Morris Minor. "And if she knows we really will be going, she'll talk me Dad round. It's him as makes the fuss about us, you see." She spoke to Charlotte, explaining.

When they left by the back door, Harry left it unlatched and took them out through the yard to the alley at the back. "Best you use this entrance for now, especially if you are bringing stuff in, and we'll see you here tomorrow evening to give you a hand."

When they had said goodbye, Harry and Charlotte went to the pub, both feeling high. They ordered drinks and laughed with the excitement of children.

"You see, it's working. I knew we could do it."

"It was actually easy. I thought it would be awful. I even wondered if they would come. Will they really do it?"

"Oh, they'll do it now if we get them some stuff. We must have a meeting with the team and get them involved. And we must start collecting. Now what have you got at home you can do without?"

"You must see to the front door lock."

"I'll buy one tomorrow and Bob can fix it. It's going to be his home."

"Oh, my God! What are we doing Harry?"

"I think we can call it social engineering. We are supposed to be agents of change, remember. Isn't that what they taught us at college? Well, agents of change change things and on my course we talked a lot about the need to focus on our own management instead of always trying to make the clients behave differently. The institutions sometimes need to change. That is what we are about."

"And when they are more or less settled, we go public, right?!"

"Absolutely. We write to the papers, the MP, the Housing Department, the City Councillors – the lot –anonymously of course!"

***

Harry bought a lock for the front door and a bolt for the kitchen door and he and Charlotte met Bob and Arlene the following evening... Bob full of enthusiasm and ideas for getting hold of this and that, Arlene nervously starting to sweep the kitchen floor and constantly shushing everyone in case someone heard them. Charlotte had brought black bin bags for the rubbish and a flask of coffee and some plastic mugs and they gradually cleared the downstairs rooms of debris, and made a list of the things they would need to do.

In the pub later Harry and Charlotte quarrelled about telling the team. Should they include Rachael? Should they include Jeanette? What about Marian, their clerk? Charlotte had moments of panic when she thought of being sacked and losing her income and possibly her flat but Harry almost looked forward to the storm to come. He appeared to welcome the idea of getting fired, talking about the fuss they would be able to make, involve the Union and the British Association of Social Workers. "It will be a marvellous fight," he said, "and Housing will never be the same again. Think of the stink we shall cause, don't worry about it." Charlotte agreed not to, but worried nevertheless.

They eventually decided it would not be fair to involve Rachael who would certainly be asked to tell all she knew once things became public. They could not expect her to lie. And Marian? She was part of the team but again, was it fair to tell her? Jeanette? Well, she would probably be annoyed to be left out.

In fact, the news began to leak out. Charlotte told Bella and Adrian what they had done and Bella told Jan. The news was received with nervous excitement but also astonished admiration, and Bella felt a rush of adrenalin as she remembered the emotion she and James had shared when they took part in the CND campaigns. To be part of something that had a political edge...

And the team were surprising. Apart from Don, who had never questioned the system in his long life in local government, and who foretold dire consequences for Charlotte and Harry, everyone was amazed and then delighted. And everyone offered to help with the things they needed.

What surprised them even more was when Harry told them he had recruited two members of Shelter, a local curate, a disaffected member of the Department of Social Security and two members of the Good Life Community which occupied an old church on the edge of town and who held all worldly goods in common (so had no problem with taking over an empty house) and where everyone was concerned with spreading peace and love. These people all helped with food, furniture and household stuff and the women from the Community had also volunteered to type the letters which were to send news of the squat to all those who needed to know.

During the next two weeks all manner of things began to arrive in the team room and the car park for onward transmission to the squat. Rachael did ask why Charlotte had two boxes of old china on her desk and a roll of carpet stuffed behind her chair.

"People just keep giving me stuff," Charlotte said, which seemed completely inadequate, but satisfied Rachael at the time. The appearance of Harry and Charlotte manipulating a fireside chair into Harry's car excited some attention from Judy Naseby who stopped to watch.

"WRVS," muttered Harry, which told nothing, but made Judy nod and smile before walking away.

Rumours did spread. Area 2 workers came into the team room more often than they usually did, clearly seeking information. They were told nothing, but the team remained edgy and nervous for the two weeks before Bob and Arlene moved in properly with their children. They only had the bare essentials but the house was a good deal cleaner. It was then that the notice was pinned on the door, the press informed and a letter, unsigned, sent to the Housing Department, the press and all the City Councillors, giving the information that this family, who had been homeless for over six months, forcing the parents to sleep in an old car, had taken over the house which had been empty for over two years, and were squatting.

On the day the local paper featured the squat in large type on the front page the Director asked the Team Leaders if any social worker was involved with this family, and in due course he sent for Harry.

The whole team was present when Harry returned. No one had gone out. Everyone was waiting. He smiled and said he supposed everyone was hungry for the possibility he had been sacked. He sat at his desk and looked round silently until Jan said, "For goodness sake tell us what happened."

"Well, he asked me if I had helped the family squat and I told him a lie. I said I hadn't, but once they were in they told me and I supplied some of the things they needed via the WRVS. I said that they told me they were desperate and I knew they were. I told him we have been talking to the Housing Department every week for months, but my main concern was for the children and making sure they were cared for properly. He said it was very unfortunate that the Department was involved at all and there might be a presumption that we had helped them take over the house. I said did it really matter if there was such a presumption. The family were in need for housing and I had seen the stress they were suffering and the strain it was having on the marriage and the children and that was the main issue. He got a bit shirty then and said that as a member of the Department it was essential we respected the law, and he would have to answer for the behaviour of his staff."

Harry paused and looked round. He said he began to feel confident at this point. He realised he could actually say all the things that bugged him. He went on, "I said squatting was not illegal and the department should be concerned for the welfare of the family and should work to get homeless people housed properly and then they wouldn't have to squat. He didn't seem to like this. He said I seemed to lack loyalty to the service which employed me. The people in Housing were my colleagues and as such deserved my support." He paused again. "I had to say it. I told him I thought that we deserved their support."

There was a small outburst of clapping at this. People were smiling and nodding, and then all talking at once, assuring themselves and each other that Harry could not be sacked. In fact no one could be sacked... could they?

But Evelyn thought it might start a squatting trend. She had a family in bed and breakfast already talking about it and she could hardly blame them, turned out of B&B at ten and not allowed back until six. How could families cope? And the mother, who was such a nice, kind woman, already shouting at the children.

Jennifer was surprisingly enthused. One could never tell with Jennifer, Bella thought. So conservative most of the time (she had a cousin who worked at Buckingham Palace) she could be startlingly radical. She thought Harry and Charlotte very brave and had heard that the Director had told Rachael that Harry should be heavily supervised in future and not involved with families with housing problems. Jennifer wondered if Rachael was supposed to creep around, spying on him in the evenings. "What nonsense," she said.

Don was the only one who was worried. He said they were all local government officers and should not work against one another. They had to be loyal to the organisation – that was what he had always been taught. But Harry was quite clear. "Times have changed," he said, "Loyalty to colleagues used to be about not rocking the boat, watching our backs, keeping everything steady and comfortable. We now have to show some of our loyalty to the clients... and if that means stirring everyone up, so much the better. Who else is going to do it?"

"In Bristol the social workers have been very vocal about the squats. Getting themselves quoted in the papers and storming around generally. Perhaps we should do that," Jan said.

But Harry knew. "I've been in touch with them and they said we should go for it. They are right behind us. Let's wait and see for the moment. The Housing Department will have to get a court order to get them out – that means more publicity and it won't do them much good to make the family homeless again, will it? They will have to re-house them!"

"But thank you all for your support. You are wonderful." Charlotte beamed at everyone as they gradually went back to their desks and the telephone on Jennifer's desk rang, joined a moment later by Jan's phone reminding her she was on duty. Adrian, who had been sitting at Bella's desk, returned to his own and Harry put his coat on and went out with Meg. Evelyn switched the kettle on and Don took the tray of dirty cups to wash. Charlotte walked up to Bella's desk and stared through the window behind her.

"Harry and Meg are going round there now," she said to Bella. "He has got hold of another gas camping light they can use but he really wants to see if the press are still round there. I think he's looking for an opportunity to be quoted."

"If he does get into print, I think we should join him, don't you?" Bella was still filled with the frisson of excitement that had run through the team while Harry was talking. "I mean, it will be important that he isn't standing alone."

"Absolutely. Oh, Bella, I know this is right and it's fantastic that we have all the team behind us. Nearly everyone is with us, aren't they?"

***

As Bella shut the front door the telephone rang. It was Adrian to say he would be too late to cook as promised, and unless she could think of something else, he would bring fish and chips on his way home, He hoped he wouldn't be too long; he was waiting for the doctor to arrive and see a client who was refusing to take his medication and getting very confused. He usually responded to the doctor but if the worst came to the worst he might need to be admitted. Bella couldn't think of anything else they could eat and said she would survive on Scotch until he arrived. She might even go to sleep. In fact she went into the garden and contemplated the bulge on the right, which she had nearly cleared of nettles and ivy the previous weekend. It was to be an arbour and there was to be a seat. Piles of weeds, and general debris waited to be taken down to the bonfire but that would mean changing her clothes and it would soon be too dark to work outside. She went back into the house and glanced at the collection of letters she had picked from the mat, immediately noticing one from Martha and a card from her mother and father who were staying with her uncle in Harrogate and suffering from colds and strong winds.

She poured a second whisky before opening Martha's letter wondering why she always felt slightly apprehensive when Martha wrote and remembering she must bring up the subject of a trip to Canada with Adrian.

In fact there was nothing to be apprehensive about in Martha's letter. It was full of superlatives. She was now working in Mapplethorpe in an Intake Team, which she seemed to like. She said the department had been re-organised. They now had teams dealing with long-term work, and she was in the Intake Team which saw all new clients and worked with them for up to three months before those which were still active were passed on to the teams dealing with long term children or adults. She said it had been a bit of a muddle at first, and they were very busy and sometimes confused, but on the whole it was a good idea. She said she was learning a lot, as they had to cope with all comers, whatever the problem, but it was interesting. And their senior was marvellous, there was terrific support. She and Luke had a new flat which was large and airy and the new furniture looked really good although it had been difficult choosing things with Luke. Rather like shopping with mother, she said, with several exclamation marks. The letter sounded breathless. Martha on a high. Well, perhaps it was going to work out.

She knew she should not just sit doing nothing. There was ironing. There was the weekend with Adrian's boys coming. She should bake a cake. There were chores to be done. The house was neglected. Newspapers lying around; shoes scattered by the kitchen door; cereal packets on the dresser from breakfast; general disorder. No longer just my home, Bella thought. So are we a couple? We don't make plans more than a week or so ahead. We don't speculate on the future. We avoid that. We just fell into this. Into bed, I suppose. But gradually it is taking hold on both of us. And not just us. Now we have the boys fairly regularly and Mum and Dad met Adrian when they came down for the weekend and Mum now thinks I am settled for life. But I'm not. I don't feel settled at all. The boys are suspicious and Jason hardly speaks to me and I have this feeling that what is happening now is temporary, even though I don't want it to end.

    She turned on the television and looked at the Radio Times. She had missed The Liver Birds. She switched channels and found a debate between four people who were talking about the significance of the prison sentences handed down to the men complicit in the Watergate scandal. She turned it off and found music on the radio. Something by Mozart she thought and sat down to listen. She would relax and wait for the fish and chips... but she thought about the team and the crisis Jan had had to deal with. A cot death? But there had been concern about the family. There were rumours that they smoked pot and Jan had sometimes found Tracey Brownley vague and strange and ignoring the baby crying in his cot. Today she had been rung by the police and had found the Brownleys at the police station, shocked and shaking, with Tracey repeating how she had found the baby this morning, cold and dead. She seemed unable to answer any questions, while the father protested they should be allowed to go home. Now they were waiting for the pathologist's report.

    Her mind drifted. The excited apprehension over the squat and the news that they were about to be re-organised again into Intake and Long-term teams – Martha is ahead of me here, she thought – and old Mrs Staples who, she thought, she was slowly killing. Bella felt herself flooded with disasters. The music did not help so she got up and switched it off and went into the kitchen, taking out the mixing bowl and ingredients for the weekend cake.

She had just broken the eggs into the bowl when Adrian came in full of apologies, putting fish and chips in the oven and moving her away from the cake in order to kiss her and then explaining. Listening to him and extracting herself to finish the cake she felt her gloom lift. They laid the table with plates and cutlery. Adrian found the half full bottle of wine on the dresser and when Bella had exchanged the fish for the cake, they sat down to eat.

Bella asked about Adrian's case. She was always interested in what he did, still feeling very unsure about mental health. He explained that the doctor was a long time coming and Tom – his client – had been very agitated and quite aggressive towards his mother. He wouldn't take his pills saying he would be quite alright if she would go away. He said she was a pain, and she was, Adrian said, a very fussy lady, constantly pressing her son to take his pills. When the doctor turned up Adrian thought they had probably lost it, but the doc sent her into the kitchen to make some tea and Tom gradually calmed down and took his pills. Adrian was surprised that the doctor had a very good relationship with Tom – they began to talk about the rugby, there was an important match last Saturday. And Tom did agree eventually that the pills would make him feel better. The doc said he would be able to cope with his mother if he kept taking them and they both laughed.

"The doc thinks he would be better away from his mother entirely, but that's not really on. He's going to try to get him into the new day centre at Millbank Ave, when it opens. God. I'm hungry... and so how was your day? And how did it go for Jan?"

So they talked and worried about the dead baby and about Jan. Bella said it could be bad. Jan had not told Rachael she wondered about drugs, and she had not put anything in the file. They speculated. And then she told him about Mrs Staples, an eighty-three-year-old diabetic whose daughter was taking too much time off work to look after her and was worried she would lose her job and her pension if it went on much longer. She came to the department and asked if she could get her mother into an old people's home. She had cried when she asked and said she didn't want her to go but didn't know what else to do.

Bella had talked to the old lady. She had taken her to see St Stephens House where there was a vacancy, and was in the process of filling in all the forms. But today, the daughter had greeted Bella with the news that she thought her mother had decided to die as she had stopped eating and would not have her insulin or get out of bed. Mrs Staples looked very frail and ill lying quietly in her bed and had simply told Bella that it was kind of her to call, but she had decided not to go anywhere. She had lived in this house for forty-five years and couldn't move now, but she was grateful for the trouble Bella had taken and sorry she had wasted her time. She didn't say she wanted to die at home, but there was a finality about the conversation which was quite clear, Bella thought. Something that had to be accepted.

"I just said I quite understood, and I did, and I thought how pleasant she was. They have such good manners, haven't they? Then I talked to the daughter in the kitchen, you know, helping her face the situation I suppose. She's about fifty and seems to have no other relatives. Her job is clearly very important and there will be a pension. I said there was no need for her to feel guilty. Her mother was making a choice as she had a right to do." Bella stopped talking and stared into space, then she said, "I didn't say so, but I'm sure I'd rather die than go into St Stephens. When we were there we sat in the lounge between an old man who was sleeping and snoring with his mouth open, and a demented soul who kept asking us if we were going to take her to the park – the staff were quite nice but the residents... and there was this odour of disinfectant and urine. I told the daughter

I thought her mother would probably prefer to die at home and we were both in tears by the time I left. I wondered how I would cope if that happened to me. And then… then, I really cheered myself up." She was silent for a minute until Adrian said, "Well, go on…"

So she told him about visiting Joan Bowen, who was pregnant and wanted an abortion, and was furious to discover her husband had to agree. He was in prison and had refused to allow it, so Joan suggested to Bella that she take the child for adoption as soon as it was born. Bella said she explained that he would have to agree to that as well, and it sounded unlikely that he would and even if he did agree, the adoption panel would not like it at all. Joan had raged at her, Bella said, asking her how she would like to have another baby when she had two already and a husband who was always in prison, and whom she was going to divorce anyway. Bella said she tried to remind her about the births of her two girls and said she had always thought she was such a good mother and when the baby was born… well … "I told her she would love it like she loved the girls. She cried then and said no one understood." Bella looked hard at Adrian and said she actually thought that perhaps we should listen to clients like Joan instead of trying to persuade them they were wrong. After all, some people did have too many children and couldn't love them all.

"Enough of this!" Adrian began to clear the table, pouring the remains of the wine into Bella's glass. "Drink up. We watch 'The Old Grey Whistle Test' in a minute and I forbid either of us to mention work again. And, yes, I've had a great idea. This weekend the boys are coming, but next weekend, we are going away."

"Where are we going?"

"I don't know. We shall decide. How about the sea? A long way away from all this crap anyway!"

"Oh, the sea would be good. Yes, I would like that. But can we afford it?

"We need to talk about us. What we are doing. Don't you think? Get right away from this atmosphere of gloom and doom. I don't know if we can afford it, but we'll go anyway. Some things one has to afford." He dried his hands and bent down to Bella, kissing her hair. "Come on. Let's have some escapism, watch the box and pretend we are still in our teens and then we will go to bed and behave like adults."

It's what I was wondering about, Bella thought. The future. What are we really doing? Adrian had been thinking about it too. She felt a wave of anxiety and wondered if she really wanted to confront this now – or even at all. But she followed him into the sitting room and slid down beside him on the sofa, letting go of the future as he drew her towards him and feeling warm and secure and wanted.

***

"Before we start let's say how glad we are that the pathologist said the baby died of natural causes. One anxiety over at least and you will all be pleased to know that the squat is over. The family is to be re-housed. Nothing very great of course. They have been given a house in Wellington Road – you know, that really scruffy area – and I think the house is pretty grotty, but still they are being re-housed."

"My God. Wellington Road! That's where the Billingtons were moved from because the house was contaminated. It's not the same house, is it?" Charlotte exclaimed.

"I don't know but it could be. They will be punished, that's for sure, but they do have a house and whatever it's like it will be better than the squat."

"Maybe it has shaken up Housing."

"It hasn't done your career prospects a lot of good, Harry."

"I know – and there was I thinking I'd be Director by the time I'm forty."

"Who will be next? Anyone got a really bad housing problem? I have a list of unoccupied council houses now," Charlotte offered.

"Before you go I have some stuff here which will really excite you." Rachael distributed papers to each desk saying, "Here is something to brighten up your day. New referral forms. Just what you all wanted. We are to try them out and feed back our reactions… AND… there is more. Mary Cope and Jason Masters are going to do a sort of Time and Motion study on all of us. It's about casework management. Now won't that be nice?"

"Who are Mary Cope and Jason Masters?"

"I believe they are the people who have just been appointed as special project officers. They will be coming to see us. The Director thinks this will make us all more efficient."

"Oh, my God. As if we haven't got enough to do."

"What would make us more efficient is to be given more staff and not more work."

"These forms are nearly twice as long as the ones we use."

"Are we really supposed to find out all this information on the first interview? I mean, name of doctor, name of health visitor, names and ages of all the children, and the schools they go to. This is really going to make clients feel at ease? Oh, and this. If moved in last two years, previous address and date of previous contact with our office. It's going to be such a help when Mrs Bloggs comes in with an electricity bill she can't pay!"

"What is all this info for?"

Rachael sighed. "I think it's supposed to help us, or so they think, and some of it will be useful. I mean we often need some of this info as cases develop."

"By the time we've got all this info the client will have forgotten why they have come."

"It makes us so bureaucratic and I thought we were supposed to be easy to contact. It's 'we are here to help you but please jump through all these hoops first'."

"We've only got to use the forms for two months, then we evaluate. They are going to send us another form for this and I think I shall be seeing each of you in turn to fill it in, so we shall have an opportunity to say what we think."

"That's what these people in City Hall do. Invent new forms. What shall we do today, they say. I say, let's invent some new referral forms. There must be lots of information those social workers can ask for which might be useful one day, and think how busy we shall be sorting it all out and making lists and producing figures."

Rachael said, "There is one other thing before you all go... The proposed Intake Team. It seems that this is going ahead and the aim is to re-organise so we can start in a couple of months."

"What does that mean?"

"Who's going to be in this new team?"

"Are we getting a choice?"

"I thought we were going to have a student. I'm supposed to be going on a student supervision course in four weeks." This from Jan who went on, "And what about our cases? Are we just handing them over to someone else because I certainly can't do that."

"Hang on. Don't panic and all talk at once. You know roughly what is proposed. We will have a team dealing with all the new work. They will be permanently on duty and the idea is that they attempt to work intensively for about three months with what comes through the door or over the phone, but when it seems the case is going to be a long term affair, they will hand it over to the long-term teams. Some stuff will go straight to long term anyway, statutory work like supervision orders, care orders and so on. Come on, you know there's always a debate about whether we should be doing duty as well as dealing with all our other work. You are always complaining that duty gets in the way of all your plans. This way the long term teams – and you could all be long-term workers – won't be trying to cope with everything.

"Personally I think it has a lot going for it and we shall be having a proper discussion when a draft of all the proposals comes out in a week or so. And you'll be glad to know that we shall be getting a Standby Team soon. We have kept on about this and it seems they have found the money, so no more evening and night duties!"

Bella felt a flood of relief at this piece of news. Being on call at night was one of her greatest bugbears. It only came round about once in two weeks, but she always dreaded it – never knowing what she might have to cope with. She remembered the last time when the police had rung at 11.30 pm, about a man called Michael Bailey threatening his family with a carving knife. They had rung the doctor and the police and the doctor had rung the psychiatrist and when Bella arrived at the house four policemen were nervously talking to a man crouched behind a chair brandishing a large knife, while three frightened relatives were pleading with him to put it down. They made way for her and told the man a social worker had come to see him, which was a mistake. He knew about them, he said, and they gave you stuff to poison you. Bella told him she had no stuff like that and wanted to help. Perhaps he could tell her what had upset him. He stood up again and began to shout at her. Everyone tells lies, he yelled. Everyone wanted to lock him up, and she could get out or he'd carve her up in small pieces so she wouldn't know who she was any more. Bella felt the tension in the young PC beside her and wanted to back away. She tried to stifle her fear and remembered Adrian talking about Dr Laing who argued that madness was a form of personal alienation with patients losing their sense of self, and she suggested to Michael that perhaps he was not quite well and would like to feel better and there were people who could help him, which sounded very weak and absurd in her own ears. So it was with relief that she heard a commotion at the door and Dr Martin Berry, the GP, and Dr Thomas Bakewell, the psychiatrist came in.

Dr Bakewell stationed himself just behind Bella and one of the policemen and said in a loud voice that he did hope no one was going to tell him that something must be done. He then said he remembered Michael and it seemed he was not very well and should go into hospital. Michael was silent for a moment, staring at the doctor, then he said it was all part of the plan and he knew what they would do because he remembered the last time and the needles. No one was going to put needles into him again. He waved the knife and stabbed the air with it, laughing.

Bella remembered telling Adrian how the psychiatrist had then turned to the GP and said to give him a shot of largactil and bring him into Ward F9, and then turned on his heels and went out, pausing for a moment to tell the relatives that the hospital would sort him out and not to worry. Everyone had stood silently for a moment, one of the women sobbing quietly and then the GP had said that if the police could disarm him he would sedate him and they could take him to hospital. No one, Bella remembered, had spoken to her.

It was strange, she remembered, Michael suddenly seemed to give in. He smiled and threw the knife on to the sofa, where it was quickly picked up by a policeman, and then they surrounded him. He made no protest or resistance when they handcuffed him and Dr Berry gave him an injection – he smiled and said needles, they always use needles – and then the police took him outside. It happens like that sometimes, Adrian had said. People who have violent episodes so often seem to know that they will go to hospital. They even want to, I think, he said. But awful for you. And that bloody doctor. That's Dr Bakewell. In and out as quickly as possible. And no thought for the relatives for whom it must have been horrific.

Bella said she and the doctor signed the necessary papers and stayed and talked to the family, who knew the system but were very upset. She then took the papers up to the hospital where Michael was already asleep. Yes, she was glad there was going to be a Standby Team for emergencies like this but it hadn't started yet, so perhaps she should read the book he had recommended – The Divided Self, wasn't it, by R. D. Laing? Adrian nodded and smiled. "Yes, you should," he said. "And then you can explain it to me!"

***

"Do you think that's enough potatoes?" Bella waved the baking tin towards Gemma. "Twenty, that's four each, and I'm not going to eat more than two, I'm out of the habit of large meals. But don't do too many sprouts, I have a cauliflower and carrots. And when we've done these I think we should have a drink."

They worked round each other, getting things out, putting things away and remembering there was bread sauce to make and the pudding to check. Gemma telling about Christmas with Josh's parents last year and how good it was to be home this year.

It is good for me too, Bella thought. It feels so comfortable to have Gemma here and good, last night, to talk. Gemma wanted to know if Adrian was coming round and dug deftly at the subject of her mother's relationship, and Bella had found it easy and satisfying to talk to her and express some of the ambivalence she felt.

"So you are just having a permanent affair?"

"I suppose I am. Although Adrian would like something more. He has talked about selling our houses and buying something together."

"And you don't want to do that?"

"We both have other lives. Other emotional entanglements. I don't think his sons would like it, and... and... well, I'm not sure I want to live with anyone else permanently." She laughed. "I think I'm getting rather set in my ways and enjoy being totally in charge of my life. We went away and talked very seriously about it and I tried to explain."

"And does Adrian understand that?"

"Well, he says he does, but I think he hopes I will change my mind."

"And if you don't, will he still be around in the future?"

"I don't know. No. I don't know."

Grace and Henry on the other hand, talked about Adrian as if he had just been called away. They were curious about him and were surprised to learn that next year when she was planning her trip to Canada, he would not be going with her. She explained that he would be taking his holiday with his sons and needed to save his holiday for them and although Grace thought it would have been such a good opportunity to get to know them, she let the subject drop. Bella thought they had expected some announcement of an engagement or a marriage but were nervous about asking too many questions in case something had gone wrong. Bella knew they wanted her to marry again, but a divorced man with children was not what they had in mind. Bella felt they would rather not think too much about it and with Gemma and Josh here, her parents, particularly her father, seemed relaxed and content. The law was such a solid and respectable profession and here were two solicitors, one of them a much loved granddaughter who was canny enough not to tell him she spent much of her time helping the feckless with their debts and housing problems.

Later, when dinner had been eaten and cleared away and Josh had brought out a Noel Coward record he had bought for Grace just in time to clash with the Queen's speech, Gemma told Bella that she had seen Martha who had been visiting Stockport. They had had lunch. It was all very unexpected but Martha was visiting a child in a foster home and wanted to talk about the progress he was making at school and what a good placement it seemed to be. "And listening to her," Gemma said, "was actually rather like listening to you on a good day." They both laughed.

"My God, we are all alike – everlastingly talking shop. But I'm glad she seemed OK. I wasn't sure it was a good idea changing profession as she did."

"She did seem fine, although Martha was always either one thing or the other. She's always either up or down. I wondered what I was going to get and I got the high, although she did say that it's a bit difficult with her mother as Luke doesn't ever want to visit. Can't say I blame him there. I could never stand Liz either, but you know that."

Chapter Six

1978

They stood in a small group outside the crematorium talking quietly and doing their best to ignore the cold. A black suited man asked Bella whether they would like to take some of the flowers or whether these should be left with the ashes. She had not thought about the ashes and suddenly realised that they were all that remained of her father. She moved across to her mother and asked her what she would like, unexpectedly shaken and tearful. Her mother wanted the cards. "I shall have to write to people, won't I?" The man in black collected the cards and gave them to Bella.

"What shall I do with the ashes?" Grace asked. They stood silently each wondering what to suggest. The man in black spoke softly. "Perhaps you would like to scatter them in the Garden of Remembrance?" He sounds so unctuous, Bella thought, wondering if official mourners were trained in unctuousness, or whether it came naturally. She was reminded of Uriah Heap, apologetic and slightly cringing.

"Oh, yes, Bella. What do you think? Shall we scatter them here?"

"Yes… yes. Why not? If you would like that. Of course, I think you could probably plant a tree as well eventually."

"Oh, that would be nice. Thank you."

"Have you asked everyone to come back to the house?" Bella moved round the groups, hoping they would and joined

Liz and Matthew who, surprisingly, had come. "But of course we came, Bella, I knew your parents when I was at school, remember?"

Her mother was very pleased to see Liz. She had always liked her. Liz was always so polite and helpful and Dad once remarked that she came from such good stock. It made her sound like a racehorse or a prize bull, Bella had thought at the time. And today Liz and Matthew had said all the right things about Henry, even although they were overflowing with the news about Martha's baby. Later back at the house Grace asked about the baby and they all glowed with the pleasure of new grandchildren and remarked how odd it was that Gemma and Martha had been born, married and given birth all within a few months of each other.

"Of course Gemma couldn't come today," Grace said. "It's not four weeks since little Susan was born. Much too soon to be travelling down here. Bella is going to take me up to see them in a few weeks. I can't believe I am a great grandmother. I'm just so sad that Henry didn't have the chance to see them – but somehow it seems comforting – one life goes and another arrives."

"Will Gemma give up her job now?" Liz asked.

"Oh, I doubt that. She's taking maternity leave – about five months I think, and then going back."

"Martha hasn't gone back yet, but she is talking about it, although Luke doesn't approve. I can't understand why she has this urge to do that sort of work. She doesn't need the money and the baby needs her."

"Perhaps she just likes her work," Bella said. "I know Gemma does. Of course babies need their mothers, but I don't think they need them all the time as long as there's a good childminder or nanny."

"Well, I can understand that the law must be very interesting but…"

Bella laughed, "You don't think social work is very nice, do you, Liz?"

Matthew interrupted at this point (probably defending Liz, Bella thought), to say that they had a long drive and really should be going, but Liz wasn't ready.

"I keep telling Martha she must arrange the christening and you must all come to that. It will be so good to see the girls together with their little ones; and then there will be Susan's christening. I don't suppose they have thought of this yet?"

"Oh, I don't imagine Gemma and Josh will have a christening. They have no religious beliefs, but I thought you knew that?"

Liz didn't see that as significant. Christenings were for babies, not parents. She went on to say she didn't know what to make of the younger generation. Sam, her son and his... his partner – that's what they say, isn't it – his partner, Marina, haven't had Jasper christened, but she didn't know why she was surprised, considering how they lived in that community place.

Grace ignored the disapproval and said, "Oh, yes, of course, you are an experienced grandmother. Tell me about this little boy, and Sam... is he back in England?"

"He has been home for the last year, but has gone back to India. He wanted Marina to go with him but I gather she isn't ready to go yet. She said that last time. I don't think she will ever be ready, but then I think Sam should stay at home and be a proper father. Marina doesn't seem to think that important. He has plenty of males to act as role models in the community, she said. I really wouldn't be surprised if she had a relationship with one of them while Sam is away. They live a most extraordinary life, apparently sharing everything... more like gypsies. I'm sure Jasper will be quite wild."

Bella felt she couldn't cope with Liz's endless disapproval of her family at the present time. She felt irritated and tired and managed to move away to other guests preparing to leave as well, so the next half hour was filled with fetching coats, kissing people goodbye who said what a nice service it had been, and who promised to keep in touch, urging Grace to let them know if there was anything they could do, and finally waving from their cars as they drove away. Only Grace's sister Florence stayed a little longer, arranging for Grace to stay with her in a month or so, giving Bella a cheque to give to Gemma for the baby and saying as she bade Bella goodbye, "Don't worry about Grace, Bella. I shall phone her and pop down when I can, and she's tough, you know. She'll be fine."

Dear Auntie Flo, Bella thought. Unmarried and still working part-time in the wool shop she had once managed, but always close to Grace and probably rather glad she won't have to contend with Henry any more.

"I only see Henry's brothers at funerals, and frankly, I didn't recognise those cousins at all," Grace remarked.

"We are not a very close family are we?" Bella commented, helping her mother clear away plates and glasses. "Apart from Auntie Flo, my relations are really just names that have cropped up throughout my life, mentioned from time to time. I mean, Uncle Robert? Dad often spoke of him but I don't think I have met him in years and that rather fat, balding man didn't really fit with the man Dad said was Grandad's favourite who was always getting him into trouble as a boy!"

"Your father always thought he was a disappointment to his father. Robert was so successful. He married money for a start whereas your father married me. Working class background and a mere primary school teacher until I had you. Even in the war, Robert was the hero. Promoted to captain by the end whereas Henry only managed a sergeant in the Pay Corps. Although that was quite sensible. He had banking experience."

"I remember him coming home. We were excited and you spent ages trying to buy the food he liked. You saved up our coupons, and then when he arrived..." Bella stopped herself from saying how disappointing it was. This strange man who had been away in Africa for three years seemed to rearrange the life she and her mother had developed. She had felt demoted to a child again. She lost her place in her mother's life and found she had to explain herself and justify her wishes and ambitions. Dad's favourite jibe was to call Bella and her mother a mutual admiration society. Because they encouraged each other, she supposed.

"It was odd. He felt he was a disappointment to his father and yet he found it very difficult to approve of me."

"Oh, Bella, he was very proud of you. When you graduated he was so pleased. He told everyone. But he never approved of the welfare state and believed people should make an effort to help themselves, although goodness knows, we benefited from the NHS, especially during this past year when he was ill."

"Oh, I know all about that," Bella smiled.

"I think you are like me. I sometimes think the war gave me opportunities to be useful, which I'd never had before."

She remembered her mother's constant activity during those years. Helping to run the rest centre for bombed out people, arranging emergency meals and accommodation, collecting blankets and household goods for people who had lost everything, and knitting... always knitting. Balaclavas for the troops, squares for blankets, baby clothes; and her mother's insistence she knitted as well. Perhaps I absorbed this imperative to be busy and to be useful, to affect the lives of other people.

She stayed two more days, removing, at her mother's request, all Henry's clothes and taking them to a charity shop. It seemed rather an abrupt ending to his life in the house he had lived in for thirty-six years, but Grace wanted Bella to do it while she was there, "because somehow I don't think I can do it." And together they moved the furniture around in the bedroom, "because I've got to make it mine now, haven't I?" Bella was surprised at the extent of her mother's pragmatism; at the speed at which she seemed to be adjusting, but then thought, she had always needed to get on with everything, to be active and it seemed as if she had decided she now had another life to live – perhaps, almost another chance.

Adrian rang before she left. He was missing her, he said and had tried to get away but he had been waiting for the result of the interview and this had just come. He had been offered the job and had just written his letter of acceptance. Bella realised she had not thought about this at all, Adrian leaving the Department and working as Manager at the new centre for mental health which had just opened. She knew he had wanted this and also saw the flat which was included as enabling him to sell his house. Still spending part of most weeks with Bella who continued to resist making their relationship permanent, he had begun to feel he could no longer afford the expense of the house and was, perhaps, Bella thought, re-organising his life and his objectives. Often recently she had thought he was going to slide gently out of her life and perhaps this was what she really wanted. But he startled her before saying goodbye.

"I still want to marry you, Bella. Nothing has changed there. Think about it. Talk to Grace. I know she likes me."

Oh, yes, I know that. Mother would like nothing better. She has said so often enough. But thinking of Grace taking charge of her life again, being practical and organising herself as a widow, Bella wondered if this attribute had also rubbed off on her. Or maybe I just have her genes! She thought of Jennifer at work, and her oft repeated belief that it was nature, not nurture that influenced behaviour. Her insistence that children were not subject to environmental conditions but inherited their attitudes from their fathers or mothers. There were often arguments in the team about this and Bella was inclined to think that nurture was most important – otherwise why did they work so hard to get the nurture right?

Chapter Seven

1980

Rensham had changed since Bella first arrived there. As she drove to work she was diverted through one-way streets that bypassed the pedestrian area which now led into the main square. She noted that a supermarket was taking shape on the ground recently cleared of an old chapel and some adjoining small houses – at least she thought there had been houses there. Once buildings had disappeared it was hard to remember them. It had not been a particularly pleasant area, but she was sure the huge L-shaped mass of brick and concrete was not an improvement, although people said it would be open until eight in the evenings which, she had to admit, would be very useful. And it was going to have its own car park. That certainly would be useful. Parking was becoming increasingly difficult. Everywhere there were yellow lines.

The Department had changed as well. In fact it had hardly got used to one change when another was on the way. The last Director – James Henderson – had only lasted two years. The one before him, Gareth Williams, had left suddenly after an illness, and now they had George Pringle, who had done the rounds, meeting everyone and had beamed and smiled and told them all what a tremendous job they did and how he was going to give them as much support as possible although, he sadly reminded them, the Department was overspent and he had to try and balance the books.

And the team had changed. It was now a long-term team, still dealing with all client groups, but Rachael had left to manage one of the new Family Centres providing day care for under fives and their mothers, and their Team Leader was now Malcolm Hardy. They had lost Evelyn to Intake, Harry to Community Work, and Don had retired. In their place they had Tina an adoption specialist, who seemed to prefer to keep herself to herself, Alan, who was about to leave and go to Norfolk, and Gordon, who was young, vigorous and very interested in adolescents. He was organising camping weekends and talking a lot about IT, which was about recommending special activities to the courts in cases where young people were in danger of custodial sentences. Intermediate Treatment – halfway between custody and home.

Stuck in traffic, Bella reflected on the weekend just past. Liz and Matthew had been to stay on their way to Cornwall, and it had been quite pleasant. Liz was very magnanimous in her praise of the garden. "My dear, how do you manage to do it all?" They had talked about the babies, exchanging photographs, seeking likenesses. And they talked about Gemma and Josh and Martha and Luke... especially Martha and Luke. Bella had expected criticism, she knew Liz didn't like Luke, but she was not prepared to be told that Liz thought the marriage over. "On the rocks... it won't last a year..." Martha, "she had said, was unhappy, although not without fault herself... and Luke... well apparently he was never at home... didn't help with little Beth..." she didn't know what to make of it. If Martha had stayed at home and not insisted on going back to work... Matthew tried to back her up. "I don't know what we did to our children," he said laughing, "although that little boy of Sam's is rather a jolly little fellow." Liz snorted. "He's almost wild, calls me Lizzie, and no one corrects him." Bella felt that Liz had difficulty putting the blame entirely on Luke – disapproving of her family came so easily – but she was sad to hear about the marriage.

Arriving at last at the office, Bella found the others talking about a notice which was on everyone's desk, including hers, announcing a NEW INITIATIVE for all council staff. Scarves and ties could now be purchased in the council's colours, blue and gold, which, it seemed to be assumed, would be worn with pride by all employees. Scarves would cost £10.00 and ties £7.50.

There was a mixture of anger, disbelief and amusement in the team. No one knew the council had colours... Gordon suggested they had missed an opportunity. There should be blazers as well. Jan thought they should have baseball caps with SS blazoned on the front, but Charlotte thought they would be attacked in the street. Jennifer was really angry.

"We are short staffed and posts are frozen and the work increases week upon week and they decide it would be nice if we all had matching ties and scarves. God! Who are these people? Do they think we are a public school or a cricket club? What nonsense."

Jan pulled her chair up to Bella's desk and said they had better discuss the Jenkins family whom they were visiting that afternoon. They had become very interested in the concept of working together, looking at the family system in which the individuals attempted to overcome problems by repetitive threats even though they solved nothing. Children faced with disapproval were often grounded, deprived of treats, forfeited pocket money to no effect at all, and yet parents continued to use these punishments ever more desperately, sometimes coming to the Department saying nothing worked and the only thing left was putting the child into care. Whereas working with the whole family unit it was possible to identify these transactions and help individual family members to look at the way they communicated and the ways they might change things to better effect.

Jan and Bella worked together so that one could sit back and listen and observe the session – seeing the way each person reacted to the conversation – while the other talked to each member separately and made sure that each person was heard by everyone else. It was, of course, an expensive way of working if one simply looked at the time spent by two social workers. It was, Bella and Jan thought, inexpensive in that it so often helped the family change sufficiently to function well, and not become one of the department's long term cases – with perhaps a child eventually in care.

Jan reminded Bella that the parents of Marcus originally complained that he was swearing, staying out late, refusing to do any chores and, they thought, stealing from his mother's purse. They had, Jan said, appeared to be in agreement about everything, but in fact, when they had last seen them, Mrs Jenkins had said she got very upset whereas Mr Jenkins was quite clear that he was very angry. This was important, Jan thought. The parents did not, in fact, react in the same way, so perhaps their behaviour to Marcus was also different.

"Being angry and being upset are different," Jan said. "It's possible that Marcus gets different messages and I wonder whether, in fact, Mrs Jenkins undermines Mr. Marcus is quite agreeable to talk to us, so how about asking him what the parents actually say and do and see if we can identify a difference between them. And in particular, let the parents hear what Marcus hears."

Bella agreed with this and thought they should also use the same technique in asking each parent what they did when the other one attempted to deal with the boy. "I think you are right. They are each so busy being upset or angry they don't think about how they affect each other. I got the impression that we were actually dealing with a marital battle. Mr J wants to be in charge and Mrs J uses tears and protests as a way of reducing his power. I think this is what makes him angry."

They made some notes about the structure of the coming interview and then continued to talk as they went to wash the cups and make coffee which Bella felt she had time to drink before her appointment with Malcolm for supervision.

They agreed they approved of Gordon, who had joined the team a few months ago and was already taking adolescents trekking in Wales. He had teamed up with someone from Brownfield Youth Club and they were planning a camping weekend. But they were sorry Alan was going. He had also been with them for less than a year and was now about to leave. Jan wished it was Tina who was leaving instead. "We were beginning to settle down as a team again, apart from her. She doesn't seem part of us at all. I have tried but I can't seem to make any kind of relationship. She's so precious about her adoption work it always feels as though one is interrupting some profound thought if one speaks to her."

Bella knew what she meant, although she had been pleased they had an adoption specialist. She always felt uneasy about playing God and having all that power, but she agreed Tina was odd. "The careful smile which hardly covers the impatient frown and the poised pen and little indrawn breaths which make one feel one must hurry. And have you noticed the lowered voice – almost a whisper when she talks about her work – it always feels quite conspiratorial."

Supervision always filled Bella with anxiety having to talk about what she was doing and yet she knew it also came as a relief to share the problems. Malcolm invariably made her feel good about herself and he had the kind of wisdom that made her feel secure. He was, today, pleased to hear about the work she and Jan were doing and said he was trying to get a room for family meetings at the Greenside Family Centre, where Rachael was now manager. And he was arranging for Steve Smith from the Workside Family Institute to come and give them a day's training on working with families. Bella remembered this was the man who had written an article on family therapy in one of the journals and she was particularly pleased about this, telling Malcolm that she and Jan had been the butt of some jokes about doing fancy social work and being elitist, from the others in the team. Malcolm said he had his critics too. Some of the other team managers seemed to think that family therapy was some kind of luxury for middle-class parents which they had not got time or resources for. "But you keep at it," he said. "In the long run it will save time... at least it will if it works." He laughed, "No, from what I read it's about getting families to change and solve their own problems... good stuff."

"And working with someone else is useful," Bella went on. "Once you have done it you realise how much you miss when you are on your own... body language... individual reactions to what is said. By yourself you can't stare at everyone."

"Of course it's not a good time to be talking about two people working one case. I understand they will freeze Alan's post for the moment and I'll have to decide what to do with his caseload. Well, actually I have decided what to do. I'm going to present his cases to the Fieldwork Director and ask him what he suggests as my team has enough to do already." Malcolm showed his exasperation and expressed his frustration with the politics of the time. He had never worked in a situation where there were enough resources, he said, and now they had Mrs Thatcher complaining that the public sector wanted money which the private sector could use and threatening to cap local government spending, although, of course if they got anything wrong they produced another set of rules and laws which cost more money anyway. "But we must concentrate on your cases and leave politics. Reviews I think you need to discuss, and we must book some dates."

So they consulted their diaries and Bella talked about Derrick Boston, age ten, who had been in voluntary care for some six months and whose mother was an alcoholic who had been visiting the foster home and making all kinds of promises to Derrick about going home. She had become quite aggressive to the foster parents when they told her to come and see her, Bella said. She thought Derrick needed more security and her efforts to get the mother to admit she had a drinking problem were getting nowhere. Before Derrick came into care he had been getting his own meals and even putting his mother to bed when she passed out. It was quite unacceptable that he went home. Bella thought they should apply to the court for a care order and as a review was due, she thought they could use this event to discuss this with the mother and the foster parents. It would be difficult, she said, as the mother would be totally opposed and Derrick probably upset, but the situation needed some stability.

Malcolm agreed with this plan, and Bella said she would be visiting the foster home tomorrow when she could make the arrangements. She thought she should invite the school to attend the review as well, as they had been very positive about Derrick's progress since he came into care.

They fixed two more reviews, Bella reminding Malcolm that the Belmonts lived at Upton Park, which was fifty minutes' drive away, so going there would involve a whole afternoon. And the Redcars, who had Jenny Simpkins, now sixteen and at work who would require an evening appointment.

Bella briefly referred to Mark Winters, up for his third offence of taking and driving away for whom she had to write a court report. Malcolm suggested she might see if he could join the car maintenance course being run by Probation, and ask the magistrates to give him another chance, and she mentioned Jimmy Phelps, a boy with severe learning difficulties who had been arrested for shoplifting. Bella said the police were suggesting a police caution and she felt this was appropriate. Then they came to the Stringers who had just been passed back to Bella from Intake, who had had a referral from the hospital where Peggy had been admitted with a miscarriage.

Bella remembered that this was the case where she had taken Adrian, years ago now, and started taking the older children to school. It had been a good idea at the time and Peggy had gradually taken heart at the progress the children made. The case was closed eventually, but had opened again when Peggy's old habits reasserted themselves. Bella had begun the process once more keeping up her visits until Billy went to school, when the case had again been closed – about a year ago, she thought. Intake had become involved recently when Peggy was admitted to hospital with a miscarriage and was found to have bruising to her stomach and shoulders, which she said had been caused by a fall. The hospital were not convinced and seemed to think she had been abused by Jack whose personality did not endear him to the hospital, or to Intake who had looked at it briefly before referring back to Bella.

When Bella discussed it with Malcolm, admitting that she was relieved that Peggy was not having another baby, he had decided he should visit with her now that people were worrying about abuse, and Bella had agreed to this willingly, knowing she was frightened of Jack. She remembered the occasion when he had opened the door to her and told her Peggy was out and she could keep her nose out of their business. "We can do without the fucking welfare interfering, so you can bugger off."

Visiting with Malcolm had been quite different. He had immediately made it clear that the Department was worried about the family and intended to visit regularly to monitor everyone's welfare and to ensure that Peggy was getting support from her husband, as this had not always been evident in the past. Jack, who was sober, had protested that he was also concerned and knew his wife needed help and they were all very upset about the miscarriage. Peggy and the children had said very little except that they were alright, although they seemed to find it difficult to respond to Jack's sudden show of interest and affection.

"I think you should visit every week for now," Malcolm said on the way back to the office. "There was a strange, almost artificial atmosphere there. If you have any worries, I want to know, and it may be we should call a case conference."

Bella thought Jack had been subdued by the presence of a man. "He frightens me," she said, "and he knows he does." But she agreed they might need to call a case conference.

Case conferences were now part of everyone's working life. The great scandal of the Maria Colwell case, which had filled the papers and the media in 1973 when Maria was killed by her stepfather, had left an indelible mark on social work. No one actually pretended that abusing children was a new feature of family life, but there was an official enquiry into the events leading up to Maria's death and the public became aware that there was now a body of people employed to ensure that all children were safe, and that on this occasion they had failed. A new vigilance took hold and the social work profession became the object of detailed scrutiny. Case conferences became an official procedure for the exchange of information between all agencies concerned with children. When an allegation was made or a suspicion arose, Social Services Departments had to be informed and they subsequently invited all agencies who were likely to be involved with the family to a meeting where all that was known was discussed and debated. It was at this meeting that a decision was made as to how work should proceed and whether the children concerned should be placed on the At Risk register and their future progress monitored.

Children were still abused, of course, but if the Social Services Department had been involved there was always someone else, besides the actual abuser, who could be held responsible.

Bella was aware that sharing information was important. Different purposes cause different perceptions. Social workers, casualty officers, nursery staff, health visitors and probation officers – they all focussed on their own work. They tried to help, encourage in their own way. Meetings helped to paint a larger picture. But even so, no one had second sight. No one, or very few, thought that breaking up families was what they should do. Case conferences and the unified decisions they reached made it easier to take the necessary action, although reaching unified decisions was not always easy. But the Stringers? She had not seen this as a possibility for them – at least, not until now. She was glad Malcolm was involved.

Bella returned to her desk feeling encouraged. The work still had to be done but she felt confirmed in her ideas and clearer about the tasks ahead. She started to eat the sandwiches she had made for her lunch and began to write the court report for Mark Winters.

Everyone else was out and the room was quiet. She read the last report she had written on the boy and was writing steadily when Jan came in saying it was time to go and see the Jenkins family, and they had better hurry up or they'd be late.

***

When she got home the phone was ringing. It was Liz to tell her that Martha's husband, Luke, had left. Bella, still in her coat and unprepared for the kind of conversation she guessed she was about to have, tried to think of a way to limit Liz's need to discuss this fact at length, but to no avail. Liz was clearly finding it difficult to totally disapprove of Luke's behaviour as she had never liked him, but she wanted Bella to ring Martha because, as she put it, "she always likes talking to you about her problems."

Her voice was heavy with the implication that for some reason Martha talked more easily to Bella than to herself. Gradually Bella extricated herself from the conversation and promised she would ring Martha, and she told Liz that if the marriage was as bad as she thought it was, perhaps a split was the best thing to happen. Liz countered this with the opinion that Martha made a great mistake in marrying Luke in the first place.

Then, still without taking off her coat, Bella rang Adrian and told him that she had to go to her mother for the weekend, as she had had a fall and hurt her knee. He was, of course, sorry about this, but had troubles of his own.

Apparently Julian had rung to say Jason was threatening to leave home after yet another row and Adrian had arranged for both boys to come to him for the weekend. He sounded depressed and worried and Bella felt inadequate. She could think of little to say that would help except to suggest, as she had done before, that Adrian attempted to talk to his ex and her new partner. He always said it was a good idea, but got nowhere. It always depressed Bella to hear about Adrian's boys. They came for weekends from time to time and Julian was a little more friendly to her now, but Jason was an unhappy boy who always made her feel in the way, which, in her own house was uncomfortable and something she seemed unable to overcome. As she put down the phone she thought how embroiled they were with their other lives.

After this Bella changed her clothes, made herself a salad and, after she had eaten, rang Gemma and told her about the weekend. Then, reluctantly she rang Martha and heard how Luke was showing less and less interest in helping with baby Beth. Martha thought she should give up work, although Luke often complained about the expenses... was often out late and seemed to want her just for decoration because he often criticised the way she dressed. And then, she found out about him seeing someone else and when she confronted him he didn't pretend.

He said he thought their relationship had died and was going to tell her. And now her mother said she must see a solicitor and she had made an appointment but it all seemed so horrible and sordid. Martha sobbed her distress, saying perhaps she should have given up work. Perhaps being a social worker had been a bad idea. Social workers were supposed to be concerned about child care, weren't they? And that meant looking after their own children didn't it? And... "Oh, Bella, it's such a mess but you understand, don't you?"

Bella did her best at understanding and consoling. She suggested that Luke must bear some of the blame and Martha had no need to castigate herself, and perhaps they needed help in making proper arrangements for the money and for contact for Beth. She thought Martha should see if there was anyone doing mediation work in the area, perhaps she could ask colleagues about this. Solicitors were needed too, but not to forget that they take sides.

Martha cried and said she really enjoyed work although it was often very hard and she adored Beth and felt guilty about leaving her and didn't know how she would get over Luke going... and on and on. Bella thought of Gemma and Josh who seemed to have a good partnership with Josh appreciating Gemma's need to keep working and both doing their best for Susan. At least that was how it seemed. But perhaps she was idealising their relationship. Who knows what really goes on inside a marriage?

***

The moon was beginning to wane but still cast a clear white light which picked out the white roses and the alyssum as Bella filled the watering can from the water butt. The air was warm and the light breeze rustled gently as she went from pot to pot letting her mind imagine the pleasure felt by the dry roots gulping down the moisture. She had forgotten them on Friday in her haste to leave and now filled can after can as she moved round the beds feeling an obligation to make up for her neglect, her eyes becoming accustomed to the darkness as she went. She paused at the viburnum which she had moved to this new place weeks ago. She felt the leaves which were dry and brittle. It was not going to survive but she watered it lavishly anyway. Some plants do not like being moved and Bella wished she had left it where it was thriving.

It was so quiet, Bella thought, so very peaceful. She sat in one of the chairs she had left by the pear tree, planted last year, and disturbed a magpie which chattered in alarm and fluttered above her for a few moments. She knew she should go in and go to bed. It had to be after one, but she sat listening to the small animal sounds which broke the silence. A bird fidgeting on its roost; a mouse perhaps, or some other small mammal in the hedge; a tiny squeak; the faint engine of a car going past the front of the house; the rustle of leaves shifting in the light warm breeze.

She and Adrian had sat out here quite late a few weeks previously, drinking wine and discussing their relationship until the alcoholic haze let the future rest. He had held her hand and kissed her fingers and said, "Perhaps we should just let the future go and live in the here and now tonight," which stilled anxiety and indecision and left her free to indulge her desire and need for him. But the here and now doesn't satisfy us for long, she now thought. Tomorrow, next week, next month, next year was still empty of plans and she realised she was not sure whether she wanted to make them.

Her mind drifted back to the weekend spent with her mother. The knee was very painful and swollen and Bella had shopped and then cooked meals for the freezer and rung up two of her mother's friends to ask them to call in, as she knew her mother would never ask anyone for help. And of course, telephoned the Day Centre to say Grace would not be able to attend for at least two weeks – during which conversation her mother interrupted constantly to say of course she would soon be better but would certainly want a week off. She promised her mother she would come up again next weekend to see how things were. She had been apprehensive about the injury, thinking of her mother's age and that injuries did not always get better when one was old. And not for the first time she wondered if one day her mother would have to live with her, something she knew her mother would not want which led to more pessimistic thoughts about having to look after her, perhaps for the rest of her life. But would that be so bad? Wouldn't that be what was right?

She only has me, Bella thought, and the alternatives were unthinkable. Her mother in care? She remembered the war years when Grace worked so hard for other people, motivated by a sense of duty and obligation. Some of that rubbed off on me, only I use different words, she thought. Mother was not into self analysis. Now we think in terms of personal reward and the guilt we feel when we fail ourselves. We don't let the side down, we let ourselves down. But in a way the roots are the same.

She realised the night air was creeping into her arms and legs. She felt chilled and suddenly very tired so she went back to the house and made cocoa to take up to bed, letting the warmth of the duvet and pillows relax her into sleep.

Chapter Eight

1981

At the end of the allocation meeting, Malcolm had arranged for the team to take part in a discussion about Gordon's camping expeditions with some of the boys with whom they had to deal. Malcolm began this by referring to some of the statistics he had researched into the family backgrounds of the children who were presenting difficulties, over 80% of whom he said, came from families where there was some form of marital breakdown or disharmony, while 38% came from families where women were coping with children on their own. He said he knew that Gordon was actually providing a service for some of these difficult and disturbed young people and wanted to point out how relevant this work was, given that working with this client group affected everyone in the team and people were often at a loss to know what was most effective.

Gordon said it began for him when he considered that the boys he had on his caseload lacked confidence and had low self-esteem. He felt, he said, that they needed the opportunity to achieve success in something. Mostly they achieved little at school and their social life took place on the streets with others like themselves where they competed to raise all kinds of mayhem against all kinds of authority. Weekend camps were not about changing their entire lifestyle. He wouldn't want to pretend they could achieve very much but they were an experience in group living and decision making and setting socially acceptable goals.

"For those of you who think this is a holiday event for social workers," he said, "let me assure you, it is hard work!

"I entice them," he said, "with the idea of living under canvas, which they mostly think will be great fun, until they have to put the tents up in the pouring rain, and give them the opportunity to set themselves goals. They use maps and make suggestions about climbing hills and walking long distances; they cook their own food. It would be good if they could do their own shopping and plan the meals, but on a weekend they really don't have enough time, but as far as possible the decisions are made by the group – and it's group pressure that deals with the mavericks and trouble makers. So far we have kept the group to eight, which is quite enough – probably too many with only two staff."

Tina interrupted at this point and said that it sounded very good, but surely it was youth club work, not social work. Gordon agreed but reminded her that youth clubs didn't run camps for difficult and delinquent boys. He said he had been talking with Malcolm and looking at the statistics he had uncovered and thought that one of the things these boys lacked was consistent male authority. A subplot for the weekends was the provision of good male models – "Me and Bill Meadows from Brownfield Youth Club," he said, laughing. "Not a lot, but we think we should try to keep the group together and plan another camp with the same boys, so there is some consistency."

There was general approval and enthusiasm from the team who asked questions about money. Gordon said the Department had agreed to use Section 1 money and there had been no problem. Time in lieu? Gordon said it was agreed, but so far not taken. Parental agreement? Gordon said they had devised a form for parents to sign giving consent. Selecting boys to go? Gordon said he and Bill interviewed boys and parents and talked to the social worker concerned. He said that four of the boys so far taken had been on his own caseload. But it was very limited of course, which brought him to his next point. He looked around smiling, and said he wanted to run a longer camp during the summer hols, and for this more volunteers would be needed, probably about eight. He thought Bill could encourage a couple more youth workers to join in and the rest... well, he hoped he would get them from the team. He was, he said, talking to the other teams the following week because they wanted women as well as men. In fact, looking to the future, they could develop mixed sex camps in time. One of the things Malcolm had identified, he said, was the fact that many delinquent boys were very aggressive towards women, even their mothers. Jennifer responded to this by saying that everyone knew what she believed and that was that aggression was a genetic inheritance – so many of these boys had aggressive fathers.

Jan said that this was true but this could be learned behaviour which could be modified.

No one actually volunteered to take part in Gordon's camps, but discussion went on until Malcolm suggested people think about it for now and talk to Gordon later on.

He then reminded the team that there was special a half-day seminar on the 14th when a Dr Marian Hastings was going to talk about sexual abuse, its diagnosis and treatment, and he wanted everyone to attend. Sexual abuse, he said, was the new priority so they had better get clued up.

Tina was particularly interested in this and said that sexual abuse was far more prevalent than once thought. She said she had been to a workshop in her last job and it made her realise that so many of the behaviour disorders she was dealing with were caused by sexual abuse.

Later, when Jan and Bella were making tea prior to going out on an evening visits, Jan brought up the question of sexual abuse again.

"It's taking over from physical abuse, have you noticed? A few years ago we had never thought of it. Now it's coming out of the woodwork. I was talking to Tina the other day and she was telling me I should be particularly vigilant about children who were wetting the bed – one of the signs, she said. I said that bed wetting was surely caused by a variety of events. My oldest girl started wetting the bed when Ruth, the youngest, was born and when we got her dry she started again when her Dad left and went to Dubai. Tina gave me a funny look and said, 'Oh, really.' I'm sure she thought I had paedophilic tendencies."

"She's a strange woman," Bella said. "She said something about going to Mass and I asked her if she had been a Catholic all her life or whether she had converted, and she gave me a strange smile and began to walk away saying she had converted during her second marriage. I felt I'd been given a present which I didn't know what to do with. She's never said a word about a husband and all of a sudden she tells us she has had two."

A few days later Bella was rung by Reception and told Peggy Stringer was in and waiting to see her. This was quite unexpected. Peggy never came to the office. Bella felt a wave of anxiety. She had been visiting the Stringers weekly during the past months and the mood in the house varied. Sometimes Peggy was apologetic about the mess... she would have got on if it wasn't for her back, or her neck, or her time of the month. Usually friendly, sometimes she seemed nervous and subdued, nearly always burning her legs by the fire and smoking endless cigarettes.

When Bella asked about Jack she said he'd just lost his job or was just going to start a new one, or was down the pub, and he didn't change much. When Bella asked if he helped her she often hesitated, sometimes looking quickly at Tracey before answering, and then forced a laugh. Well, sometimes, she said.

When the children were at home, the youngest boy, Billy, now about seven, hung around Bella, often holding her arm and asking if she would take him for a ride in her car. Sometimes this caused his older brother Lenny to shout at Bella that Billy was bad and didn't get treats, which would bring Tracey to Billy's defence, telling Lenny to shut his mouth. Lenny, Bella knew, didn't have much in the way of conversational skills and showed a good deal of aggression towards the girls. She also began to think that Tracey, the oldest girl, now in platform shoes and a mini skirt, was doing some of the mothering. She was protective towards Billy and sometimes put her arm round her mother, and once Bella had found her brushing Marigold's hair and putting it in a pony tail.

She had told Malcolm she felt she did nothing to improve life for any of them, but he always said that this was really a case of monitoring, almost playing a policing role, making sure they knew the Social Services were keeping an eye so things didn't get worse. "We don't know what goes on in families, Bella, and we can only find out if something goes terribly wrong. But you can be a regular presence, particularly if you go unannounced. And I guess Peggy trusts you."

Following the phone message, Bella went out to Reception and immediately knew that something was terribly wrong. Peggy was sitting with her arm round Billy, in a corner of the room, her face tearstained and badly bruised. Their clothes were grubby and stained and their hair dishevelled. Bella took them into an interview room and Billy began to sob while Peggy clasped Bella's hand and talked to her through tears.

She couldn't go back, she said. Couldn't take no more. Couldn't let him hurt Billy again. And must get the other children out when they came home from school. "You will, won't you, Mrs Wingfield," she sobbed. "Get the children. Make them safe... and then she stuttered out that Jack had never accepted Billy was his child. Accused her of going with someone else, which, she said, was a lie, and now he'd hurt him again. She pulled the little boy to her and kissed him. "We won't let him do it again Billy. Mrs Wingfield will help us now."

Bella got cups of tea for them and then went to see Malcolm in his office. She told him the story she had just heard, that Jack had come home from the pub drunk and wanted to know why Billy wasn't at school. He shouted at him and shook him and told him to get going. Peggy had tried to explain that Billy wasn't well, but Jack would have none of it and seized hold of the boy and forced him to the door. Peggy, Bella said, had apparently pulled him back and Jack punched her in the face and then hit Billy, throwing him through the front door. He shouted at Peggy and punched her again. She got past him and out of the house and caught up with Billy and began to run with him – to come here, Bella supposed – with Jack shouting after her, swearing and cursing.

"She has just told me that Jack has never believed Billy is his child," Bella said. "She has never said that before or perhaps I would have been more aware. And now she's frightened and wants us to get the other children out when they come home from school." Bella knew she was talking too fast and said she was sorry for babbling and then sat silently.

"This is a police matter now, Bella, and we must get her and Billy to the doctor. Her GP if possible. If we can get Jack arrested, she will be able to go home." Malcolm paused and looked out of the window, thinking. "You sort out the GP and I'll ring the police. I think that's the best thing to do first."

Bella found Peggy frightened when she told her what they were going to do. She did not want to involve the police. Jack would never forgive her. Even if they arrested him he would get her one day. It was hard to persuade her that this was now the only way to deal with what was obviously a serious assault, but they went eventually to the doctor, Malcolm joining them with a WPC who told them that officers were visiting Jack at home.

It was a long and difficult afternoon. Bella and the WPC saw the bruises on Peggy's shoulders and the remains of old bruises on her arms but Bella was not prepared for the state of Billy's small white body with fading grey and yellowing patches on his back and buttocks and finger bruises on his arms. "These are some days old," the doctor said. "Looks like you've been in the wars. How did you get all these bruises?"

Billy, still tearful, said, "Our Dad did it. Our Dad hits me all the time, doesn't he, Mum? An' he hits our Mum as well. I hope he goes to prison for ever. That's what. I hate him."

"I think we should get an X-ray, see if there's anything else. So how would you like your picture taken, young man?" The doctor smiled at Billy. "We must arrange a trip to the hospital for that. No need for tears, Mrs Stringer. Just making sure."

It was after seven when Bella got home. Malcolm, who had stayed with her most of the day, arrived in his car shortly after her. The police had arrested Jack and Bella had taken a very reluctant Peggy home with Billy, Peggy insisting that Jack would get them eventually and needing much persuasion. She was told Jack would be kept in the cells tonight and be in court tomorrow, charged with assault, and probably remanded. The police were emphatic that he would not be allowed home, even if he got bail.

Bella had stayed with them for a while, sending Tracey for fish and chips while Peggy kept going to the window and looking out in case Jack appeared. The children asked questions which Bella answered as well as she could. She wanted to read to them but no one could find a book with all the pages intact so she managed to get the younger ones drawing at the kitchen table.

At home she felt very cold and tired. Her hands were shaking as she poured drinks for herself and Malcolm. They sat on the sofa and Malcolm put his arm round her shoulders but she turned away. "No, Malcolm, I'm sorry. Don't be nice to me. I shall cry. It's so good of you to come back with me but I think I might cry and I don't want to fall to pieces."

He moved his arm and said it might do her good if she did. She smiled weakly and shook her head. "I'll be alright in a minute. I just can't help thinking of those bruises on Billy. I have been visiting and not realising it was happening. I knew Jack was a revolting man but no one said anything, although I should have... I keep remembering something that Lenny said about Billy being bad. Poor Lenny. He just copies Jack. And the way Tracey cared for Peggy. She thought she was protecting her Mum, and in a way she was."

Malcolm said that families had their own rules and sometimes things had to get worse before they could get better. He didn't think she could have done anything until Peggy was prepared to talk and now this had happened there was a good case. There was plenty of evidence. "Nothing on the X-ray," he said "thankfully, but photographs of all those bruises... and be pleased, Bella, Mum is home with the kids and Jack is in the cells." He patted her arm and said he could do with another drink.

After he left, Bella boiled herself an egg and then ate a bowl of cereal. Nursery food, she thought. Comforting. Then she rang Adrian but there was no answer and she felt a wave of tearfulness at being alone and wanting someone. She poured herself another drink, switched on the television, which seemed only to be showing people laughing and shouting or playing games. Everyone was absurdly happy and it jarred so she turned it off. Wanting the day to end she ran a bath and lay soaking in hot water with her eyes shut. But she still saw the thin little body with the bruises and the red-eyed snivelling child who hoped his Dad would stay in prison for ever.

***

September 1981

Martha and Bella walked up Middleton Hill and Martha remembered the day they had done this before when she had been doing teaching practice. She remembered too the visit Bella had made to the children who had been left alone. She thought this was when she had decided she would like to be a social worker. Bella remembered as well. "Your mother thinks I'm responsible for your change of career," she said, "and I suppose in a way, I am."

Martha could not agree with that. Her mother never gave her any credit for making decisions. If it hadn't been that occasion it would have been something else. She was sure, although she often wondered if it had been the right thing to do. She seemed, she said, to make a mess of everything and she didn't suppose being a depressed teacher meant she would have had a successful and happy marriage. She needed to talk about the marriage, as Bella knew she would, so she heard again that Luke had not wanted a wife with opinions of her own; that he didn't really want her to work, although he was pleased enough that she earned money; that he, Luke, was really only interested in making money. Martha thought her mother had been right about that, and it was obvious that he had no time for Sam, Martha's brother living in an ashram in India. Helping other people was not his thing at all, Martha said, but being rejected for someone else as she had been made her feel a complete failure.

Martha had invited herself for the weekend, leaving her little daughter Beth with her grandmother. Bella had actually intended going to see Gemma indulging herself in being a grandmother for the weekend. She needed normality, or at least what passed for normality in her life, but had not felt able to tell Martha it was not convenient. She could after all, go to Gemma any time and she knew from Martha's phone call that Martha wanted – perhaps needed – to talk to her. She was, however, beginning to find the endless recital of the marriage breakdown rather tedious. Martha, depressed and endlessly self-critical, was hard work and Bella was tired. She seemed to have been tired for weeks, ever since the Stringer case had blown up, but she knew that broken marriages had to be talked over and over and analysed and justified ad infinitum so she listened and sympathised. She thought it was too soon to talk about the advantages of being a single parent – Martha was not ready for this – so she nodded, and cooked meals, suggested walks, and nodded some more.

When she said goodbye, Martha said it had helped; told Bella in fact that Bella was always wise, and that she felt better and more positive. And although Bella did not believe her, she felt some satisfaction. She had always loved Martha and was always sad when things went wrong for her, and she knew she felt better when people like Martha told her she was helpful. That's what I do it for, she thought. So people tell me how useful I am.

***

Jan came into the team room pale faced, with an oddly dishevelled appearance and something in her hair. She sat at her desk, dumping her bag on the floor, and rested her head on her hands. Bella knew something was wrong and moved over to her desk and asked her if she was OK.

She looked up at Bella and smiled, although Bella thought her near to tears. She said people should tell you when they were going to try to kill themselves. It was Rosie Denver. She had phoned about nine thirty and left a message with Reception asking her to call. But she didn't get round there until about twelve, when she had found the front door open, which was just as well otherwise Rosie might have bled to death.

Bella called to Gordon to make some tea and pulled up a chair beside Jan, taking one of her hands. "Do you want to talk about it now?" she asked, and Jan shook her head and then nodded. She forced a laugh and for a moment rested her head on Bella's shoulder. "I think I nearly panicked but you can't do that, can you? I mean, I found her lying in bed, blood everywhere, and she said, 'I thought you were never coming.' I don't know whether she cut herself because I didn't arrive, or whether she had done it before. Oh, Bella, it was frightful…"

Gradually calming down, drinking the tea Gordon had made, she told them how she had rushed down the road to the phone box, called an ambulance and then rushed back and somehow, when the ambulance arrived, they had got Rosie to hospital. She paused and then went on angrily saying that the hospital was not exactly sympathetic. Even the staff nurse made sarcastic remarks and the doctor told her they were there to heal the sick, not patch up the stupid. But, she said, they dealt with her and found out where her husband worked. "I left then and tore down to the factory where he worked and told him what had happened and that the mess must be cleared up before the children came home from school. Poor man, he was in such a state but he left work and went back to the house with me."

They had done what they could in the bedroom, getting the sheets off the bed and into the bath where he tried to wash out the blood, and they got the blood off the floor as far as they could. Eventually he left to go to the school and told them he would be back to fetch the kids and take them to his sister.

"I think you have blood in your hair, and some on the inside of this arm," Bella said.

"Oh, God! I had it all over my jacket which I've left in the car. I'll have to go home and have a bath." Jan managed a small smile, touching her hair. "She's done it before. Not cut herself, but overdosed. I should have thought… she doesn't mean to kill herself... at least I don't think so... she gets down, especially when she's had a row with the kids, or Jeff."

Bella insisted she went home and offered to go with her. Jan agreed, but said that Jeb would be back about five and she would be alright on her own. The others in the team gathered round offering help, worrying about her driving. But she seemed more calm and said she would rather be on her own. Bella said she would call on her way home to make sure she was alright and she and Gordon walked with her to the car.

As she prepared to drive off she suddenly remembered she had a visit arranged with a foster mother at 4.30. Bella said they would ring and explain, well, not exactly explain, perhaps make some excuse.

At their tea break later, they talked about the messy nature of their job. They thought of the children returning to a blood soaked mother after school if Jan had not been there – and not everyone who cut themselves up had social workers calling – and they made jokes about some of the unsavoury aspects of their work.

Gordon said the office was sometimes like the accident department. He recalled how last week, Frances from Area 2 had had a lady in who had insisted on taking off her false leg to show Frances how sore her shin was. And Frances was, he said, apparently not good at amputations and she had had to help the woman put her leg back again. Just hearing about it quite put him off his lunch as he was not entirely comfortable with amputations either.

Even Jennifer joined in. She asked if anyone remembered Bert, the old man who used to come in to see Don and find out if he could go into a home. "He liked to have a chat but one day he insisted on taking off his shoes to show me how bad his toes were. I was on duty," Jennifer shuddered. "I told him that I thought he should go home and give them a good soak. He said he only wanted a new pair of shoes and water did them no good. Oh! My, the smell!

"I'm sure it was good of Jan to help with washing the sheets, but it really isn't social work, is it?" Tina commented. "I mean, don't you think families should cope with the consequences of their behaviour themselves? Otherwise how do they learn? There used to be Family Service Units that did the housework with the clients, but I don't think that's what we are here for."

"Cue for brainstorm on What Is Social Work?" Gordon suggested.

"I did a placement at a Family Service Unit," Bella said. "They believed that when people were shocked or depressed practical help was what was needed. It made sense to me. I mean, sometimes we all need that kind of support, don't we?"

"Of course, but our job is to help them find that amongst themselves, not provide it, surely?" Tina insisted.

"I don't think Jeff would have appreciated Jan sitting and talking to him about where he got help from, or about why Rosie cut herself up. He had a mess of blood to clear up and children to think about. I think social work is based on recognising that there are all kinds of ways to help people and some of them are practical," Jennifer retorted.

"Perhaps." Tina bent her head and took up her pen signalling her participation in the conversation was over.

"So you worked in FSU?" Gordon asked Bella. "Heard about them when I was training. They called them the Scrubbers Up. Sounded like ladies of the night. Never really knew what they did. You must tell me about them."

People began returning to their work. Bella went through the papers on her desk and made some notes, then suddenly remembered. "Gordon, do you remember me talking to you about two boys who I thought might benefit from one of your camps?" Gordon said he did, and told her that another weekend was being planned and he could consider them if she wanted. If she gave him a note he would arrange to visit the parents and the boys to see what he thought.

Bella agreed to do that, and was then startled at Gordon's suggestion that she might like to join the expedition. He said he was trying to recruit women!

She was not at all tempted by the idea of a tented camp and told him she thought he should really be looking for younger women, it wasn't really her scene. She suddenly thought of the camping holiday she and James had had when Gemma was about four. It had rained and rained, she remembered, and she had hated cooking meals on her knees over a camping stove. And the lavatories on the camp site were across a muddy field. No.

"Rubbish," Gordon said. "Anyone would think you were too old. I think we need mature women. But if I can't tempt you…"

Bella was sorry but she didn't think he could.

Chapter Nine

1982

Grace opened her eyes and blinking in the light, closed them again. She had seen a blurred face beside her. She blinked again and again, trying to focus and heard Bella's voice saying something. Bella. Why was Bella there? She knew something had happened. She had pain and her head throbbed. She felt Bella take her hand and saw her face bending towards her. She tried to speak, but the words did not come properly and then the mist cleared and she heard Bella talking, felt Bella kiss her cheek, heard her say, "You are waking up, Mum. You are in hospital. There was an accident. Do you remember?"

"An accident?" Grace tried to make sense of the word. "An accident? What accident?"

Bella patted the hand she held and said, "Well you had one, but don't worry about that now. You are going to get better soon, then you'll remember. You have to have a lot of rest now."

Grace moved her head slightly and frowned. "The vegetables. I was going for the vegetables. May and Jim are coming. I forgot them, you see."

"It's alright, May and Jim know you are in hospital. They sent their love. They will come and see you."

Grace touched the bandage on her head. "I've hurt my head, haven't I? It aches so." She closed her eyes. "I'm very tired."

Bella watched as Grace lay with her eyes closed and appeared to go to sleep. A nurse came in to check the drip and told Bella that her daughter had arrived and was in the relatives' room.

"Go and see her. Your mother will probably sleep for a while now."

As she hugged Gemma, Bella felt a wave of comfort overwhelm her. She was close to tears, The fear and loneliness of the last few hours faded in the warmth of her daughter's arms.

"But you shouldn't have come. With a baby on the way. Are you alright, Gemma? Not too tired?"

She told Gemma the hospital had rung her at the office. Grace had her number down as next of kin, and she had driven up straight away. "I rang you, and auntie Flo and the people next door who will tell anyone who calls, and just got in the car. She's very badly injured. Broken arm and probably her hip; badly cut head. They are going to do an X-ray and she may have to have an operation, but they are worried about her blood pressure. She has drifted in and out of consciousness but doesn't seem to remember anything. As far as the hospital knows it was just a road traffic accident. Head on collision at the crossroads by Colleson Avenue. The driver of the other car is dead. It's appalling. I keep wondering if it was her fault... but that doesn't help. I think all we can do is wait. Flo said she would get here by about six and I suppose she and I will stay at the house tonight. Perhaps you as well? But how are you? It's such a long drive. Are you alright? Have you had anything to eat?" Bella held Gemma close to her and began to weep. "Oh, Gemma, I don't want her to die. She seemed so fit... getting on with her life..."

Adrian rang about eight in the evening when they were back at the house. Bella told him that it was just about waiting. Her mother had drifted in and out of consciousness and the doctor said they wanted to stabilise her before taking her for an X-ray. "It was awful not being able to do anything. We just sat with her, or waited outside. Flo came and she's with us now. They seem to think they will be able to do the X-ray tomorrow. They will ring us if we are needed of course... yes, I'm alright, I suppose. No... I'm shattered. I think she might die and I feel as if I can't cope with that. Yes... I know... it's kind of you to ring. Gemma is taking care of me, and Flo. Yes, of course, I'll let you know."

There was a fish pie in the fridge ready for May and Jim's arrival. They heated it and ate what they could. No one was hungry. There was a large plastic container full of soup and two tins of small iced cakes, prepared, they thought for the day centre tomorrow. Day centre staff rang up at intervals, and Bella said she would take the food down to them in the morning. Gemma took the call from the vicar who said he knew Grace from the centre. "'We didn't see her at church, but I know she was a good Christian woman,'" Gemma reported, adding, "They have to assume people are Christians because they are good, don't they? Grandma would have laughed at that. He said he would be praying for her as well. I can just imagine her saying, 'And a fat lot of good that will do'."

"Don't mock, Gemma," Flo said. "Praying is something one can do when there is nothing else."

The house seemed to be waiting. It felt empty and yet in a state of preparation. Washing on the line. A tablecloth ready to be unfolded and spread on the dining room table. Two cups in the sink, newspapers on a chair in the living room. The Radio Times opened on the kitchen table. In Grace's bedroom her dressing gown lay on the bed, some clothes on a chair. A book was open and face down on the night table. Bella stood for a moment, but did not go in. Flo made up beds in the two spare rooms, a single in the small room and two singles in the room which had once been Bella's. "Gemma and I will go in there, if you have the other room," she said.

Bella slept fitfully, getting up at 3.15 and making herself some tea. She began to think that her mother would now be an invalid, needing care. Her care. Living with her? Which would mean giving up work. Or needing nursing care and having to go into some residential home. Or perhaps she would die which would mean dealing with a funeral, the house. The things. She looked about her, imagining clearing out the kitchen. What does one do with all the stuff? And selling the house? This house where she had grown up. Which had always been there. She had never felt any great affection for the house, but it was a fixture. Always there. Totally familiar. Part of her. Growing old means discarding things. Reducing the responsibilities. Loss. Not seeing her mother any more... loss.

She looked at her watch, 3.40. She knew that the middle of the night was a bad time for solving problems, although the misery would not leave her. She went back to bed.

They took the food to the day centre in the morning and took away the good wishes and love of the staff and clients with messages for Grace and even a bunch of flowers somehow obtained so early in the day.

At the hospital they were told that Grace was having an X-ray. She had had a peaceful night and her blood pressure was down. They waited. Cheered a little by the news, they talked about how they would cope with what would be a long recovery. Flo would be able to stay with her, at least for a while. Bella could go back to work, but come and go. The weekends could be covered easily.

Perhaps she could stay with Bella as she got better. "Perhaps I will need to have some months' leave in order to look after her," Bella said. But there would be some community care. District nurses calling. Perhaps rehabilitation at a day centre. Bella smiled as she thought how her mother would resent being a patient at a day centre.

Thinking, as they were, about recuperation which would lead to recovery and buoyed up by the news that there had been a small improvement, they were not immediately aware that the doctor who approached them was solemn and tense. They heard his words, "I am so sorry..." at first without understanding; then as the words penetrated, with cold fear and a desperate desire to disbelieve. "As we finished the X-ray her heart just stopped. She just closed her eyes. She felt no pain. We tried to revive her. She was very badly injured of course. Almost certainly some internal damage. I am so sorry. So very sorry."

***

They went back to the house where they made some tea and wandered from room to room hardly speaking. Bella felt her mind had frozen. She felt detached from everything about her. Unable to think of what she must do, she plumped up cushions on the sofa, tidied the papers away, emptied the bin and then, walking round the garden, pulled up a few weeds. She kept touching her mother's wedding ring which they had given her, and which she had put on the same finger as the one she had worn since her wedding to James, and she saw it in her mind on her mother's hand where it had always been, a thin gold band which would not slide across the knuckle. She heard her mother say, 'I can't get it off any more, even with soap. I suppose if it gets too tight, I shall have to have it cut off.' Did hands shrink she wondered, when one was dead?

The telephone brought the world back. Gemma crying as she told Josh, Flo talking to her colleague at the shop; the day centre manager ringing for news, and then next door calling, and someone from across the road. Bella rang Malcolm, and Flo found Grace's telephone book and said they must ring this person and that. Telling the story mechanically and dry-eyed, somehow finding the words, and then telling it again. Bella wished people would stop saying that it was probably a happy release as Grace would have hated being an invalid. Was this supposed to help? What did they know of Grace and her great determination to get the best out of life? When Adrian rang later in the evening and told her how he had loved and admired Grace and how he would miss her, a surge of sadness suddenly filled her and as she said goodbye she began to weep at first quietly and then with great sobs of misery. Gemma sat and hugged her, and they cried together. Flo fluttered about saying it was always good to cry, a kind of release, and then she made some more tea and said she thought she would scramble some eggs, because they really ought to eat something.

Adrian arrived at Bella's house on the day she returned to Renshaw. The house had felt strangely lonely and cold and when he arrived with a large bunch of flowers and a bottle of wine she felt comforted and glad. She had had no appetite although she had stopped and bought a few groceries, but opening a tin of soup and putting a quiche in the oven made her realise she had eaten very little that day, and getting food for someone else seemed to give her energy she had lacked.

They talked about his work at the Half-way House he managed and when he asked her about her mother and the funeral, she was glad to tell him about the last week.

"One of the things I hadn't anticipated was this feeling I now have that there is nothing between me and death! I mean, while mother was alive she was a sort of barrier and now she has gone," Bella told him, and then described the funeral. She said they had probably astonished, and possibly shocked all those good women from the day centre. No religion. "Well, Mother was quite definite about not having a religious one. When Dad died she said they must have a traditional funeral because that was what he'd have wanted, 'but don't you do that for me, Bella', she said. So I didn't. The minister who was involved with the centre came round and hoped we would have the funeral at his church, even though Mum wasn't a regular attender. Regular! She wasn't an attender at all. The vicar was rather sad, but seemed resigned. C of E ministers are a wet lot, aren't they? Anyway," she said, "we had the music she most liked. The stuff that was all the rage during the war. Stardust, by Hoagy Carmichael, and something by Carrol Gibbons which I found on her tape recorder. And then," she said, "we were a bit more serious. John McCormack singing Somewhere a Voice is Calling, which she was always playing. She always said he had perfect diction – and then an Etude by Chopin at the end." Her sister Flo surprised us all. She said she wanted to talk about her and she was amazing. Told stories about them growing up and then made me cry talking about the work she did during the war. How unselfish she was and always there for people who had suffered." Bella sniffed back tears and said that no funerals are exactly enjoyable, but it seemed right for her. She said James' parents were there – her in-laws – and they were nice. They said it was so appropriate for Ma and how they'd admired her.

"Of course, some people are a bit sniffy." Bella went on, "My oldest friend, Liz, was definitely disapproving, although she didn't actually say so, but one can always tell with Liz. 'How very avant guarde of you' she said, and one of the helpers from the day centre said she thought it very odd and that Grace deserved better, which if he hadn't made me laugh, was really rather offensive."

After they'd washed up, Bella opened the letters which had lain on the mat since she arrived. Colleagues had written and some of her neighbours had sent notes or cards – a mixture of kind thoughts and formal commiserations. She put them on the mantelpiece in the sitting room, feeling comforted and warmed. Less lonely. And then Gemma rang to see if she was alright.

Adrian stayed and they sat quietly, finishing the wine and talking until quite late, and then, when they were in bed, she felt all restraint leave her and began to weep.

She didn't return to work until the following Monday, spending the time in the garden, writing letters and making phone calls.

People were very kind and sympathetic when she returned; Ellen had rung her every day to make sure she was alright and had called twice with flowers, and the neighbours had been solicitous, asking her for meals which she had found difficulty in accepting, but which somehow helped to emphasise the fact that she was back where she belonged. But at work within an hour the work engulfed her, pushing her private problems into the background.

There was an immediate furore when Jennifer's car was stolen by Charlie Henderson, who was on a Supervision Order. She had put her keys on the table in the interview room and then been interrupted by Reception. After Charlie left she realised the keys were gone and reached the car park in time to see her car disappearing down the road. She said, "Well, thank heavens it wasn't my house keys as well or he'd have had the TV." Her anger dominated the room while she phoned the police, but Malcolm came in and asked for someone to go down to the police station where they had a baby in a pushchair they had taken from his father, Joe Roskin, who was reeling down the middle of the road either extremely drunk or high on drugs. The Roskin family was one of Alan's cases, which Malcolm was holding as the post was still frozen. Joe was a single parent, his wife having left soon after the baby was born.

"Drunk in charge of a child! That's an offence under the 1933 Act. I remember that from college," Gordon said. "I thought at the time that it was chance really that I didn't end up in care. I used to have to sit outside the pub with a lemonade while Mum and Dad were inside and Dad was often several times over the eight as we drove home. I used to think it rather exciting as he was always in such a good mood and drove the car so fast. OK, Malcolm, I'll go, but I'd better find a foster home first, I suppose, in case he takes a long time to sober up. Any ideas, anyone? Or would one of you ladies like to go and fetch a baby?"

Bella did not volunteer. She was reading through her in-tray when Marian put some papers on her desk and then said she probably didn't know about Malcolm's son, who was in the Navy and who was out in the Falklands. Bella realised she had not thought about the war which was taking place on the other side of the world and she was startled to realise that its impact had reached the team. Malcolm's son on a destroyer in a war! They had all been so appalled by this invasion of the Falklands. "Do men really have to die to safeguard the freedom of a few hundred islanders – can't we be pragmatic and move them to another island somewhere?" Jan had said, countered by Tina who believed we should always fight aggression and defend freedom. "I mean, what would have happened to us if we hadn't fought Hitler?" There had been quite a dispute with Gordon suggesting that Margaret Thatcher thought she was Churchill and enjoyed the idea of war.

Malcolm, of course, had been hoping his son would not be involved. She remembered him saying how the boy had seen the Navy as a way of seeing the world and having a great life; he never imagined he would be part of a war. Her own problems had erased this from her mind. She felt guilty. She had not asked him how things were and he had been so kind to her; but these thoughts were overtaken by Reception ringing to say that Betty Martin, health visitor, wanted to see her urgently about Carol Pritchard so she went downstairs, not knowing that the whole of the day was to be used up by Carol, who was not on her list.

Bella and the health visitor had discussed Carol before and today she told Bella that her anxiety had increased. Carol was vague and inclined to giggle when she visited. The children were not properly dressed and Carol had nothing for their lunch. There was a pair of man's shoes on the floor which Carol said belonged to her boyfriend, but he was only visiting. Bella said she had also been worried and wondered if Carol was taking drugs and she agreed to visit today and assess the situation.

When she arrived, the oldest child, Maureen, who was about four, opened the door. In the hall, three-year-old Cheryl stood sucking her thumb. She stared at Bella, took the thumb out and said, "Mummy is very tired." In the living room Davey, about fifteen months, and not yet properly on his feet, had a wet nappy trailing round his knees. Maureen said they hadn't had their dinner and Davey needed changing. Bella made her way to the kitchen where Carol was sitting at the table, her head on her arms, apparently asleep. Resting against a cupboard, the young man called Pete who had been in the house when Bella last called, sat on the floor, the remains of a cigarette held between stained brown fingers. The room reeked with a heavy sickly smell combined, Bella thought, with dirt and urine. Peter grinned at her and said, "Hi ya."

The children had followed her and Maureen reached for a bottle on the draining board. "Davey's," she said. "It needs some milk in. Sometimes there is some but I couldn't find any." Davey, crawling now, began to cry. Bella picked him up, discarding the wet nappy. She opened the fridge which was empty except for a lump of mouldering cheese, half a packet of margarine, two bottles of light ale and two empty milk bottles. She put the crying baby down on the floor and opened cupboards, finding flour, curry powder, a packet of sugar and some teabags. She took the bottle from Maureen and washed it out at the sink, repeatedly speaking to Carol. She filled the bottle with water from the kettle, fastened the teat and gave the bottle to Maureen saying she expected she could give Davey a drink.

Maureen handed the bottle to Davey who grasped it with grubby fingers and began sucking greedily.

Bella knew she couldn't cope with the situation on her own. She thought the children should be moved and fed but couldn't manage this by herself. She was reluctant to leave the house, but she had to telephone the office so she told Pete that she had to go out and telephone for help and he must try to look after the children while she was gone. She spoke sternly and told him that he and Carol could be in serious trouble if the children were not looked after. She said she might have to call the police. At this, he stopped grinning and seemed quite alarmed. He'd done nothing wrong, he said. No need to get the police. He'd look after them, he got on well with them. He picked up Davey, still sucking the bottle, and began jogging him up and down. Davey stopped sucking for a moment and smiled, so, slightly encouraged, Bella told the children she was going out for a very short time and left the house.

Outside she looked up and down the road, but there was no telephone box. Someone, she thought, will have a telephone. She went next door and rang the bell. No, they didn't have one, but across the road, No 34, Mrs Jowles, she had one.

So Bella asked Mrs Jowles and then talked to Malcolm and he said he would send Jilly the welfare assistant to join her. This was the new welfare assistant – Meg had at last been seconded for social work training. Malcolm said he would look for the file – it's on my desk, Bella said – and try to find a magistrate to whom he could apply for a Place of Safety Order. Bella agreed that they needed to take this step. So she waited at the house where Carol remained dull and sleepy and Peter made anxious attempts to tidy the kitchen and shake off his lethargy, talking to the children and trying to create the impression that he was good at caring. None of which made much impression on Bella who found what she could in the way of clothes for Davey and tried to prepare the children for a car ride. When Jilly arrived they tried to talk to Carol and explain what they were doing but to little effect. Carol lolled about on her chair and ignored both Maureen and Cheryl who tried to get her to speak to them, while Pete kept saying it was a good idea to take them away for now as Carol was certainly out of her mind.

They eventually got the children ready and persuaded Maureen to go with Davey in Jilly's car as she had a child's seat for Davey. Bella told Cheryl she was going in her car and they would follow Jilly all the way.

While they were sorting out clothes and toys, Jilly asked Bella what a Place of Safety Order involved. Bella explained that one had to persuade a magistrate to sign an order removing the children into care because they were in moral or physical danger. The order was for twenty-eight days, after which the Department either went to court and applied for a Supervision Order or a Care Order, or agreed to let the Place of Safety Order lapse. She said she thought it likely that they would apply for a Care Order, but if Carol got herself together and seemed capable again, they could let the children go home.

"And if you get a Care Order, how long does it last?"

"Well, it can last until they are eighteen, but either the parents or the department can apply to the court to have it revoked whenever there is enough evidence that things have improved," Bella explained.

Later the team room was a mess of fish and chips, chocolate, orange drinks, milk and toys spread around the desks while Gordon, Jan, Jennifer, Jilly and Bella fed, played and talked with the children. On his second bottle of milk Davey went to sleep on Jan's lap and cushions and a blanket were found and a bed made for him on the floor by the filing cabinet. Tina, who was writing at her desk, wondered how one was supposed to work with all the noise and paid little attention to the children. Gordon suggested she used Malcolm's office as he had gone to see a magistrate about the Place of Safety Order, and she gathered up her papers and retreated.

"You know, I don't think she likes children," Gordon said.

"I don't think she likes anyone very much."

"How do you get a job like this if you don't like children? And why would she want to work here?"

"When you arrived with them, Bella, she said she thought you should have got the police to take a Place of Safety, rather than bringing them here."

"And then we would have had to fetch them from the police station." Bella was exasperated. "What sort of help would that be? I think she just has to disapprove. She doesn't feel part of the team at all. Thank God the rest of you are so helpful. Now I need Homes Finding to help as well. They were very pessimistic about finding somewhere they could all be together, but we can't separate them... I mean, they are so young."

"Well, Mary Weston will probably have them. She can always find room for one more," Jennifer said. "Shall I ring her?"

"Mary would be wonderful. She handles emergencies so well. But... well, it's not one more, it's three, and Homes Finding will have tried her, won't they?"

Jennifer said she would ring anyway, because she could explain and Mary liked a challenge. Bella did not argue, she knew Jennifer had a way with foster parents. But she suggested Homes Finding would not like it, at which Jennifer just snorted.

When Bella got home it was after eight. She took her whisky into the garden and sat by the tree, weariness in every limb. She and Jilly had taken the children to Mary Weston and stayed there a while, the children clinging to her and wanting to go home. Promising to bring Mummy tomorrow they eventually left and Bella went back with the Place of Safety Order to see Carol and Pete. Carol was very tearful and agitated and Pete was asleep on the sofa. The Place of Safety Order frightened Carol.

She blamed Pete for getting her on drugs and said she was going to throw him out the next day and she would never take drugs again if only Bella would bring the children back. Bella, tired and angry, told her she was in danger of losing the children for good, ignored the pleading and the tears and suggested that if Pete was a bad influence on her and the children she should indeed break up with him, reminding Carol that she could have called the police about the drugs and would certainly do so if ever she found they were using them again. She told Carol to be ready to visit the children at 2 p.m. the next day. She could stay with them for about an hour and she must tell them they were to stay with Mary Weston a little while until she, Carol, was better. She felt herself being officious and quite aggressive, as she had been when Juliet from Homes Finding discovered that Jennifer had arranged for all three children to go to Mary Weston, whereas she had just arranged for the children to be split between two foster homes. She told Bella that Homes Finding found foster homes, not social workers who had no business putting pressure on marvellous foster mothers like Mary.

"But this way they won't be split up. Surely you can see that is better. For God's sake, foster homes are for children not Home Finding Officers. You people just think in terms of empty places and forget we are dealing with little minds who have been taken away from their mothers. And you don't know the children. I do and Mary is just right for them."

She had been irritated and frustrated and close to losing her temper completely. Juliet had replied in a careful, modulated voice saying that one of the reasons they had a Homes Finding Section was because social workers often got so close to the children that they didn't think enough about foster parents and their feelings and capabilities. And, she reminded Bella, Homes Finding was serving all the teams and had to take a wide view. She said she would accept the present situation for now as Mary would have made all kinds of arrangements but she would be talking to Malcolm tomorrow. After which speech she left the room, Gordon making a rude sign as the door closed.

I should retire, Bella thought. Twice today I have nearly lost my temper and there is not enough time to do anything properly and not enough resources when we need them.

Adrian had rung and told her she should take some sick leave. "The doctor will give you the necessary notes and don't tell me," he said, "that your mother always said that if you pretended to be ill you were just tempting fate. You need a break." Which made Bella smile, but also made her think of her mother. Mother. Mother's house. Things to see to. Clear it out. Put it on the market. See solicitor. She looked round in the half light of evening, seeing the grass was long and the roses needed dead-heading.

As she ran a bath she thought perhaps she would take tomorrow off and then remembered she was taking Carol to see the children. She had also arranged to visit Peggy Stringer who had sent her such a kind card when she heard Bella's mother had died. Poor Peggy, who dreaded Jack coming out of prison. No, not tomorrow. Perhaps in a day or two…

***

It was Gemma who persuaded her to get her priorities sorted out and Bella began to realise it was good to have a daughter who suddenly seemed stronger and better organised than she was herself. Gemma, who talked about Bella retiring, reminding her that she would have some money when the house was sold, suggesting it was time for new plans to be made, long holidays taken, a month or so in Canada with Sim?

So they gradually cleared the house and eventually sold it for a sum of money that would have astounded her father who had often said how the £2000 he had paid for it had been so hard to find. And it was strange and rather sad when, having cleared it of all the furniture, they left it for the last time. It seemed so shabby and cold. Bella went from room to room refurnishing it in her mind and replaying scenes of the life that she had lived there. She dug up the azalea she had given Grace when Henry died and then dug the erigeron and a lump of tradescantia. Gemma decided she wanted the cistus and also one of the astilbes and finally some rock plants. They packed them in boxes of earth and covered them with plastic bags, hoping they would survive. They packed both cars with the china and glass they decided to keep, and Gemma took a small table, a rush seated chair and two garden chairs, while Bella managed to fit in the good garden tools she found in the shed and the two cushions covered by Grace's embroidery as well as a box of linen and towels. Useful, practical things, Bella remarked, which was what they had liked. Dad and Mother thought in terms of a thing's use and its cost. It did not really matter what it looked like if it filled a need and had been *reasonable*, by which they meant not expensive. Bella felt some nostalgia for the contents of the house in which she had grown up, but could not escape the thought that she and Gemma were obliterating the lives of her parents as they stripped the house down to an empty shell.

Chapter Ten

1983

The house was sold for a large sum of money, which Bella divided up between herself, Gemma and her mother's sister, Flo. She also sent a cheque to Martha who rang her from time to time, either depressed, or excitedly high, but who was managing as a single mother and still working. Liz had been to stay for a weekend and had decried the fact that Martha was now in the middle of a divorce and that her little girl was being bundled back and forth between her parents. So no change there, Bella thought, unable to share Liz's anxiety and buoyed up by the birth of her second grandchild and the fact the Gemma had seemed to want her to go up as much as possible.

She was at present looking at Gemma kneeling on the floor, changing the baby who was squirming and kicking and, she thought, looking quite adorable.

"Before I came away I had a phone call from Martha who seems to have come to terms with single life and has become the gay divorcee. She seemed very high and talked about her new friends. There's a man called Bruce and another called Mervyn. I wasn't sure who was the favourite but Liz doesn't like Bruce at all and isn't very keen on Mervyn either. Martha said she really didn't care. Her mother disapproves of everything she does, so there's no point in worrying about it," Bella said.

"Well, that's true, isn't it? Liz is a pain, isn't she? I have never cared much for Martha, but I do sympathise with her, having a mother like Liz who is so critical. Thank God you are not like that." Gemma smiled at Bella while attaching the ends of a new nappy around the baby boy lying on the changing mat on the floor. This is a good time, Bella thought, taking the soiled clothes and nappy into the kitchen. This is being happy. And having a purpose. Twice babies had arrived to fill the gaps which death had made.

In the kitchen she began to prepare the evening meal and then looking at the clock, rushed out to fetch Susan from school. She came back admiring the drawings Susan was clutching and listening to the opinions and advice given by Mrs Penning, the teacher, who had become the fount of all wisdom in Susan's life. She had today said that it was not a good thing to pick wild flowers as they needed to sow their seeds as they died so they could grow some more baby flowers next year. Bella said she thought Mrs Penning sounded very nice and very wise.

But later, when they had cleared up the toys, and washed up the dishes from their meal, Josh said he wondered if Bella had thought about moving up to Stockport or nearby when she retired. And talking of retirement, when was she going to stop working?

"Well, not until I'm 60 and that will be in three years. I need to stay until then to get my pension. And moving... well I haven't really thought about it." Which wasn't exactly true. Bella knew that Gemma and Josh would like it, at least at the present time.

Grandmothers were useful especially if they lived nearby. And new mothers needed help. If she had learned anything from working as a social worker, it was that. But she did not want to move or, if she was quite honest, to give up work. It was about independence and control of her life. The same feelings she had had when Adrian wanted them to live together. Something of the struggle for personal survival which she had experienced when James had died was still there. "I must cope by myself. I must manage." She remembered how this had been a mantra which pushed her through the months of loneliness and grief. *Perhaps I still need it,* she thought, *because I like managing, being in control. Although I also like being here, close to Gemma. We get on so well. But she likes being in control too. We are alike in that so would we get on well if we were together a lot more?*

***

My dear Sim,

I think it must be months since you wrote and I didn't answer – but thank you so much for the tiny T-shirts you sent for Stuart. Gemma asks me to apologise for not writing, but Stuart is just big enough to wear them and they are much admired. You are quite right. It has been good to have a baby in the family again and I go up as often as I can, where I mostly pay attention to Susan, who is, of course, quite jealous, and told me that she loves him but wishes he would go away when she gets home from school! They want me to move to be near them and I am tempted but have decided to see my time out at Rensham. The dilemma of the old! To move when one can still get about and make new friends etc but not in need of care and still enjoying friends and being at home, or leave it until it becomes a necessity, one is in one's dotage, unable to get about or do anything except stare at the wall. Perhaps I am being silly, but here I am Bella Wingfield, there I shall lose my identity and just be Gemma's mother – and, of course, I can't bear the thought of losing the garden. The idea of someone else messing it about is awful.

Work continues to be in a state of flux. We are being told that specialisation is coming back and we now have a team for children leaving care and another one is being planned for children with learning difficulties. There is also talk of a young offenders team. Clients get shuffled around in every re-organisation... and we were all trained to believe that good social work was about making relationships. Actually a working party has been mooted which will probably last for a year or so, so I may be gone before I get reshuffled again. They are supposed to be studying the way the Department should evolve, a sort of 'Whither social work!' Whither indeed – Malcolm says it is withering away and child care will become a statutory matter only eventually with a team working exclusively with children at risk. Social policemen. I don't think I want to be part of that.

We've sold mother's house and divided the money between Aunty Flo, Gemma and me so we are now all rolling in money. I went into town the week the cheque arrived and bought myself a dress for £80 and a suit for £155 and I am getting a man in to take down the two plum trees which take all the sun from the end of the garden so I can grow vegetables. I suppose I shall be depriving the wasps of the plums, but then the slugs will thrive on my lettuces! And yes... I aim to have another trip to Canada if you can bear it. Next spring, I thought. Would that be possible for you?

Politically it is awful. Mrs Thatcher is privatising everything and constantly accusing the public sector of being wasteful. They are selling the council houses so the homeless are less and less likely to be re-housed. The ghastly war in the Falklands is over (Malcolm's son came home OK) but the unions are raging and roaring at her. It was planned that new social workers were going to do a three-year training programme before qualifying, but that has been put off because of expense, although nothing stops the criticism of social workers every time there is publicity about an abused child. Then we are all too young and badly trained but the idea of spending money on local government workers appals Mrs T. She is a nightmare, but apparently here for ever, advocating individualism and getting rich quick. Our department has been capped – which means we can only spend so much and cannot raise rates if we need more money, which we always do. And our managers seem to think that there must be a way we can re-organise which will save money, hence the everlasting changes, which, of course, cause confusion to the clients, depress the workers and usually finish up costing more!

Sorry to go on... I just get so angry thinking about it, but when that woman talks about us being wasteful and we are everlastingly short of staff and have to work so hard...!

I do hope you are all well and the children are thriving. I am longing to see you again. Do give my love to everyone and tell me if you think you could bear a visit next year... love to you all...

***

Tina hesitated by Bella's desk as she returned from replacing a file in the filing cabinet and Bella smiled, which was fleetingly returned. But Tina did not stop. They hardly ever spoke, Bella thought. She hardly speaks to anyone, except about work, although she had very briefly, told Bella she was sorry to hear of her mother's death. Without any eye contact, Bella had noted. She was looking past me at the time. So Bella was surprised when having placed the file on her desk, Tina walked back to Bella and said, "So how was your visit to the new baby? It's a boy, isn't it?"

As Bella told her about Stuart and Sue, she was aware that Tina was making an effort. She is not really interested, Bella thought, although she smiles and nods and makes a few appropriate remarks. So she was quite startled when Tina suddenly changed the subject and said, "I do wish we could be friends, Bella."

It's as if I have been resisting the idea, Bella thought, not sure how to reply. "Well, yes, I'm sure we could if we got to know each other..." This felt inadequate, not quite right, but Tina smiled and suggested they might have a meal together one evening. She knew an Italian restaurant which looked rather nice. So they made an arrangement for the following week and Bella noted it in her diary, not entirely enthusiastic, but curious. Friends? Well, who knows?

The week passed in the usual way, although Bella kept to her new resolution of going home more or less on time. She was conscious of a new attitude. Less worry about work, more concern with other things. Maybe it's the money, she thought or am I mentally preparing myself for retirement? Today she was particularly preoccupied with the plum trees.

Two men arrived with ropes and power saws, with a van towing a trailer. "For the trunks, missus. You won't want two big trunks littering the garden now, will you?" Bella had not thought of them taking the trees away. She had decided she wanted them cut into two or three pieces and laid on top of each other against the end wall. She had a slight argument with the men, who failed to appreciate Bella's wish to provide a good environment for insects and hedgehogs as the wood slowly rotted away. She also realised they probably wanted to sell them as logs, but she was quite insistent and watched as one man circled himself and the trunk with a rope and trod his way up the first tree. Near the top he fixed the rope he was carrying round the tree and dropped it down to his partner. There was not much room and Bella decided that the garden would be ruined as the trees were felled, but she was impressed by the skilful way they pulled the tree down in pieces to fall where there was space, and apart from side branches spreading across the remains of rudbeckia daisies and breaking some of the stems, little damage was caused. The power saws quickly cut up the trunks which were stacked in a heap on the grass. By the time the second tree was down, Bella realised she would only have room for half the wood, and compromised with the men, who took the trunk in pieces out to the trailer.

"I can't get over how light it is now," said Ellen, who had come to watch. "I think the garden looks bigger, don't you?" Bella wasn't sure she liked it at all. There was now such a gap. She no longer felt the garden closed around her; she was conscious of the traffic using the road the other side of her fence, and she felt sad about the trees. They had been growing there for so long and she had killed them. "I can see now what a good space you will have for a vegetable garden, and the morning sun will come right through there. And those old trees weren't up to much, were they?" Ellen was quite enthusiastic.

"The birds enjoyed the plums," said Bella. "The only ones I ever ate were those on the ground, and they were mostly bruised. Yes, of course, you are right. Plenty of room now for vegetables. Now, how about some tea. It is getting quite cold out here. Let's go in."

***

On the day of the meal in the Italian restaurant she became more involved than she had intended in a marital fight between Derek and Jasmine Cleaver. She had held a Matrimonial Supervision Order on their children, Jay and Marsha, since the divorce, so when Derek came in and complained about Jasmine's refusal to let him take the children out for the day, she arranged to see them both together at Jasmine's house to discuss contact arrangements. This was a mistake. From the moment he arrived, and started poking around looking at everything and asking why this and that had been changed, the situation was explosive. The children were playing with friends next door, but the parents did not get round to talking about them going out with their father. Jasmine became aggressively territorial about the house, telling Derek to mind his own business and he countered by reminding her that she would not have half the things she had if it had not been for him working his butt off! Bella's attempts to stick to the original agenda disappeared in the waves of hostility between them as Jasmine accused her ex of trying to set the children against her. He answered by saying that she was the one who was alienating the children who were confused by finding different 'uncles' in Mummy's bed in the morning, which was proof enough that she was unfit to have them. This accusation had an electrifying effect on Jasmine. She screamed at him to get out and never come near her or the children again. He said he was going and turned to Bella saying he was going back to court to get custody and to tell the judge that the fucking Matrimonial Supervision Order was doing no fucking good as his ex-wife apparently fucked any Tom, Dick or Harry and nothing was ever done about it.

Bella stayed with Jasmine for a while after he had left and explained that the Matrimonial Supervision Order obliged her to help them sort out contact arrangements. She said that she had made a mistake in deciding the meeting should take place at her house. They should have met on neutral ground – perhaps at the office. They had some tea and Jasmine calmed down but remained very hostile towards Derek, which, Bella thought, was hardly surprising. Bella told her she would see Derek again and arrange another meeting, as it would be far better to come to some peaceful arrangement than go back to court.

When she and Tina had settled at their table and ordered food, Bella wondered what Tina thought about Matrimonial Supervision Orders. "We get these from the divorce courts on the whim of a judge who, it seems to me, never explains what they are supposed to be for and without our prior agreement most of the time. And no proper explanation is made to the parents about learning to co-operate with each other or the supervising officer. I think the judge senses that the divorce is messy and is not entirely happy about the children and slaps on an MSO as a sort of safety net..." but Bella realised that Tina was not listening.

"This cannelloni is almost cold," she said, pushing her plate away and looking round for a waiter. She pushed at the pancake with her fork. "The first one I ate was tepid, but this one is cold. Probably just out of the freezer. Yes," she said to the waiter who responded to her wave. "This is cold. It hasn't been heated at all. Its quite disgraceful." The plate was removed and the waiter apologised and said he would get it heated. "You'll do no such thing," Tina said. "I am not eating food which has been half-heated and then heated again. Don't you know the danger of food poisoning?" She picked up her glass and emptied it and refilled it from the carafe that stood between them.

The waiter said he would speak to the chef and took the offending plate away.

"Is yours alright? I'm so sorry I brought you here. I thought it looked the sort of place one could get good food. And then to suggest re-heating it! Are you sure yours is hot?"

Bella reassured her and then tried to eat as slowly as possible giving Tina time, she hoped, to catch up. She searched for another topic of conversation, watching Tina inspecting the cutlery. She tried holidays, but Tina had not been to France, or Italy and concluded the subject by saying, "To save you going through the map of Europe, Bella, I haven't been abroad since I was married, when we went to Spain. Since then, it's been impossible."

"Was that the first time you were married?" Bella asked.

"Oh, so this is going to be exploration of my life, is it?" Tina stared at Bella.

"Of course not. I didn't intend to offend you."

"You don't know how lucky you are, Bella. Your mother dying as she did was a shock, but such a release for you."

"I'm sorry. I don't understand."

"No people like you never understand. I live with my mother you see. She had polio when I was seventeen and is disabled. She has always been there. I'm one of those good people who care for their elderly," she laughed harshly. "You should thank your lucky stars you don't have to care for yours."

"Oh, I see," Bella swallowed the last of her wine. "She's difficult?"

"You could say so. Yes. She's difficult. Bloody awful most of the time. I have fantasies about killing her. Don't look so shocked. I don't expect I will... but... oh, don't social work me, please, Bella. One makes one's bed..." She smiled too brightly. "Oh here comes my dinner."

"The chef apologises, madam," the waiter said, putting down the plate. Tina pulled it nearer to her and flinched as she withdrew her hand. "I see I am to be punished for complaining by being burnt," she said. The waiter rolled his eyes at Bella as he walked away and Bella smiled.

"I see it amuses you," Tina said. "And, yes, I am a bad tempered woman, I know that."

"But you have had a lot to put up with, I expect."

"You could say that. Two marriages ruined. No children. No holidays abroad."

"Because of your mother? It seems reasonable to be angry, I'm sorry."

She had finished her meal and as Tina drank the dregs from her glass, Bella called the waiter to bring another carafe."

***

Jan invited Bella for a meal two days later and Bella told her it had been an odd experience having dinner with Tina. She supposed she should not talk about it, but, well, she had to tell someone but although Tina did not ask for confidentiality, Bella asked Jan to keep it to herself.

"She ate her cannelloni as fast as she could, considering it was too hot, but she drank all the wine and she talked. I think she probably gets by on booze a good deal of the time. It would explain the awful mood she is in in the mornings. Probably hung over I guess. But the mother sounds like a witch. Demanding and complaining and keeping Tina on a sort of leash, always ready with a reason why she was needed at home. The first husband couldn't cope at all and left and when she met the second he gave her an ultimatum. She either left her mother and just lived with him or he was off too. Apparently Tina did leave, but her mother never left her alone and after about nine months she went back and there was a divorce. It sounds quite crazy but. I suppose there was a lot of guilt there and now she is just full of resentment."

"So now we know. But at least she talked about it. Did she relax at all?"

"Not really. She apologised for talking too much and said she rarely did, because she couldn't stand it when people were sympathetic. "Sympathy doesn't help," she said, "and I don't want suggestions about the best way to deal with her, so please don't go down that road... which more or less cancelled out anything I thought of saying, and I thought referring to Gemma or the grandchildren wasn't really on and she doesn't like gardening... so... we talked a bit about cooking and television, and we had pudding – rather nice crème brulee, which she actually liked – and somehow we got to the end of the meal."

"You should have asked her why she became a social worker."

"I didn't think of that. Yes, that would be interesting although I don't think she likes social work, so it probably would have only led to more resentment. It was a funny evening."

"So are you two now going to be friends?"

Bella laughed. "I doubt it. Friendship either happens or it doesn't, don't you think? The 'will you be my friend' approach reminds me of the playground. And I don't really want more friends with major problems. Makes me feel like an ambulance."

Chapter Eleven

1984

It was a surprise when Adrian rang and asked her to have dinner with him. They saw each other infrequently and Bella knew he had accepted her reluctance to live with him – we meet as old friends now, she thought. Old friends with an unspoken agreement not to talk about the past, although it was always there between them, limiting their conversation. It made her feel lonely and sad at times as now he never came to the house. She often thought she would like to cook for him and woke sometimes in the night, wanting to feel him beside her. But it had been her decision. I made a choice, she thought, but I am always pleased to see him and dinner would be nice. But there was a formal deliberation in his invitation; it was not the usual casual suggestion. He said it was important so they fixed a place and a date and she took care in getting ready. Almost as if this is a celebration, she thought. And yet, what could we be celebrating?

They talked about her trip to Canada and Sim's family and how the children had grown, and then they shared views on the miners' strike and spent a few minutes discussing the repressed fury social workers felt at the continuing diatribes that came from Mrs T, who apparently thought all local government staff spent their time wasting money. But Bella knew that this was not why they were there; they were marking time. Nevertheless she was not really ready when he said, "But I didn't ask you to dinner to talk politics."

She smiled. She didn't expect so. "I'm waiting to hear. What are you going to tell me?"

He expected she knew Clara, his deputy? She nodded. "Of course, I met her when I last visited you. Has something happened to her?"

"Well, yes and no. We have become close, very close. We are more or less living together. Well, we still have our own accommodation... at the moment..."

Bella said nothing. Completely unprepared she just stared at him, frowning. For some moments he didn't speak, then, "Actually we are buying a house together and plan to get married."

Bella forced a smile on her face. "Well, it is a surprise, but... that sounds like a happy situation... it will take me a minute to get used to the idea, but... well... of course I hope it works out. I mean... well, I mean I feel very odd about it. But that's my problem, isn't it?" Her laugh was as forced as her smile.

He reached across the table and took her hand. "Sitting here with you, I also feel odd about it. But I wanted to tell you before someone else did. You are still very important, Bella. I've told Clara about us and that our past together is always there for me."

Bella withdrew her hand. The fact that Clara knew about her was offensive. They had talked about her. She felt exposed and vulnerable. Angry. But it had to be hidden, this loss she felt. It was her doing after all. Did she expect Adrian to always be there, wanting her and waiting? She made the necessary effort.

"So, all kinds of plans then. And where are you planning to live? And how are the boys? Jason must have finished college and Julian, what is he doing? He wanted to do languages, didn't he, and didn't he take off for South America a few months ago?

That must be a marvellous opportunity. We didn't have opportunities like that, did we?"

They got through dinner talking about children and grandchildren. Bella made sure there were no more opportunities for talk about Clara or the proposed marriage. There was nothing to say. She couldn't ask questions – there was nothing she wanted to know. She was, she realised, frightened of hearing anything else.

She knew she was prattling and over-bright and when they had finished eating she said she thought she ought to go home... things to do. She started to put on her coat, fiddled with her bag and then she went for her car. He hurried after her and when they reached the parked car, held her briefly and kissed her cheek. She smiled lightly, said goodbye, closed the door with a bang and started the engine. He stood by the kerb but she didn't look round and as she drove home she began to cry.

Chapter Twelve

1985

She got dressed while the Today programme talked about Mr Gorbachev and his visit to Mr Reagan. She was not listening properly. She discarded the blue skirt for grey slacks and a pink sweater, then changed her mind again and took the new green one from the wardrobe, but as she pulled it over her head she realised the Today programme had moved on and she began to concentrate.

'The judge concluded his summing up with a severe criticism of the Social Services, who, he said, failed to see the child on the last two occasions social workers had visited. This little boy had suffered considerably for several weeks before he died and while the mother was culpable in that she gave false explanations for the child's absence from the house, the reports from neighbours and the history of violent behaviour on the part of the stepfather should have been a sufficient reason for the social worker to insist on seeing the child...'

About to start brushing her hair she stopped, walked to the bedside table and turned the tuning dial, finding music which was discordant and obscure before returning to getting ready for work. Hearing a judge slamming into social workers filled her with a mixture of anxiety and anger. She didn't want to hear any more. It hurt her to listen... people make mistakes... everyone is wrong sometimes... so this lot were wrong... but it rankled... It seemed, she thought, that we are supposed to always get things right. The music was not helping either so she turned it off. The parents killed the child but it was the social workers who were to blame and it's always assumed they were inexperienced and too young. Well, perhaps they were, but they were in a large city where the caseloads were heavy and complex.

She made herself some toast but had no appetite so she cut it up into small pieces, went into the garden and put it on the bird table. Then she began to water the pots, pulling the weeds which grew so quickly round the plants. Walking to the compost heap she saw that the row of tiny lettuces in the new vegetable plot, which had looked so promising yesterday, had been reduced to mangled leaves by slugs or snails. There were signs that the onions were growing, uneaten, but what to do about the lettuces? She looked at her watch and knew she must go to work, but wished she could stay and dig over the rest of the bed with the manure she had collected from the stables at Grindley Hall. She was still affected by the newscast, thinking she had begun to hate hearing about child abuse, thinking it was time to stop working.

The rest of the bed needed preparing for the beans growing well in pots in the cold frame, ready to plant, which meant buying long canes. But she must get going. Malcolm was off sick and she had been asked to supervise Jon Havers who had taken Alan's place and was still fairly new. Malcolm had suggested she hand over Carol Pritchard's family to him soon – "We must start to think about where your cases will be going. It won't be long now until you retire and this one could do with a long handover." A remark which startled her into realising that retiring was not just leaving work, but leaving the people with whom she was involved.

"I feel rather sad at handing Maureen, Cheryl and Davey over to you," she said later to Jon handing him the file. "You will see that I first took them into care when Carol and her boyfriend were out of their minds on LSD – at least I think it was LSD – and quite incapable – must be over a year ago. Her husband was in prison and she was divorcing him. At the time I believed she was frightened of losing the children, although I had been concerned about her parenting for some time. She never seemed to have much time for Davey, the youngest. She either shouted at him or ignored him when he cried for attention and I did attempt to modify this. I took a behaviouristic approach, persuading her to respond to him consistently, play with him more and divert him with his toys when she was too busy to be involved. But without much success. Her mood swings began to concern me and I did wonder if she was using drugs. And then, of course, this was confirmed on the day I found her and a boyfriend stoned."

Jon asked if it was then she had applied for Care Orders and Bella said no, not at that stage. They had taken Place of Safety Orders, but let them lapse. Carol seemed to get herself together and she had been so frightened she'd lose the children she seemed determined to get things straight and never touch drugs again.

The children were placed together at first with Mary Weston for a couple of weeks, but were moved at the insistence of Homes Finding – the girls went to the Morrisons and Davey to Mrs Forsyth, but because they were separated, and the conditions at home improved with Carol making a real effort, visiting the children regularly and swearing that she would never take drugs again, we let them go home after about three months; but things quickly deteriorated. Davey was very unsettled and the girls began to look neglected and there came the day when she had found Carol dreamy and giggly and the same young man reappeared lying on the sofa in the sitting room, apparently asleep.

"By some miracle," she said, "the Morrisons and the Forsyths were still available and we applied for Care Orders on all three children and moved them back to the foster homes."

She said she would take him to visit the children and the foster parents, whom she was sure he would like.

"What about Dad?" Jon asked. "Is he still in prison?"

Bella told him that the children's father had come to see her soon after she had obtained the Care Orders, expressing his disgust at his wife and his intention to make a home for the children. He was full of good intentions. He would get a job, a place to live, and make it all up to them. She said she told him he would have to get to know the children first, and he promised to keep in touch. Since when, she said, she had heard nothing from him at all. Post prison good intentions, she thought. No, she did not have his address, and no, she had not contacted Probation, who, Jon suggested, might have kept in touch with him as an after-care case. Bella, actually thought it a waste of time to try to contact him, but did not say so. Jon said he thought they should make an effort to find the father. Children did want to know these things eventually. Bella wondered then if she had neglected this aspect of the family. Jon, newly-qualified, had made an important point – she had made a judgement about the father, but had perhaps not thought it through. She offered no argument.

They talked about dates to make introductory visits, and Bella said she thought he should see Carol, who, she said, appeared these days to be having her adolescence. She had lost her house through rent arrears, and now lived in a bedsit. She was still using drugs and although she kept promising to go to the drug rehabilitation unit which Bella had urged her to do she had not done so.

Jon asked about the mother's contact with the children, and Bella said she only went now if she was taken and although Bella made arrangements to do this, Carol invariably missed appointments. She made the point to Jon that the children were no longer told of arranged visits, as they were so upset when she did not arrive. She did tell him, however, that the Morrisons and the Forsyths had been splendid at keeping the children in touch with each other.

Jon asked about other relatives, and Bella told him about Carol's mother, who was into her third marriage and had never shown much interest in her grandchildren. She said she believed there was an aunt somewhere, but Carol had lost her address.

Jon was enthusiastic and had several ideas. He thought Carol might respond to one of the parenting groups which the Family Centres were running and perhaps, he said, the children should visit her, rather than wait for her to visit them. Or perhaps they could have family outings.

Bella nodded, encouragingly, and said that a change of social worker might be a good time to try a change of tactics, but privately thought that these children would be staying in care. She had felt for some time that Carol had lost interest in them and dulled any pain she might have felt at losing them with drugs. Bella always found it difficult to get inside the head of a mother who seemed to have stopped caring for her children but she thought it likely that Carol had not had much experience of good mothering herself and had no model of parenting that would guide her own role as a mother. And with a natural father she had barely known (her mother divorced him before Carol was a year old), and two stepfathers, it was perhaps, not surprising that her choice of a husband had been less than ideal. She knew Jon had a point in wanting to ignite the relationship between Carol and her children, but she actually thought it would now be best for the children to be brought up in good foster homes. She wanted to urge Jon not to raise the children's expectations because she was sure they would be disappointed, but she said nothing more and they went on to look at his other work.

He was again full of ideas and enthusiasm. He talked about social work methods, a cognitive approach, task centred work, behaviourism and systems theory, at which point Bella told him that she and Jan were into systemic work whenever they could find the time. She found herself needing to tell him that she too had thought of different ways of dealing with the work and was not to be patronised, but then was gratified that he was interested and said he would like to hear more about it sometime. Perhaps he might even observe a session. "I've got to take advantage of you while you are still here. You seem to know so much. Can't imagine how we will cope when both you and Jennifer go."

***

"It seems the nearer I get to retirement, the busier I become," Jennifer was walking with Bella to their cars. "There isn't going to be a replacement for me before I go and I still have to hand over thirteen children. Malcolm suggested I talk to Jon and Gordon about some of them, but I must say I feel very uneasy. I would like Jan to take on the Faulkner girls. They are in Rumsey House and should have a woman. Nearly all the staff there are men... which reminds me. Belinda Millen is in voluntary care with Mrs Courtney. Do you know her? She's a splendid foster mum and she loves Belinda, whose mother died and who was living with her grandmother until this old lady developed dreadful arthritis and felt she couldn't cope with a very active five-year-old. Belinda is now eight years old and I think she will be in care long term. I wondered if you could take her. It's not a busy case. I keep Belinda in touch with the granny and there are two aunts. Dad remarried some years ago and has gradually dropped out of the picture. Belinda knows him, but there's no real attachment there, although she likes to receive his birthday present, which he never forgets."

Bella reminded Jennifer that she too would be retiring in less than two years' time, long before Belinda had grown up, but... well, she knew it was inevitable, they were so short staffed... she said she would have a word with Malcolm and if he agreed...

***

As they assembled in the team room for Jennifer's retirement party they passed the blackboard which was still standing inside the door, today exclaiming boldly:

MAKE GOD LAUGH. PLAN FOR THE FUTURE

The Director, George Pringle, had come to the event and he made a speech. He started off by saying how nice it was to visit an area team and how he wished he could come more often, which Bella remembered, was what James Henderson had said at Judith Naseby's retirement do three years earlier. But Malcolm had briefed him about Jennifer and he eulogised about her long period of service to children and how he knew she would be sadly missed, especially by all the foster parents to whom she had given so much support. He mentioned the changes which were coming and said he was personally rather pleased that specialisation was coming back but realised that staff were anxious about the future, wondering how the Department would look in five years time, when thankfully, he said, he would have also retired.

We all wonder about that, Bella thought, but the team were rather anxious about Jennifer's future. They knew that her whole life was her work. Although they were often irritated by her accounts of weekends spent taking children out or to visit relatives. She had no family to speak of and all her conversation was about the children whom she worked for now and the ones she had worked for in the past. Everyone also knew that she probably worked harder than anyone else and made important, lasting relationships with those children who for one reason or another had no parents or family they could call their own. They were going to miss her. There were not many single women left nowadays who filled their lives with other people's children, whereas once it was only single women who had been there for the children who needed care and support. But Jennifer was her usual practical, cheerful self, thanking everyone for her presents and then surprising her colleagues by suggesting to the Director that one of the things he might do before he retired was to persuade the Social Services Committee to pay the foster parents an adequate allowance for all the hard work they did, instead of the pittance they received at the moment. Everyone cheered at this. Even the Director managed a smile.

Bella and Jan helped Jennifer pack her car which took longer than it should have done because Jennifer kept remembering things she needed to tell Marian and Gordon and Malcolm, and before she finally left, Reception called and told Bella there was a Tracey Meredew waiting to see her.

Bella thought she knew the name but could not remember why. When she walked into Reception she recognised the face but could not at first place the very pregnant woman in her late twenties with a small child about three in a pushchair, who smiled and said, "Remember me, Mrs Wingfield?"

"I couldn't think, but of course I do. Tracey. You were fostered and then you went home to your Mum and after a year or so I had the Care Order revoked. Goodness. That was years ago. How are you?"

"Well as you can see, I'm expecting and this is Darren, he's nearly three. I'm alright. I always remember you letting me go home. I couldn't stand that old witch Mrs Cummings though me and me Mum didn't really get along. But she took me to the Family Planning Clinic which was a surprise, but what really surprised me most was when she told me it was your idea."

Bella smiled and nodded and Tracey went on. "I left home after a couple of years and got a room with Milly, my friend, but then I lived with a guy called Jack and Darren is his. But he buggered off soon after Darren was born and I've got married now. Benny Fulbright his name is. I used my old name just now. Thought you might remember it. But Benny's alright. Good with Darren and looking forward to his own baby coming. That's why I'm here."

"Right. Go on."

"Well, he's just got a job. Been out of work for ages, but working now and can't risk losing it by taking time off when the baby is born, and my Mum's no use and I thought perhaps you could take Darren into care for a week while I has the baby. I can't really believe I'm askin'. I always swore I'd never let one of mine go into care, but then I thought of you and I know you wouldn't try to keep him, and it would only be for a week or so..."

We used to do a lot of this, Bella thought. When I first started, in the late 60s we often took children into care while mother had the next baby, and then someone wrote an article entitled 'Recidivism in Child Care' about the ease with which child care officers responded to requests during confinements, and policy began to change. We used to think that it was always better for children to have nice foster parents to look after them rather than friends or relatives whose standards might not be very high. Some children were coming into care every two or three years. Care became an easy option for families who had temporary difficulties of whatever kind. She remembered Judy saying that it was always best to help where one could – so much better for the children, she would say. We were so arrogant, Bella remembered. Never mind that children were dumped with people they did not know. Judy was certain that fostering at least gave them a taste of nice middle-class values. Something for them to aspire to later on.

So when she told Malcolm she had already arranged for Darren to come into care when Tracey had the baby, she was not surprised that he was not exactly pleased. She said she had explored the possibility of friends and relatives, who were either working or were unacceptable to Tracey. She had had a battle with Homes Finding but they had found a foster home willing to take Darren. She was quite confident that Tracey was a good mum and her new husband was a sincere person who helped her as much as he could.

Malcolm muttered about employers needing to understand that sometimes men had to be at home to help and it was time attitudes changed, but he accepted what she had done. "What goes around comes around," she said, still surprised at the request but rather pleased that her original decision, so long ago now, had probably worked out rather well.

Chapter Thirteen

1990

Bella picked up two bunches of wallflowers and put them in the trolley with the tulip bulbs while gazing at the great splash of colour made by the pansies covering a whole stand, and then shook off the temptation to buy some for the pots. They are like peas and strawberries, she thought, beguiling but out of season. I want the garden to acknowledge that flowers do not bloom riotously in the winter.

As she walked to the cash desk she noticed a familiar figure with a small boy standing by the indoor plants. Brenda Forsyth, foster mother, and... could that be Davey? The small boy was wearing a school blazer and cap and a large bag hung from his shoulders. Bella paused and then went to pay for her plants. While she was paying she kept glancing at the two figures who were laughing and talking together. She nearly went over to speak to them but decided not to. The reluctance to become involved in any way with the past was still there, and she knew Davey was doing well with the Forsyths, still seeing his sisters and very occasionally his mother. When she had met Jon in the supermarket a few months ago, he had told her about them still being in care and Davey now at school. He had given her some insight into the Department's attitudes as well.

"The new Fieldwork Manager has been looking at files and sent me a note asking why these children had not been considered for adoption. I believe other people have had similar notes. Adoption is the new priority. Permanent homes for children now in care. I expect you have heard some of the politicians on about it. The Home Secretary is apparently very concerned that there are so many children in long term care who could, he thinks, be adopted. I sent a note back to the Fieldwork guy saying that the foster parents didn't want to adopt and the children were so well settled it would be very damaging to think about moving them now – to which he replied that he wanted to be invited to the next reviews as I probably knew that the Department's policy was to ensure no children were deprived of the opportunity to have permanent homes. By which he really meant, adoption would be cheaper."

"So what's happening," Bella asked.

"Well, so far, I've forgotten to invite him to a review and at present he seems to have forgotten as well. But don't worry. We shall fight this if we have to and I have the foster parents on my side. These children are settled and reasonably happy. It would be awful to move them again. Don't worry. Over my dead body!"

Bella remembered an earlier time when the powers that be had decided that more children should be adopted and social workers should pay more attention to this resource. Everything comes around again eventually, she reflected, recalling that the team had thought at the time that it was more about saving money on foster parent allowances than about the welfare of children. Adoptive parents did not receive allowances. The children became their sole responsibility and many foster parents – if not all – could not afford to adopt. There was also an apparent disregard for the children concerned. Most had been moved more than once. Some had been moved several times – all had been in some way or another neglected, rejected or abused by their natural parents.

And another important factor was the fact that children in foster care were usually over five years old, sometimes over ten and had memories of their families – relations which were still important with whom they could, and often did, maintain some contact – but adoptive parents were often unable to accept that children who were now theirs would continue to see their original kin. Even Jennifer, who was a great believer in adoption, had agreed with this point.

On the other hand Bella knew that children who remembered something of their families and kept relationships going, even if only intermittently, were easier to settle when they were moved. They were more secure. We all need to know something of our origins, she thought, and Jon had reminded her that there was a strong movement towards 'open adoptions' these days. Keeping adopted children in touch with the past. Helping adoptive parents to understand that this was in the children's long term interest. Not just placing them for adoption because it sounded better, because it was politically a good idea to ensure children had permanent homes or because it was cheaper.

Jon was right, she thought, they had been here before and it was about money and it would be dreadfully damaging to consider moving the likes of Davey who had made a strong relationship with Mrs Forsyth, who wanted to keep him, and almost certainly thought he was going to stay with her permanently.

She spent the afternoon gardening, planting the wallflowers and the bulbs. She dug up the runner beans, stored the canes and composted the bed. Then she remembered that Jan was coming round in the evening, so she put the tools away and went inside to clean herself up and finish preparing the meal. My day for recollections, she thought. Jan was retiring in a few months' time with much to tell.

So they sat and gossiped and recalled the cases they both knew and Bella learned, for the first time, that Tina's mother had died. Tina rang Bella occasionally and they sometimes had a meal together. Tina had never asked her to visit at home, so Bella thought it best they confined their socialising to restaurants. Nothing had been said about the offending mother when Bella last saw her, so she was surprised, but not as much as the team had been when confronted with the grief stricken Tina who was in tears when she told them and who had now handed in her notice, was in the process of selling her house and arranging to go on a cruise, all with an air of deep unhappiness and a 'life's not worth living anymore' attitude.

"She has been on sick leave for the past two weeks," Jan said, "which is a relief really. I mean... well, you know Tina. Nothing we could say was any help and she created an aura of gloom over the team. Extraordinary woman."

So they speculated about that and Bella thought she should write to her. "But do I say I'm sorry her mother has died, when I can remember so clearly how she told me she wanted to kill her? Oh well, I suppose I can manage something."

"Don't forget it's my last day on 1st December. You must come to the party," Jan reminded Bella as she got into her car, which brought back thoughts of her own retirement party when the director hadn't come and the new Assistant Director had told everyone he had heard so much about her and the splendid work she had done – all rubbish, Bella thought. He had never heard of her, but everyone else had been very pleasant and people from the past had been there. Harry, Don, Judy, Jennifer and Adrian, and so many foster parents – all promising to keep in touch. Bella remembered how she had smiled and laughed her way through the evening feeling strange. She had been sad and glad in equal parts, looking forward and looking back, tugged in each direction with regret and anticipation. As she had staggered round the back of the house with the birch tree they had given her which she intended to plant where the plums had been because the fence still looked bare. She had suddenly felt lonely and afraid. Instead of a life of reaction to events, the future was to be made up as she went along.

But the desolation of that time soon passed, Gemma had been delighted that her mother was no longer working and could be asked to look after the children from time to time. And Bella, of course, was delighted to go. Then as Susan and Stuart got older they had started coming to her for short periods without their parents. They had been with her for a week this summer and she had taken them to the old gravel pits where there was a sailing school. This had been a great success, she told Jan. Both children said it was absolutely wicked, and a great improvement on the City Museum which Susan said, she supposed was very educational but rather gross. Bella had been terrified they would drown or fall in and get pneumonia and knew she was far more nervous about her grandchildren than she had been about her daughter. But it had done her good, she said, and when they had both fallen in and she had seen how well they could swim, she began to think it pretty wicked as well. They were going to have some more lessons next time they came and when Josh came to fetch them they asked him if he would buy them a boat.

Chapter Fourteen

2000

Easter

"Actually," Bella said, "that happened to me. Your mother started life when I was at college."

Susan was surprised. "You mean you were pregnant with Mum while you were studying. I didn't know that." She turned to Gemma.

"Well," Gemma said. "I don't really remember the details. But, yes, I did know eventually. It didn't seem to matter then." Gemma smiled. "But I suppose we could say that it has become a family custom, although of course my mother was married at the time."

"Oh, here we go," Susan said. "They always manage to get around to marriage. Well, Martin finishes his degree this summer and he should get a job and then, when we have enough money, we shall probably get married… But that's not really important, getting married, I mean… like it's the most respectable thing to do. No one cares whether you're married or not these days but I'd be rubbish at college while I'm carrying the baby and even worse afterwards when it actually arrives. But… like, I'll go back and get my degree eventually – you did Gran, didn't you and look how successful you've been."

"I don't know about successful, but I never regretted it. Babies so absorb you, take you over completely. I'm sure I should have been rubbish too if I'd stayed on."

Gemma had been shocked and, Bella thought, rather disappointed, when she had broken the news about Sue's pregnancy. She has this conventional streak, Bella thought. But during her Easter visit, she found the family relaxed and rather excited about the prospect of the coming baby. Josh wanted them to marry because, he said, financially Sue would be more secure, which Gemma said was less the influence of his legal mind than an acceptable way of expressing his jealousy about his precious daughter. But he seemed content to wait now and was less sceptical about Martin's prospects and his general reliability than he had been at first.

It was not just the prospect of Sue having a baby and needing family support that brought about the combined assault on Bella's independence. It had been going on since she retired, although sometimes Bella thought they had accepted that she was managing rather well. She prattled on about her life, telling them that she was meeting old colleagues. Jennifer had developed the habit of calling in unexpectedly and staying for hours. There was Jan, and although Maggie and Jason had moved from next door, they came over for meals and she and Maggie sometimes went to the cinema together. Then of course, there were the visits to Canada – she had been over twice and Sim had brought the family to England two years earlier. I am always busy with something, she thought, and there is always the garden. She had joined the local gardening club and had learned how to graft roses from a member called Jack, who was quite an expert. And of course, there was Ellen to visit, who was becoming rather frail and forgetful – my bit of voluntary work, she reflected.

But they had started to comment on the fact that although she insisted on weeding the garden she tired easily and seemed to experience pain in her back when getting up from a chair. So they talked about her moving and rather alarmed her during this visit, when they said they thought they could adapt the house and provide her with a 'granny flat' over the garage. She lay awake a long time at night, thinking about this, hating the expression 'granny flat' and yet knowing she enjoyed being there. They suggested she would be available to help Sue and if she sold the house she could contribute to the building plans and have money in the bank as well. She told them she would think very hard about it. Perhaps make a decision when the baby was born.

When she went home after Easter for a while she felt old and lonely and wondered why it was so difficult to change this life for the uncomplicated, secure and sociable one she could have in Stockport. But the telephone began to ring and arrangements were made with friends, and she walked down the road and called on Ellen. Before she went away she had arranged for another neighbour to do Ellen's shopping and Ellen expressed immediate relief that Bella had now returned. The neighbour had done her best, Ellen said, but she got the wrong biscuits and couldn't find the right cereal.

Every surface in the kitchen in which they sat was covered with papers, envelopes and plastic bags, which Bella knew would be full of something Ellen was saving. She managed to secretly remove some tired-looking bacon from the top of the fridge and the remains of a quiche which was dried up and a rather bad colour and she stepped over first one cat and then another, strange looking tabby, which she didn't recognise. Ellen explained that he had adopted her and was obviously not fed properly. Bella knew better than to argue so they chatted and Bella made a list of the shopping Ellen wanted, and left eventually worrying a little about Ellen's capacity to cope. She seemed rather unsteady.

Back at home she decided to clean the kitchen which was neglected and untidy. She found cobwebs lacing among the wine glasses, and spent a whole day turning out, throwing away and washing down. Looking at her work before she went to bed she felt a glow of satisfaction at the order and cleanliness, and lying awake later, she thought it would be a good idea to have new dining room curtains and maybe a new carpet in the bedroom. I have a home, she decided. I don't want a granny flat.

October 2000

It had taken several phone calls to and from Liz before the arrangements were made for Martha to come to stay with Bella. Martha had been reluctant and difficult, Liz said, and eventually it was apparently Matthew who had persuaded her. He had brought her down in the car three days earlier. Bella thought of the thin white-faced woman who had hugged her tightly, muttering it was so good to be with her and then communicating with small nods and strained smiles, saying almost nothing.

This is the fourth night I have slept badly, Bella thought, as she groped for the clock. Just after three. She would have to get up and go to the loo. As she felt for her slippers she thought that waking in the middle of the night was a sign of depression. That makes two of us, she thought, how will we get over all this?

They had walked, shopped and Bella had cooked and chatted on about family and friends. She had asked no questions thinking that the best thing was to wait for Martha to feel able to talk, but she was feeling the strain of living with this almost mute woman who was in such misery. But the middle of the night is not the best time to solve problems and she had to get back to sleep. Perhaps a cup of tea would help.

She felt her heel slip on the stair and grabbed for the banister, steadying herself and imagining falling and landing in a heap at the bottom, perhaps unconscious, perhaps with broken bones. Lying there alone for hours. Then she remembered she wasn't alone, and a light in the kitchen told her Martha was up as well. She stood for a moment in the hall half inclined to go back to bed but she wanted tea and it was probable that Martha needed company. People sometimes talk more easily in the middle of the night.

"Did I disturb you?" Martha was sitting at the table, a glass of water in front of her.

"No, I didn't know you were up. I got up for the loo and then thought I'd like a cup of tea." Bella moved to the tap and began filling the kettle. "Shall I make you one?"

"No. No thanks."

Bella sat at the table, seeking something useful to say, but it was Martha who spoke.

"I sleep for a while and then I wake. Usually about three." She looked at her watch. "Its 3.20 now. Then my mind races."

"And you can't stop it. Yes, I think I know how awful it is to start thinking in the middle of the night. Everything seems so dreadful, and one's mind is on a sort of circular railway. Do you think it would help to talk?"

Since Martha had arrived she had not said anything about the child who had died. She had tended to sit staring out of the window or walking in the garden. Bella had carried on with the household chores, chatting about her life, the family, food, shopping and even the weather, not expecting conversation, asking no questions. The only time Martha had really talked had been about her brother Sam. He came home from India every two or three years and had been back the previous year. Martha spoke of him with affection and, Bella thought, some envy. He kept in touch with his son Jasper and had apparently worked out something with Jasper's mother, Marina, who accepted the contact and occasional visits. She had always refused to go to India, and she knew that Sam had another partner there now. An

Indian woman called Meta, and there was also a young girl, their daughter.

Martha said that Liz always found the subject of Sam difficult. She was always pleased to see him but he knew how she disapproved and was, Martha said, gently amused. "He's a very gentle person, actually. He always seems so calm and kind. I think India has done this for him," she said. Bella asked if she had written to him and told him about things, but Martha said she couldn't write, not now, although she expected that Liz had. She thought Liz had suggested he come back now and see her. But, she said, he wouldn't be able to help.

Sitting at the kitchen table in the middle of the night was not what Bella would have planned but the question came almost without her thinking about it. The response however, was quite predictable.

"I can't, Bella. I can't talk. I know if I start to talk I shall... shall..." she shook her head, and covered her eyes.

"When we shut things inside ourselves they can get distorted. They need to be out in the world where other people can contribute and perhaps help. I think you know that," Bella said.

Martha uncovered her face and stared at Bella, fearful and agitated. "Yes, I suppose I do, but I can't do that. I can't. I know you want to help and I'm so grateful to you, but, Bella, please don't make me talk because I can't. Not now." She got up and went to the door.

"I'm going back to bed. Goodnight."

Bella got to her feet and caught hold of Martha's hand. "I think I understand." She smiled. "Goodnight, Martha."

Liz had sent local newspaper cuttings before Martha had arrived, so Bella knew what had happened. A four-year-old girl had died from a brain injury, her mother and stepfather had been arrested and charged with murder and the neighbours had been free with their remarks to the press that they knew something was wrong and had kept informing the Social Services who, apparently did nothing. They were, of course, all devastated and remembered little Alison as such a pretty, happy, little girl before all this happened. There was a quote from the Director of Social Services too. He said he couldn't say anything at this stage, but they were conducting an internal inquiry.

And then Liz on the telephone, fierce in support of her daughter who, she said, did not have the support she needed and who was, anyway, as she had always thought, not suited for this type of work. She is not like you, Liz said to Bella, not tough and hard enough. You ought to have known that when you encouraged her to train as a social worker.

Bella had half expected that, and felt her hackles rising. That is not true, she wanted to say and telling Martha as she knew Liz probably had, that she was not strong enough for the work was really a way of holding her responsible for whatever failings had occurred, and unlikely to help. She had not responded, of course. Liz was far too upset to cope with an argument and her job now, she thought, was to help Martha cope with the present and the future. And she had felt defeated. Tonight, at 3.30 a.m. she felt very tired and helpless. How to do this? Something had happened that could not be reversed. This is a pain that will not go away and I am supposed to have left all this behind. I can do without it. She made tea and carried it upstairs to her bedroom, resenting the problem she had brought upon herself, hoping for sleep.

***

Martha received a letter when she had been with Bella five days. She did not open it when Bella gave it to her, fingering the envelope and then walking about in the garden. She came back into the kitchen and made for the door still holding the letter and Bella, herself exasperated at the delay, asked her, rather sharply, if it wouldn't be better if she actually opened it and read it, rather than agonising about the contents. Rather to her surprise, Martha sat at the table and tore open the envelope.

"It's from Kay Berwick, my supervisor. She wants me to go back and take part in the inquiry," she said.

Bella said she thought that was reasonable and was what she would have expected. Things have to move on and the Department will need to establish the facts and develop a point of view. She added that she thought it might, in the long run, be better for Martha to go through the case with colleagues. Martha stared at her and began to tremble. She shook her head and left the room. Bella heard her go upstairs.

Although she continued with household chores, tidying the kitchen and trying to think about meals and the shopping she must do, Bella could not stifle her anxiety. She kept thinking that Martha had already tried to kill herself and ought not to be left alone, but the silence of this woman daunted her and perhaps, if left to herself, she would be able to move towards the future. The letter could motivate her, help her to think, help her to talk about it.

Unable to settle properly to anything, Bella rang Gemma. This was a good time. Gemma had rung twice but each time Martha had been within earshot and the conversation had been restricted. She could talk more easily with Martha upstairs, so she poured out some of her anxiety and told Gemma she felt helpless and wondered if she should call the doctor, or at least somebody who could help this unhappy woman.

Gemma listened and worried with her. She said that Bella knew more about potential suicides than she did, but perhaps it was too soon to make assumptions. After all, Martha was simply keeping things to herself. She wasn't threatening anything. Having a legal mind, Gemma said she wondered if Martha actually needed a solicitor and they talked about that, but Bella believed Martha would be very resistant to talking to a solicitor.

That might be necessary at some time, but perhaps not now. Gemma said that perhaps Bella should be more assertive with her. Being there for her was fine, but didn't she need pushing? Kindness and acceptance was all very well but this couldn't go on for ever. Bella had, after all, been quite assertive about opening the letter and that had worked. "And Martha went to you for help, didn't she? Perhaps you should be more insistent about helping her. Ask her want she wants you to do," she suggested.

When Bella went up to Martha an hour or so later, she found her lying on her bed staring at the ceiling. No, she said, she didn't want anything thank you. No, she wasn't hungry... she would come down later.

But she didn't appear downstairs and Bella made a sandwich for her lunch which she didn't want, and then made tea and took a cup upstairs. She had been thinking about Gemma's remarks and had also decided that she would not be able to cope much longer with the present situation. She felt tired. Her back ached and the feeling of helplessness was confusing her. Martha was turned to one side, her eyes shut. Bella put down the tea and said she wanted to talk, and would Martha please listen.

It was hard to remember the exact sequence of the conversation which had taken place. It had been very distressing, at times explosive and there had been a lot of tears. But, Bella thought, Martha had talked. Almost incoherently at first when Bella had said calmly and carefully that she really didn't know how she could help if Martha remained silent. Martha had turned her head away at this saying she was sorry and beginning to cry. It was then I became persistent, Bella remembered, telling Martha that her silence was wearing her down and doing Martha no good at all. She said that she thought Martha should tell her what had happened at work and why she felt so terrible about it, and then said, "Whatever happened has to be faced. Hiding won't help. It has to be faced, Martha. You know this. This is what you have had to do with your clients – help them face the facts however awful they are. This is what I believe I have to do now with you."

Martha had lain in silence and Bella sat quietly for a few minutes before saying she did know that a child had been killed and the parents arrested, and that Martha had reacted to the news by trying to kill herself, so she had assumed that Martha felt in some way responsible. Perhaps Martha should tell her why she felt this way. In what way had she been involved? "Tell me about it," she said.

After a moment Martha began to sob. Something seemed to erupt within her as she made a choking sound and began to weep in great gulps and gasps, tears streaming through the fingers she pressed to her face, shoulders heaving as she flung herself on the pillow, pulling up her legs beneath her, banging clenched fists on her head, rolling from side to side as though pain gripped her whole body. She cried out as she twisted on the bed, bellowing her grief, her strangled voice seeming to tear through her throat.

Bella sat on the end of the bed watching this explosion with something like relief, but as Martha's cries diminished to the sobbing of a hurt child, she bent down and held her, pulling her up until she collapsed in her arms. She felt the wet face against her own and gradually the crying stopped.

Bella persuaded her to drink the tea which seemed to calm her. She looked suddenly at Bella and said, "It was my fault. It was my fault, Bella, that Alison died."

For a moment Bella said nothing, then, "No, Martha. She was killed by one of her parents, but perhaps you think you might have prevented it, which is different."

Martha shook her head. "Is it? Is it really different?"

Bella replied that it was different, and perhaps Martha should tell her exactly how involved she had been and why she had been seeing the family in the first place.

It had been a referral from the next door neighbour, Martha said, who rang to say that she was worried about the child next door who often cried at night.

The neighbour said the little girl had been happy and sociable and very lively until the mother's new boyfriend moved in. Now she looked pale and thin and didn't visit them any more.

Martha had visited and seen the mother and the child who, the mother said, had been a bit upset when her boyfriend had started living with them. She started wetting the bed, the mother said, and it upset her and she would wake up and cry when this happened, although she was never cross with her. She used to change the bed and tell her not to worry. The mother had also said that it was a pity the neighbour didn't talk to her before ringing the welfare.

Martha had talked to the child who had been shy and rather withdrawn but agreed by nods that it was difficult sharing her Mum with the boyfriend. She also said she tried not to wet the bed, but it came anyway. Martha said, "I wasn't really worried about it. The mother was quite friendly and open and seemed affectionate towards Alison and she was quite responsive when we talked about dealing with bedwetting by not making a fuss about it."

"So at that time you didn't visit again?" Bella asked, and Martha replied that they were too busy and her supervisor closed the case.

It seemed a month or so went by before the neighbour rang again. Martha went to see the mother, who was angry at what she called the nosey interference from next door and then said that Alison was not there as she was staying with her Gran for a few days after falling downstairs and bruising herself. Martha supposed she should have found out where the grandmother lived and gone to see Alison, but, she said, she didn't ask for the address and got so taken up with other work. But that was important, wasn't it... because, of course, she probably wasn't with her Gran at all.

And then the neighbour came to the office saying that something must be done about the child who lived next door. There was constant crying and yet they hardly ever saw her and they didn't like the look of the boyfriend and often heard him shouting, although he was very smarmy and friendly if they bumped into him in the street. The duty officer saw her on this occasion and left a note for Martha who talked to Kay Berwick, her supervisor, who said Martha should visit again and see the child. Which she did, although again, Alison was apparently not there. Her mother said she was playing with friends and was fine. She went on and on about the neighbour, saying that she was a troublemaker and was constantly making complaints about other people. She thought it had started when Kenny, the boyfriend, had parked his motorbike outside their house because he was mending a friend's car outside his own. It was not as if the neighbours had a car themselves, they hadn't, jealous they were, that was it, that was when the complaints started.

Martha seemed confused at this point. She said that she knew neighbours fought about silly things, she thought that perhaps she had been taken in by this story. She should have taken more notice about Alison falling downstairs and getting bruised. She knew now she should have insisted on seeing Alison, waited for her to return home although of course, she now knew she wasn't playing with anyone. She said she told Kay about the visit and Kay said she should go again, perhaps tomorrow, early in the morning and insist on seeing the child, and then, when she remembered another appointment she had made for the morning, Kay said well go the next day, and perhaps she should ring the health visitor and ask her to call.

Martha did ring the health visitor, but she was not available. She left a message asking her to ring and when she did, the following day, Martha herself was out. She rang her again and again the health visitor was not there, and when she arrived at work the following day, the day she was to visit Alison, Kay took her immediately into her room and said they had had a call from Accident and Emergency, who said that Alison had been admitted in the early hours of the morning and died soon afterwards of multiple injuries.

Martha said she heard what Kay said, and how the ambulance had been called by Alison's mother and they had found the child lying at the foot of the stairs; and how Alison's mother had said Kenny had thrown her down the stairs because she had wet the bed. They had of course, called the police... but it was like a kind of dream, Martha said. The words seemed to float in the air, the room was shaking... she supposed she was shaking... she began to shake as she spoke. "Inside part of me was saying no... no... not dead... oh, God, Bella, it was awful... it's still awful... dead... you can't do anything about dead. I only saw her once and she said the bedwetting just came. And he threw her downstairs... she was so little..."

They gradually coped with the horror of Martha's story. Bella cried with her and told her it was good she had explained what had happened. That was a brave thing to do, she said, and Martha must now try to remember that it was not she who had killed the child, and anything she might have done earlier might still not have prevented it happening, although she understood how Martha felt culpable. Yes, she understood that. And all the while she was picturing the little girl lying at the foot of the stairs, and seeing again in her mind the yellow and grey bruises on the back of Billy Stringer. So nearly a tragedy because she had not read the signs either. But then she forced herself to be practical, suggesting Martha had a bath and then perhaps she could come down for something to eat. Martha, calmer now, got off the bed and began to smooth the covers, saying she would.

Martha had some soup but nothing else and they didn't speak of the dead child until Martha put down her spoon and said there would be a trial and she would have to give evidence. "How will I do that?" she asked. "The neighbours will be there too. How will I do that?"

"I'm going to tell you what I think I heard you telling me," Bella said. "I think you need to hear it as you remember it... You were doing your job. You were working hard. It's a difficult job. None of us is clairvoyant. We make judgements as we go along. Now you are in shock and that will take a little time to get over, but you will recover – people always do."

Bella said that the trial would be months ahead but now, while it was still fresh in her mind, she was going to go over the facts as Martha had told them.

So she went through the case slowly, repeating what Martha had told her, talking calmly and carefully, avoiding emphasising the failures and omissions, and reminding Martha that the trial would be months ahead and she would not be alone. There would be her colleagues and her supervisor and at home there would be Beth, her daughter, who, Bella thought, was probably worrying about her.

As she spoke Bella felt uneasy. Was this the right thing to do? Might it be better to say little and leave the subject alone for the moment? Yet although it was a kind of emotional blackmail to go through the case again, and talk about Beth, Martha really needed to think about her daughter, and she also needed to listen and to hear and be able to talk herself. Bella was afraid that Martha could easily shut herself up again.

Martha began to wash the plates, saying nothing at first and then through more tears, she said she felt dreadful about Beth, and would ring her this evening, and she must go home. Tomorrow, she said, she would go home tomorrow.

Bella said nothing about the request that Martha go back to work and take part in the discussion. But she knew Martha had done some packing in the evening and when she got up the following day, she found her already having breakfast in the kitchen with bags packed in the hall. She told Bella she had rung the station and there was a train at 11.10 and she had ordered a taxi for 10.30. She was smiling brightly but there was an urgency about her which seemed to be suppressing agitation.

"Beth is expecting me. She's going to come home early this afternoon. I haven't rung mother though. I can't face that yet. But Bella, you know how grateful I am. I've been such a trial to you. I'm so sorry!" Her words came faster and faster and tears began to well up in her eyes.

Bella told her she was doing the right thing and she had been pleased to have her and she hadn't been a trial at all. She poured out some cereal, determined to be practical, aware that there was relief that this episode was over but still fearful for Martha. She said Martha must ring her and no, if Liz rang, she would not tell her, although it would be difficult to keep this up Martha said she would contact her mother in a day or so.

Somehow they kept control and managed to chat until the taxi arrived, which seemed sooner than Bella expected. It is happening so fast now, she thought. I wasn't prepared for it to happen so quickly. Then they were saying goodbye, both fighting back tears and smiling determinedly, and Martha was gone.

The house seemed so quiet and empty. Bella poured herself some more tea and sat for a moment at the table, but got up again and began putting things away, thinking of yesterday and that long disjointed description of what Martha had done and not done; of what she had thought and not thought. There were loose ends left. There was more to think about, more to say. A process started but not really completed. But was it her task? It wasn't her problem. It wasn't something to be solved. Only something to be lived through and Martha had to do that.

She wanted the comfort of conversation and rang Gemma who was not available. In a way she was glad. Gemma would probably be too pragmatic, too sensible for what she needed. She thought of all the other people she had worked with. She rang Rachael. They had kept in touch but only loosely and in the event her husband said she was away. She thought of Malcolm her last senior, who had died suddenly last year. It would have been good to speak to him. But in the end she rang Adrian. They saw each other seldom these days, but as the years had gone by it had become easier and the old feelings had gone. When she met him she rather wondered at the intensity of the feelings she once had. He was overweight and looked rather old. But she knew he would understand how she felt, and she had to talk to someone.

So she rang him. He was busy, but offered to come round later and she agreed, surprised, but glad. When he came, carrying a bottle of wine (which caused some kind of pang, some old memory) she was still pleased.

She said she was sorry that she was going to talk shop and he laughed and said, well, we always did, didn't we? And so how could he help?

So she told him Martha's story and he sat quietly, understanding the waves of inadequacy she expressed, the doubts and the anxiety and finally he said, "Bella, what a dreadful business. And dealing with it on your own. My God! I wouldn't have wanted to be faced with a situation like that, but you helped her get through it. That's all you could do. All anyone could do. But for her it had to be the right person, and that was you. You couldn't alter anything. It's what we do, Bella, isn't it? Help people get through whatever crisis they have to deal with. She made mistakes. Her judgement was faulty. We have to face that, but like the rest of us she wasn't blessed with second sight and the British Press won't forgive her for that. But you were there when she needed you and you handled it amazingly well."

As Adrian was leaving, the phone rang, which limited the time they needed to spend saying goodbye and which Bella thought, was probably a good thing. When she answered it Gemma was calling, asking how things were. Bella told her, briefly, and said that Martha had gone home now, which Gemma was pleased to hear. She hoped Bella was not too tired by it all, as the baby was expected in three weeks' time and they were expecting her to come to Stockport.

The time had gone so quickly, Bella said, she could hardly believe it was now only three weeks. They talked on about what had been bought, and what needed to be bought and how excited Gemma was at becoming a grandmother. After the call, Bella decided it was still light enough to do some gardening and, she said to herself, "make myself feel normal again."

She collected the bin from outside the kitchen and carried it down to the compost heap, feeling the muscles in her back contract and only just getting there before dropping it to the ground. She upended it onto the nearest heap and covered it with grass cuttings to suppress the smell, and then uncovered the second heap which she turned over with a fork. It was loose and finely rotted and she pushed her hand inside, feeling the warmth, pleased that it would soon be ready.

She wandered back towards the house wondering whether to mow the grass or continue weeding, when she heard the telephone. She went into the kitchen and rinsed her hands, hoping the ringing would stop. But it didn't and when she picked up the receiver it was Liz who had found out Martha was home and thought Bella should have told her. Liz had rung twice while Martha was with her, seeking information, prodding Bella to talk, but Bella had resisted, saying little except that Martha was resting and taking her time. Now, Bella thought, she expects me to tell her everything, but she actually told Liz that she thought it best if Martha talked to her in her own time. "I've done nothing. Martha is much better, I think," she said. "She will be getting support from her colleagues and although it's a very painful business, she knows she must face it. Try not to worry too much."

Liz said that it was easy to say that, but she and Matthew were worried out of their minds. But Sam had now arrived home and had gone to stay with Martha, so at least her children were now in the same country, but what did Bella think? Surely she had an opinion? Was Martha really involved in the child's death?

"It's not an easy job, Liz," Bella said. "I don't think we can easily imagine a parent killing a child…" But Liz interrupted. "Well, of course I know that, but Martha should never have taken it on. She's not strong enough. You can surely appreciate that now."

It was a long conversation which Bella found difficult and exhausting. She felt too tired to do the garden when she finally put down the phone and instead poured herself a large whisky and sat, staring into space in the living room, thinking how Liz always managed to make her feel responsible for Martha's problems or… perhaps… how she always did feel slightly responsible, whether Liz meant her to or not.

***

During the next two weeks Bella found herself recovering. Gardening is my therapy, she thought, cutting things back, splitting shrubs and planting bulbs in the two tubs nearest the house. She sowed seeds for garlic and sweet peas and dug over the vegetable bed, ignoring her backache and spreading barrow loads of compost. Martha had rung, sounding quite steady, and told her that the meetings at work had been bearable and useful and colleagues had been wonderful and very supportive. She said Sam wanted to take her to India for a holiday and she thought she might go for a few weeks. "Especially as Daddy has offered to pay my fare." And then Gemma rang to say that Sue had gone into labour and Martin had just taken her to hospital, so stand by... "You are almost a great grandmother."

And the following morning the phone rang again and Bella found that she had a great granddaughter called Lucy and all was well with the baby and the mother.

She went to Stockport, of course, and spent a week visiting the new baby and Sue; shopping for baby clothes that were not really needed; cooking for Gemma and Josh and talking about the wedding that now seemed to be arranged for January next year. As far as she could remember, they didn't talk about Martha at all.

Chapter Fifteen

October 2001

As she left the supermarket, Bella passed the newspaper stand and the words jumped at her from a tabloid paper:

JUDGE SLAMS SOCIAL SERVICES.
ALISON'S MURDERER GETS LIFE

It's as bad as it could be, she thought. She stood still looking at the headline feeling shocked and cold and then went out to her car. Her hands trembled so much that as she started to open the door she dropped the keys.

For a week she had been listening to the news of the trial. Liz had rung her after Martha had given evidence, saying that Sam was back in England again and looking after her. She had become very withdrawn, but even so, the newspaper headline was still appalling. Bella knew the judge had been critical of the social worker, the social worker's manager and the health visitor. She had expected that. She had, she supposed, forgotten how awful it would look in the press. She wasn't prepared for that this morning.

She wasn't prepared for the telephone calls either. At home, later, first Gemma rang, then Adrian, then granddaughter Sue. It's as if I have been on trial, Bella thought. People are so kind. And then Jack, from the Gardening Club rang and said he had been thinning out the cowslips that grew under his apple tree and wondered if Bella would like some.

He came round later and wondered if they would go under the birch. "They do well in the shade," he said, offering to put them in for her. So she got a trowel and fork and agreed they would go well under the tree.

"I expect you've been hearing about that nasty case in the north where that child was killed," he said. "Can't believe a man would kill a child. I expect you are glad to be out of it."

"Yes," Bella replied, then, "I think I'll get some snowdrop bulbs and plant them among the cowslips. They'll look good in the spring."